Craved
by the

(Stonefire Dragons #11)

Jessie Donovan

This book is a work of fiction. Names, characters, places, and incidents are either the product of the writer's imagination or are used fictitiously, and any resemblance to actual persons, living or dead, business establishments, events, or locales is entirely coincidental.

Craved by the Dragon
Copyright © 2018 Laura Hoak-Kagey
Mythical Lake Press, LLC
First Print Edition

Cover Art by Clarissa Yeo of Yocla Designs
ISBN: 978-1942211617

Other Books by Jessie Donovan

Stonefire Dragons
Sacrificed to the Dragon
Seducing the Dragon
Revealing the Dragons
Healed by the Dragon
Reawakening the Dragon
Loved by the Dragon
Surrendering to the Dragon
Cured by the Dragon
Aiding the Dragon
Finding the Dragon
Craved by the Dragon

Lochguard Highland Dragons
The Dragon's Dilemma
The Dragon Guardian
The Dragon's Heart
The Dragon Warrior
The Dragon Family (May 2018)

Kelderan Runic Warriors
The Conquest
The Barren
The Heir
The Forbidden (Summer 2018)

Asylums for Magical Threats
Blaze of Secrets
Frozen Desires
Shadow of Temptation
Flare of Promise

Cascade Shifters
Convincing the Cougar
Reclaiming the Wolf
Cougar's First Christmas
Resisting the Cougar

CHAPTER ONE

*B*renna Rossi readjusted the red strap of material over her shoulder for the fifteenth time.

Her mating ceremony should've started by now.

Maybe her intended, Killian O'Shea—the Clan Glenlough Irish dragon-shifter male who'd lost his dragon and his memory—had had a change of heart. After all, it had been over a week since she'd last seen him and their agreement to mate had been one of convenience rather than of love. If Killian didn't mate her, then Brenna would have to return to her clan, Stonefire, in Northern England; all non-Irish dragon-shifters were being banished from the Republic of Ireland for the foreseeable future.

And Brenna wanted to stay in Ireland more than anything.

Her inner dragon spoke up. There are any number of reasons for the delay. Remember, Teagan is using this as an opportunity to unite the clan and release some of their stress over recent events.

All Killian gains from this mating is a guard he doesn't hate. The scales are tipped in my favor, and he could easily back out.

Given how he looked at us the last time we saw him, I think Killian has other reasons for agreeing.

The memory of Killian slowly perusing her body before meeting her gaze, his eyes full of heat, flashed into her mind. I haven't agreed to sex. It's not part of our deal.

Her beast huffed. There's nothing wrong with gaining a little experience and enjoying ourselves in the process. Not all males are like Cedric.

No, don't bring up Cedric. He doesn't deserve our time.

I agree. But his actions still affect you today.

Not wanting to tarnish the present with the dragon male from three years ago, Brenna inhaled deeply and straightened her shoulders. No matter. I'll kiss Killian once, as it's expected. Then we can each live our own lives.

And any time we're in public. The clan must believe this is a true mating, or the Irish Department of Dragon Affairs will send us away.

Only Clan Glenlough's leader, Teagan O'Shea, and a handful of others knew of the farce. Okay, then in public as well. But no more. I don't need to make our lives any more complicated.

Her beast chuckled. You say that as if you can resist him.

Of course I can. I'm a Protector, after all. Being able to maintain control is one of the most important requirements for the job.

Before her beast could argue further, a tap on the door sounded and it opened inward to reveal the gray-haired, slightly wrinkled and stooped form of Orla Kelly—Glenlough's former clan leader and grandmother to both Killian and Teagan O'Shea.

Entering the room, Orla tapped her cane a few times before saying, "Not sure I care for the red. It'll only remind everyone where you're from."

Each dragon clan wore a certain color for formal events.

Stonefire wore red, whereas Glenlough wore green. "Seeing as my accent already gives me away, the red is negligible."

"Once this is over, you'll be wearing green, child." Orla paused before adding, "Are you sure this is what you want?"

During a recent leadership trial that had gone wrong, which had ended with a dragon fight, two dead Irish dragon clan leaders, and another in prison, Brenna had worked closely with Orla. The older dragonwoman was more like the grandmother Brenna had never had. "This is the only way I can stay here, Orla."

"He's a bit of a bastard without his memories and dragon, you know."

She raised her brows. "Such love for your grandson you have there."

Orla waved a hand. "It's because I love him that I'm being honest. His dragon may never return. And if Teagan can't manage to secure alliances with all the dragon clans in Ireland, foreigners may not be allowed to stay here legally for who knows how many years to come. Are you willing to saddle yourself to him for that long?"

Rather than explain herself, she probed, "Did Teagan send you here to change my mind?"

Leaning on her cane, Orla replied, "She doesn't know I'm here. I came because you're a rare female, Brenna Rossi. You're talented and unafraid to use your intelligence, no matter what the other males think. However, I know you fancied Killian before he lost his memory, and I don't want you hurt." She tilted her head. "More than that, I don't want to see the fight go out of you. A broken heart can do that, child. I've seen it before."

She frowned. "Who? Not you, from everything I've heard about your late mate."

"No, not me, but my predecessor. Even males can have their hearts broken when a true mate denies them."

Brenna smoothed her skirts. "Well, that shouldn't be a problem. I don't think Killian is my true mate."

"Aye, well, you're old enough to make your own decisions. After all, in my time, a female would have had several children by your age." Standing tall, Orla thumped her cane. "Come to me if you ever need to, Brenna. There are things I can do that Teagan can't since she's clan leader."

"Such as?"

She shrugged a shoulder. "For starters, I can have my grandson tied up and tossed into the dungeon to cool off."

Smiling, she shook her head. "That shouldn't be necessary. I can look after myself."

"The offer stands, regardless."

Another knock sounded, and the green-eyed, dark-haired form of Teagan O'Shea entered the room. Glenlough's leader glanced at her grandmother and narrowed her eyes. "Do I want to know why you're here instead of in the audience as I asked?"

"It's better for all involved if I say no," Orla replied without hesitation.

Teagan sighed. "Fine." She looked at Brenna. "Are you ready? Sorry for the delay, but Aaron's been having a bit of a problem getting Killian to follow orders."

Aaron Caruso was also originally from Stonefire. He was also Brenna's distant cousin and Teagan's mate, although their mating still remained secret from most of the clan for the time being. "Do I want to know?"

"Something about Killian bringing his own cuff to give you, with something other than his name engraved on it in the old language."

At a mating ceremony, dragon-shifters exchanged engraved arm cuffs. The custom was to place each other's name on the other, the name being written in the old dragon language of Mersae. "What does Killian's cuff say? Because

Aaron would only make a fuss if it was inappropriate."

"It simply says 'mine' in the Irish language."

She frowned. "I didn't think you spoke Irish regularly. At least, I've not heard it."

"We don't as a rule, but we learn it as children. But that's not important. The proclamation will cause a stir. It'll appear as if I endorse changing even more things about the status quo than what is already going on."

"I don't think he's out to do it purposefully," Brenna stated.

Teagan raised her brows. "Is that so?"

Even a few weeks ago, Brenna never would've thought to challenge Teagan so freely. However, after being Glenlough's temporary head Protector, questioning Teagan was part of the job description. "Killian doesn't remember who he is and answers to the name because it's the only one we've given him. 'Mine' is almost simpler for him."

Teagan tilted her head. "I hadn't thought of it that way."

She smiled. "You're busy with more than any leader should be saddled with right now. I'll overlook it this once."

Teagan snorted. "I never thought I'd be listening to someone fourteen years my junior."

She shrugged. "Age shouldn't matter as long as the advice or information is sound."

"Once this is finished and you've settled in to your new life here, we need to chat about your long-term role within the Protectors." Teagan turned toward the door. "Come out onto the stage in three minutes, unless I come back. Killian should be waiting for you in the great hall by then." She nodded and Teagan switched her gaze to her grandmother. "Let's go, Gran. Mating ceremonies are always between two people. Not even your personality or surplus of stubbornness will change that."

Orla huffed. "I didn't say I was going to insert myself, did

I? I'm starting to think regular sex is addling your brain."

"Gran," Teagan growled in warning.

"Don't worry. I'll have a chat with Caruso later," Orla said dismissively.

"Talking about my sex life with my mate is none of your concern, Gran."

"If you say so," Orla murmured, although her tone belied a different belief.

As the pair left, silence fell, and Brenna almost wished for them to come back. Their banter was familiar and she knew what to expect. It was also a fantastic distraction.

Her beast sighed. It's a mating ceremony, not a hanging.

She ignored her dragon and glanced at the clock on the wall. All that was left to do was count down the seconds until her life changed forever.

⁂

Killian O'Shea stood on the raised dais in front of several hundred people he didn't know and tried his best not to give a fuck.

Seeing as he had no memory of them and only recognized a handful from pictures and recent interactions, it was fairly easy to do.

However, when the female he'd discovered was supposedly his sister returned to the audience and met his gaze, he saw the split second of sadness there.

Concern he didn't understand flooded his body, but he quickly pushed it back. He may be marrying a woman he didn't know in some sort of strange ceremony, but it was his choice. Given how little of that he'd had in the last week, he wasn't about to allow bloody strangers and their emotions to interfere with his decision.

Besides, mating Brenna meant she'd have to stop

avoiding him. He'd been dreaming of the female all week, wondering what her smaller frame would feel like under him.

True, he'd agreed to mate her to keep her around. Brenna was the only one who didn't try to force the past on him. He'd long given up cursing clan members who thought yelling or pushing a picture closer to his face would return his memories.

As bitter as he was, he looked forward to seeing a friendly face every day.

It was then that he noticed Brenna Rossi emerging from a side entrance, wearing a simple, flowing dress and everyone else faded away. The red material made her olive skin tone more beautiful, if that were possible.

Perusing her body, he nearly growled at how the material clung to her curves and valleys. Her hips were made to be gripped and held in place as he took her from behind.

And her tits would fit perfectly into his hands.

As much as he would enjoy staring at her fine arse every day, the cocking of one eyebrow reminded him of why he'd agreed to this. She didn't hold back with questions or arguments, or try to convince him of who he should be.

Strange as it was, Brenna accepted him as is. He was angry and lost with everyone else, but not her. With the English woman, he forgot to remember his amnesia and complete lack of memory. He simply lived in the brief moments.

He resisted a frown. Bloody hell. He was turning into a philosophical idiot.

Clearing his throat, he raised his own eyebrow and Brenna rolled her eyes. He would goad her further if not for the room of strangers. Her cheeks flushed when she was angry, and it was easier to focus on that than on the rest of the world, let alone his own future.

She stopped about a meter away from him, on the other side of the stool just behind where they stood, which held the silver arm cuffs in a black box.

The cuff he'd worked so hard to keep lying there, a reminder that he could occasionally win a battle inside the bloody clan.

Smiling, she clasped her hands in front of her and Killian quickly remembered his role as doting boyfriend. He did his best to appear smitten as her voice rang out, "Killian O'Shea, our time together has been short, but from the moment you returned to us, something fell into place. You are the male I've been waiting for. And while others see nothing but the harsh exterior and the male you used to be, I see a strong, intelligent male discovering who he is. For whatever reason, you've allowed me to join you on the journey and asked me to be your mate. As I stand in front of all Glenlough, I make my claim. No matter how rough the road is ahead, I will stand at your side." She picked up the silver band with her name supposedly engraved in strange symbols and moved closer so she could gently place it on his bicep, the one all but healed from the tattoo removal. Murmurs whispered through the room, but she paid them zero attention. "Do you accept my claim?"

He tried his best not to think of her words and merely replied, "I do."

Taking his cue, Killian took one of Brenna's hands in his. As he rubbed the back of it with his thumb, her pupils flashed several times between round and slitted. He wondered what her dragon was saying. Probably out of kindness, she hadn't mentioned the bloody thing beyond one explanation. But that was one of the many things he hoped to change once they were alone and living together. Learning about the strange voices in dragon-shifters' heads might help him better understand what he used to be.

Pushing aside all other thoughts, he focused back on the moment. It was time to bring out the charm.

He raised his voice. "Brenna Rossi, you treat me as a male of worth. As I struggle to learn who I am, you do your best to support me. The thought of you leaving is unbearable. Therefore, I stake my claim in front of the entire gathering. Do you accept it?"

She searched his gaze for a second before replying, "I do."

Picking up the cool, silver band of metal, he slid it over her tattoo-free bicep and took a moment to trace the Irish word for mine.

Even if it were a damn lie, it was nice to pretend something belonged to him. And in words he actually understood.

Reaching out an arm, he pulled her up against his body. His instructions had been to give a chaste kiss and face the crowd. But as her warmth pressed against him, he tossed aside the order and traced her jaw. He swore he heard her heart rate tick up.

Moving his finger to her plump bottom lip, he traced it and her lips parted. With a growl, he closed the distance and kissed her.

With her lips open, he easily slid his tongue inside her mouth and groaned at the sweet taste. Within seconds, Brenna threaded her fingers into his hair and met each of his strokes with her own.

Suddenly, her mouth wasn't enough. Running a hand down her back, then her arse, and finally to her upper thigh, he gently lifted her leg until she cradled him and he pressed against her center. Even through her fucking dress, he could feel her hot and wet for him.

He was about to run his hand under her skirt and up her thigh when something hard and sharp pelted his head. Ignoring it, he took the kiss deeper only to be hit again.

Tearing his lips from Brenna's, he growled and searched for the source.

Standing just below the dais was the old woman who claimed to be his grandmother, Orla Kelly. And she held up another blasted rock, one with a wicked point.

Brenna's whisper filled his ear. "Let me go. Everyone is watching."

He didn't care for the embarrassment in her voice. He met her gaze. "Why does it matter?"

"Not here, Killian."

"Just know this isn't finished, Brenna. Not by a long shot."

He released her and quickly swept her off her feet. Facing the crowd, he bellowed, "Enjoy the celebration. Excuse us for not staying. As you can see, I can't keep my hands off my beautiful bride."

Before Brenna could do more than squeak, he stalked across the dais and into the side room where he'd waited before the ceremony. Once through the door, he placed her on the ground, shut the door, and quickly moved her so that her back was to the door.

Placing a hand on either side of her head, he murmured, "Is this better, darling?"

Brenna smiled slowly before she promptly kneed him in the bollocks.

⚬⚬⚬⚬⚬⚬

Some might feel bad about Killian kneeling over and holding himself, but satisfaction coursed through Brenna's body, helping to alleviate the anger. "You're a bastard, but yes, this is better."

He glared up at her. "Coward."

She blinked. "What the hell are you talking about?"

16

Killian managed to stand mostly upright, although his voice was still a bit gravelly as he said, "If not for that old woman trying to give me a head injury, you would've gladly taken it further. I heeded your request, took you someplace else, and you fucking attacked me."

She crossed her arms over her chest, hoping the action would dissuade Killian from touching her again.

Her dragon huffed. You are a coward.

Ignoring her beast, Brenna raised her chin. "Our agreement is to make requests. I never said to kiss and fondle me in front of the entire clan."

He nodded toward the armband. "I just put the word 'mine' on your bloody arm. A man would have to be a fool to do that and not kiss his wife properly in front of the entire assembly. You wanted this to appear real, and I was complying, darling."

"Real is one thing, but your hand was going under my dress. You might be an exhibitionist, but I'm certainly not."

He stood to his full height, and Brenna both loved and hated that she had to look up to meet his gaze. "Are you sure about that? My nose is sensitive, so I know you wanted me."

She willed her cheeks not to flush. "Talking about scents is what dragon-shifters do. Have you decided to accept you were one?"

He moved closer, but Brenna refused to retreat. "You're changing the subject, Brenna." He raised a hand and barely brushed her cheek. The whisper of skin against hers sent a rush of heat through her body.

Killian smiled smugly. "You want me, so why fight it?"

Her dragon spoke up. Yes, yes, give in. He will do nicely for some stress relief. All that self-hatred and frustration will translate into the best sex of our lives.

Given we've had sex with one male until now, that's not

hard to do.

That's not the point. Kiss him. He'll need some time to recover from you kneeing him, but maybe he'll put his fingers and tongue to good use in the meantime.

One of her dreams from a few days ago, where Killian had kneeled before her and made her come with just his tongue, flashed into her head.

The male in question leaned down, his voice snapping her back to the present. "Tell me what you're thinking, darling. I'm curious what makes your breath hitch and cheeks flush."

Killian's masculine scent filled her nose, as his heat engulfed her body. It would be easy to tell him. Honesty had always garnered the best response from him.

Of course, that would mean sharing her body with another male. And if her past were any indication, it would end up derailing her focus and she'd crave more, to the point she'd start to lose herself.

Her dragon said, It will be different this time. He isn't trying to manipulate us so that he can take over our duties and position.

The memory of Cedric luring her with pretty words and eventually threatening her with naked pictures he'd snapped without her permission cooled any desire she had. Brenna pushed against Killian's chest with all her might and said, "No. Sex isn't part of the deal."

She expected Killian to growl and call her a coward again. However, he merely searched her eyes and said, "I don't know what your secret is, but I intend to find it out."

"Sharing secrets isn't part of the deal, either."

"No, but that doesn't mean I won't try."

As she tried to think of a way to extricate herself from the great hall without drawing suspicion, a loud pounding on the door behind her made her jump. Aaron's voice carried through the door. "Open up, or I will break down this fucking door."

Killian opened his mouth, but Brenna answered first, "In a minute." She glanced at Killian and whispered, "Move so I can open the door."

For a second, she thought he'd refuse her order to make a point. But Killian walked to the far end of the room and sat down in the plush chair in the corner. The image of the sexy, strong male sprawled out nonchalantly made her stomach flip.

"Brenna," Aaron growled.

Opening the door, she barked, "What?"

"Don't play that game with me, Brenna Rossi."

Killian interjected, "It should be Brenna O'Shea now, aye?"

"I never said I was changing my name." She focused back on Aaron. "And you can stop shouting. I'm standing right here."

Aaron entered the room, and Brenna shut the door for some privacy.

Her dragon chimed in. Strange you want privacy now, when you were all but grinding against Killian in the great hall.

Not wanting to deal with an opinionated dragon on top of two alpha males, she quickly constructed a mental prison and tossed her beast inside.

With silence inside her head, she turned toward Aaron and Killian and cursed. Aaron gripped Killian's hair with one hand and pressed a talon at his throat with another. Aaron growled, "I should challenge you right now for disrespecting Brenna. She deserves better."

Closing the distance, she gripped the wrist of his talon-wielding hand and yanked it back. "I can take care of myself."

Aaron never moved his gaze from Killian. "He's unpredictable, Brenna. And given how you were kissing him back out there, I'm not sure you can."

She quickly twisted Aaron's arm behind his back and tugged. Hard.

"What the fuck, Brenna?" Aaron yelled.

Increasing the pressure on his arm, she replied, "Release him." After two beats, Aaron complied, and she continued. "If I need help, I'll ask. But if you think I'm going to allow you to start telling me what I can or can't do, then you've clearly gone mad."

"We don't know who he is, Brenna. And whether you want to admit it or not, that's dangerous."

From the corner of her eye, she noticed Killian's jaw tighten and a desire to protect him surged through her body.

Releasing Aaron's arm, she stepped between the two males. "Do you not trust me enough to judge what's dangerous or not? Kissing isn't going to hurt anyone. Or, are you hurting Teagan every time you do it?"

"That's different and you know it. I love Teagan and she feels the same about me." Aaron motioned toward Killian. "He clearly doesn't love you."

Killian's voice boomed inside the small room. "I may not love her, but she at least treats me as a fucking person and not a child. If you think I'm going to hurt the one person who doesn't make me question everything, then you're clearly not as intelligent as I thought you were."

Aaron took a step, but Brenna kept herself between the males. "Unless you have something related to the clan to tell me, you should probably go, Aaron."

She tried to read her cousin's expression, but Aaron was as good as any dragon-shifter male Protector when it came to keeping their faces neutral. "Teagan wants you two to at least have one dance with the clan, to keep up appearances.

And tomorrow, she wants an audience with you, Brenna. Since there is no real post-mating bliss to account for, there are plenty of jobs she wants done by those she trusts." She nodded, and Aaron added softly, "Reach out to me if you need it, Brenna. No matter what it is."

Some of her irritation faded at his tone. "Of course I will."

Aaron looked at Killian one more time before he left the room.

Killian spoke behind her. "Thank you for standing up for me."

Taking a deep breath, she glanced over her shoulder. The usual anger and frustration in Killian's eyes were nowhere to be seen. "You're welcome. But piss me off again, and I may reconsider."

The corner of his mouth kicked up. "I would say I won't, but it's too much fun."

She battled a smile. "Well, if you're looking for fun, then our dance awaits us."

"Dancing is not fun."

While she should bite back her remark, the words escaped before she could stop them. "It means you get to hold me close and touch me freely. I thought you liked that."

Heat flashed in Killian's eyes.

If she didn't leave, she might do something stupid, such as close the distance between them and kiss the bastard.

Not wanting to tempt herself, she opened the door and stepped into the hall. "Follow me when you're ready. I'll let them know you need a moment to recharge yourself after our interlude."

He grunted. "My cock and balls still hurt."

"Good."

With that, Brenna dashed down the hall and toward the great hall again.

Her dragon would say she was being a coward. And this

time, Brenna agreed. But she had to keep her distance. The thought of becoming the doting fool she'd been with Cedric made her stomach churn. Only once she'd achieved her goal of becoming either the second-in-command or head Protector of a dragon clan would she allow herself a chance to fall for a male, and not before.

Picking up her pace, she pasted on a smile and entered the great hall.

CHAPTER TWO

Killian watched Brenna exit the room before he glanced down at his hand. The tip of Aaron's finger had turned into a sharp clawlike thing that reminded him of a bird's talon. Considering humans couldn't do that, it should've scared him.

However, the bastard extending the talon and making threats didn't seem anything out of the ordinary.

It was one thing for everyone to tell him he'd been a dragon-shifter. But it was another thing entirely to accept it.

Given his supersensitive hearing, sense of smell, quick healing ability, and almost indifference to flashing pupils and fingers turning into claws, Killian was starting to think he had been like one of these strange dragon people.

If only he could remember something from his life before waking up a little over a week ago.

He'd been putting off asking about who he had been out of anger. He still wouldn't give a bastard like Aaron Caruso the satisfaction of telling him who and what he'd been. Brenna, on the other hand, would tell him the truth and hopefully not try to force it.

He nearly barked a laugh at how quickly the day had changed. One moment he'd wanted to kiss the living shit out of Brenna and take her against a wall. The next, he was toying with the fact he wasn't human after all.

Not that he was going to dwell on it for the time being. Brenna had tempted him with a dance. And while he couldn't care less about formalities or following protocol, he wasn't going to pass up the chance to hold the strong, beautiful female close.

After striding down the corridor and to one of the side entrances of the great hall, Killian stood in the doorway and took a second to watch the scene inside the room.

Everyone wore some shade of green. The women were in one-shoulder dresses like Brenna's and the men were in something resembling a kilt, with part of the material tossed over one shoulder to cross over their bare chests.

The dancing area was in the center of the room, with tables along the edges, filled with people eating, drinking, and laughing.

If what he'd been told was true, almost every single person in the room could change into a dragon. One misstep and any number of them could pin him down and threaten him with talons.

However, his gut told him they wouldn't do that unprovoked. Over the last week and a bit, he'd learned to trust his gut over most anything else.

Putting aside his observations, he moved again. Brenna would be a welcome distraction.

Since she was the only female in a red dress, she was easy to spot, and he made a beeline for her.

As he closed in, he couldn't help but stare at her long neck and the place where it met her shoulder. He wanted nothing more than to come up behind her and nibble the spot before slowly licking the sting with his tongue. No doubt her scent would be strong there, and hers was one he'd never tire of.

Fuck, he wanted her. More than his memories, he wanted the feisty yet vulnerable female naked and under him. He could too easily forget about everything but her soft, warm presence as she came, squeezing his cock tightly until he joined her.

She might think sex was off the table, but Killian knew she was as attracted to him as he was to her. He would find out the reason for the flash of wariness earlier, when they'd been alone. Someone had hurt her, he was certain of it.

He nearly missed a step. Apparently he'd been able to read facial expressions and emotions in his previous life. Add in the muscles and scars of his body, and he wondered if he'd been one of the dragon warriors he'd heard mentioned once or twice. Although why they used a pretentious name like Protectors, he had no idea.

Careful to keep his steps light, he was nearly to Brenna when her shoulders straightened and she looked back at him. "If you're trying to be stealthy, you're doing a horrible job."

"Maybe I'm just trying to practice some of my moves en route, to prepare for our dance."

She closed the distance between them and tilted her head. "You're a terrible liar."

He wanted to ask if he'd been a good one before, but resisted. Instead, he reached out and placed a hand on her lower back. "You should be praising to the sky how lucky you are, then. I'm told honesty makes for the best couples."

"There is such a thing as being too honest."

Not caring who stared, he raised a hand to her hair and lightly brushed some of the short strands. "Such as if I mentioned how you have a tiny mole just past your hairline and suggest we take a look to see if any hair is growing out of it."

"You have one on your lower back, so maybe we should check yours first."

He smiled slowly. "So you've been staring at my back."

Pink flushed her cheeks and it took everything he had not to lean down and kiss the flushed skin. "It's hard to miss, what with you not wearing a shirt and being so tall."

He leaned down. "You're a terrible liar yourself. I bet I could ask anyone walking by about my back, and none would notice the mole." Moving his head until he could nuzzle his cheek against hers, he murmured, "And you know what? It makes me happy that you notice things about my body. Maybe one day you'll explore every inch with your fingers and lips."

Her breath hitched, and Killian took that as his cue to pull back and put out his hand, palm upward. "Shall we?"

She glanced at his hand and studied it. He had no idea what was so significant about one dance, but she eventually slid her palm into his and he tightened his grip. "I have no idea if I remember the steps or not, so watch your toes, darling."

The next song began, and Killian pulled Brenna close. He'd taken a few steps without thinking, his body somehow remembering the motions, when pain raced through his head.

The sharp jabs only intensified until he gripped the side of his head and fell to his knees with a roar. Killian tried his best to push it away, but in the next second, the world went black.

꩜꩜꩜

Brenna knelt next to Killian's body on the floor and placed a finger at his carotid artery. At the steady, if not slightly fast, pulse, her initial fears melted away. She'd barely established Killian was alive before Teagan, Aaron, and Glenlough's head doctor, Dr. Ronan O'Brien, were also kneeling around Killian.

Moving aside to allow the physician to do his work, Brenna studied Killian's face until Teagan's voice garnered her attention. "Tell me what happened, Brenna."

Taking a deep breath, she met Teagan's gaze. The steadiness there helped to calm her own nerves. "I don't know. One second we were dancing, and the next he was roaring in pain."

"Did his pupils change?" Aaron asked.

"No, they remained round. Although he shut them when he gripped his head, so anything could've happened after that point." The doctor looked up and she couldn't hold back her curiosity. "Do you think this is an aftereffect of the drugs that stole his memory?"

Dr. O'Brien grunted. "Probably. The moss antidote that's worked with the others doesn't seem to be helping Killian. I need to get him back to the surgery and run a series of tests."

Orla Kelly's voice came from behind Brenna. "Tests are all well and good, but we need more information about the stuff that did this to him in the first place."

Caitlin O'Shea, mother to Killian and Teagan, said softly, "Let them do their work, Mother. You're not a doctor."

Brenna glanced at Teagan. At the slight nod, granting permission, she answered, "Something similar happened to the sister of a member of Stonefire recently. Teagan should reach out to Bram and see if anyone can provide Dr. O'Brien with more information."

The female in question had been Delia Owens, the half sister of Stonefire's head Protector and a member of Clan Snowridge in Wales. Unlike Killian, they had found her shortly after being injected with drugs and the doctors had been able to flush her system. There were some lingering side effects, but none were anywhere near the same degree as Killian's.

Teagan spoke up. "You reach out to Stonefire, Brenna, and I'll have Aaron reach out to Snowridge."

The request wasn't anything out of the ordinary. Ever since the debacle with the other dragon leaders recently, Teagan had been giving Brenna a variety of sensitive tasks to complete.

Still, glancing down at Killian's still form, she wondered what he'd feel like if he woke up alone, without her at his side. She wasn't foolish enough to think they were more than acquaintances who were attracted to each other. However, every time one of the clan members demanded Killian remember them or a certain memory, it only made Killian angrier. She'd agreed to mate him to stay on Glenlough, yes, but she also wanted to protect the strong male who hadn't blinked twice at accepting a new female Protector into the clan all those months ago.

Teagan placed a hand on Brenna's arm. "My mother and gran can sit with him until you finish your task. I would do it myself, but I need to soothe the clan's nerves."

Brenna looked around and noticed the various clan members standing, staring, and whispering. What had meant to be a celebration to ease nerves and relax them had turned into another stressful situation.

If they were to continue accepting her, she needed to do her job and allow others to look after Killian.

Brenna bobbed her head. "I'll talk to Bram and Stonefire's doctors and see what I can find out. Just let me know if he wakes up." She lowered her voice. "If his mate doesn't check on him often, there will be talk."

Teagan looked at Dr. O'Brien. "Do what you need to

do, Ronan, and keep us updated. Once your examination is finished, my gran and mother will sit with him."

Dr. O'Brien raised an eyebrow and glanced at Orla. "You'll heed my instructions or I'll toss you out, Orla. And no weapons of any kind in the surgery. I saw you tossing rocks earlier, during the mating ceremony."

Orla tapped her cane. "Fine, fine. One of the nurses can pat me down, if need be. Let's just get moving. I want to know what's wrong with my grandson."

Teagan signaled two Protectors in the room and they gently lifted Killian by the legs and armpits before carrying him away, Dr. O'Brien following close on their heels.

After everything Killian had endured already, she only hoped his condition wouldn't worsen. There was a chance he could wake up without memories again, or possibly go insane. After all, when Dr. Sid on Stonefire had lost her inner dragon, she'd come close to a mental breakdown.

Her beast grunted. *That took twenty years to happen.*

Keep in mind that she wasn't injected with drugs that were created to harm dragon-shifters, either.

Teagan's voice prevented her dragon from replying. "Let's all get to work and remember to keep each other informed." Brenna turned toward the exit, but Teagan's hand on her shoulder stayed her. "You're family now, Brenna. Don't hesitate to seek me out if you need anything."

With a nod, Brenna exited the great hall and headed toward the central command building of the Protectors.

As she walked, Brenna slowly packed away her feelings. No matter what happened with Killian, being a Protector was the only certain thing in her life. She hadn't worked hard to earn Teagan's trust and be made temporary head Protector of Glenlough for nothing. She needed to trust the clan to have her back.

It was time to get to work.

Killian stood next to a lake surrounded by rolling hills, the grass bright green and the sun high in the blue sky.

A shadow passed over him, and he looked up to see a small winged creature, its mostly blue hide glinting in the sun. The white patches scattered across its skin were iridescent in the sunshine.

The small creature flapped its wings and made a clumsy landing not more than a few meters from Killian. The snout, sharp teeth, wings, hide, and talons were that of a little dragon, perhaps a baby one. Not that he knew the difference.

The wee thing took awkward steps toward Killian and canted its head. "Who are you?" the dragon asked.

Without thinking, Killian reached out a hand and gently scratched the dragon behind an ear. The beast hummed and leaned into the touch. "To be honest? I don't know."

After a few seconds, the dragon spoke again. "Do you want to be my friend?"

"Dragons have friends?"

The little beast tilted his head one way and then the other in an avian manner. "I think so. I haven't met anyone here. It's just me and flying by myself is lonely."

At the dragon's words, Killian noticed the eerie quiet, not to mention unnatural stillness of both the air and surface of the lake. "Where are we?"

"I don't know. I woke up here one day and haven't been able to leave."

At the sadness in the dragon's eyes, Killian scratched his hide some more. The idea of the beast being sad made him want to do something about it. "I think this is a dream.

So when I wake up, you won't exist."

"Are you sure? I remember many days here, before you came."

He had no idea where the question came from, but he asked, "What were you doing right before this?"

The little dragon flapped his wings once. "I came to the barrier and tried to scratch my way out."

"Where is this barrier?"

"On the other side of the lake. Maybe you can get through. I'll meet you there."

The little blue and white beast jumped and flapped a few times before soaring across the sky, to the other side of the lake.

Killian ran around it, afraid to touch the still, glass-looking water of the lake. He soon caught up with the little dragon and the beast leaned forward and scratched what should be air. The second he did, it felt as if something sliced his brain.

The dragon jumped back and tottered off, jumping into the lake. The surface broke into a thousand pieces of glass before reassembling.

It took a few minutes for Killian to breathe through the pain. As soon as he could stand again, he moved to the lake's surface. He gingerly tapped a foot on the surface, but unlike with the dragon, it remained solid. He tried standing on it, jumping, and even pounding the surface, but nothing happened.

Since he couldn't escape the same way, Killian went to the barrier the dragon had scratched. However, when he raised a hand to touch it, his hand felt nothing but air. He easily walked past the supposed barrier. Each step away from the lake made his eyelids heavy until he dropped to the ground and fell asleep.

CHAPTER THREE

*B*renna couldn't help but smile as Bram Moore-Llewellyn's dark hair, blue eyes, and friendly face appeared on the screen, with Dr. Sid Jackson and Dr. Gregor Innes at his side. As much as she loved Glenlough, she missed many of the people from her home clan of Stonefire.

True to the leader of Stonefire's character, Bram didn't waste time on small talk. "Brenna. What's so urgent, lass?"

Since she knew that Bram wouldn't answer an urgent summons without securing the line, she quickly explained Killian's outburst and subsequent unconsciousness before asking, "Have you found out anything new, related to Delia's recovery from the drug injections?"

Sid spoke up. "She's awake, but her dragon is acting as a young, shy child, as if they were strangers and meeting for the first time. The doctors in Wales are running their own series of tests and will share the information later. In the meantime, Gregor and I have been running tests here with Trahern's help on both Delia's blood and some of the chemicals recently recovered from the farm near the Welsh clan." A group of humans had been manufacturing and selling the dragon-harming drug via the dark channels of the internet. "But it's going to take time to pinpoint what chemical or combinations of chemicals caused the dragon's regression. And even longer to find a cure, if it exists."

Gregor, Sid's Scottish mate, added, "Once Glenlough's doctor finishes his own series of tests, have him send the information to us. We received the initial data, but is there anything else about Killian's behavior that you can share? Has he experienced any sort of pounding or other signs of communication from his dragon? Even the smallest detail could help us find a cure."

"I don't think his dragon has made a sound," Brenna said. "To be honest, everyone has avoided talking with him about inner dragons, even me."

"Right, then when he regains consciousness, start asking questions," Sid stated. "I know it won't be easy, as losing your dragon is hard enough without the additional tragedy of losing your memory, but if we've any chance of bringing his dragon back, we need to look for the smallest sign that his inner beast still survives."

Brenna said what everyone else had to be thinking. "It's possible that the drugs killed his dragon and he'll never return."

Sid answered with hesitation. "Yes. But I'm not about to give up so easily. Remember, it took twenty years for me to find mine again. I hope it won't take as long with Killian, but it's far too soon to make any sort of foregone conclusion about his inner beast."

Sid had lost her inner dragon as a teenager, after an overdose of the dragon slumber drug. Only once she found her true mate and went through the frenzy had her beast returned.

That gave Brenna an idea. "What if I try to find his true mate? Do you think that could help?"

Gregor frowned. "Maybe, maybe not. Although, it couldn't hurt to locate her and try."

Bram spoke again. "Do you know who it is?"

"It's not me," she stated simply.

Concern flashed in Bram's eyes, but it was quickly replaced by a neutral expression. "While finding his true mate could help, lass, the odds of finding her are low."

She shook her head. "His grandmother once mentioned to me that his true mate had come and gone years ago. I'll talk with her and see if it's possible to locate the female. Even though she probably doesn't want him, we can restrain Killian for as long as needed, if her kiss does indeed work, and then move the female to someplace safe."

Her dragon growled. *I don't like the idea of giving him to a female who overlooked his worth.*

We don't know the full story, dragon. So don't judge so harshly.

Bram's voice prevented her beast from replying. "Let me know if you need any help. We might not be able to set foot in Ireland just now, but if the female in question is somewhere in the UK, we'll do whatever we can to locate her."

Sid jumped in. "But just know that kissing his true mate may have no effect, Brenna. There are old tales of dragon-shifters losing their inner dragons through poisoning in times long past. While I don't have the scientific evidence to substantiate any of it, some of the old stories have kernels of truth to them. We'll even ask some of the teachers and historians to helps us locate any pertinent information."

Gregor added, "And one more thing—if you can't locate his true mate, there is another option. I've been studying how the human and dragon halves interact with one another. Since Killian is now mated to you, he is allowed to come to Stonefire. I'm not saying Dr. O'Brien isn't skilled, but thanks to Cassidy in my life, I've made this study one of my top priorities."

She smiled. Gregor was the only one who called Sid by her full name. "I'll keep that in mind. I'd love nothing more than to give Bram more paperwork to fill out for the transfer."

Bram grunted. "It's worth it if it means we can save your mate."

Stonefire's leader was one of the few who knew the truth of her mating to Killian. So the fact he was willing to go to such lengths to help her made Brenna slightly homesick.

Her dragon huffed. *Of course he'd help us. We have two families now, both here and in England. Taking Killian to Stonefire might be better in the short run. No one knows him there and would accept him as is.*

Maybe. But let's see if we can locate his true mate first. That will probably be more helpful.

Her beast growled. *I don't like how easily you want to hand him over to another female.*

I never said that. But we need to look at all the options. She paused and added, *And remember, he's not ours. Not really.*

Believe that if you wish.

Brenna focused back on Bram and the doctors. "I'll call again tomorrow, if possible. I can't thank you all enough for your help."

Bram frowned. "Of course we'd bloody help you. Just because Teagan O'Shea has charmed you into staying doesn't make me care any less about you, lass. Not to mention your parents are back from Italy for the foreseeable future and anxious to talk with you."

Brenna's father was from an Italian dragon clan, but her mother was originally from Stonefire. She hadn't spoken to them since she'd run away to join the army at eighteen.

She had her reasons, although she had and still missed her dad.

Pushing aside her regret, she cleared her throat. "Once things calm down, I'll call them, I promise."

"See that you do. Evie's maternal instincts have kicked up a thousand-fold as of late, and she's determined to reunite all the families she can."

Evie was Bram's human mate. "I sense you aren't telling me something, Bram."

When he remained silent, Sid rolled her eyes. "Evie is pregnant again and Bram is terrified despite the fact a lot of progress has been made studying Gina MacDonald's blood."

Gina MacDonald was a human female who lived on Clan Lochguard, in the Scottish Highlands. She'd given birth to a half-dragon-shifter baby without any complications, which was rare for humans to do. A blood test had revealed that she'd been given a dragon's blood infusion at some point, to cure an illness. Dr. Sid and Gregor believed it could work for other human females and they had been testing out small injections on any pregnant humans on Stonefire.

Brenna nodded. "Trust the doctors, Bram. Besides, Evie is as stubborn as they come. All will work out in the end."

"I hope so," he murmured. He sat taller. "However, we're talking about you right now. You'll hear more from me soon."

After everyone said their goodbyes, the screen went dark.

And of course her bloody dragon decided to talk again. *Taking him to Stonefire might be the best idea yet.*

Right, and then I give up my hard-earned position here to go back to the lower ranks of Protectors on Stonefire?

That's a weak excuse and you know it. Nikki Gray is now second-in-command of the Protectors, and she and Kai will give us a worthy position. I think you're more

36

concerned about avoiding Mum and Dad.

As she debated how to reply to that, her mobile beeped. Checking her messages, she had one from Dr. O'Brien:

Killian is awake and asking for you.

Dashing out of the room, Brenna made her way to the surgery. Seeing Killian would ease her own worries a fraction, but she also needed to start asking him the difficult questions. Sid never would've suggested she do so unless it was important.

She only hoped Killian didn't resent her for bringing up the male he used to be.

⌒⌒⌒⌒⌒

Killian could do nothing but lay there as Orla, Caitlin, and Dr. O'Brien all hovered around his bed. He felt akin to a bug trapped under glass, simply there for observation.

Dr. O'Brien frowned at him. "I can't help you if you don't tell me what you remember. You muttered something whilst unconscious. Did you dream?"

Killian repeated his request. "I want to see Brenna."

Orla leaned forward. "Can't you do something to make him talk?"

Dr. O'Brien sighed. "For the last time, no. Truth-telling serums have been outlawed for over fifty years and you know that."

"Hmph. Special circumstances call for extreme measures," Orla stated.

Caitlin, the woman who claimed to be his mother, stepped between him and Orla. "No, Mother. Killian is my son and I won't allow you to harm him."

"My, my, the soft-hearted one has claws after all," Orla drawled.

Caitlin stood tall. "There is nothing wrong with being

kind. But even if he doesn't remember me, I will do whatever it takes to protect Killian."

As he studied the back of Caitlin O'Shea, he willed for a memory to come forth. The female seemed to care for him and guilt threaded his heart that he was causing her pain.

Not that it was his bloody fault.

Dr. O'Brien pricked him with a needle and drew more blood. He wanted to tell the doctor enough, but he barely had the strength to do anything but move his head.

Thankfully Brenna's dark-haired form rushed into the room. Her eyes instantly found his and a sense of calmness came over him.

For all that they were near-strangers, she was more familiar than anything else in his life.

She pushed her way to his side and laid a hand on his forehead. The warm, smooth skin of her fingers stroked, and he relaxed a fraction. "What happened?"

"I don't know. I was dreaming, but I can't remember about what."

Searching his gaze, she asked, "Are you still in pain?"

He smiled. "Why? Are you going to nurse me back to health?"

"Killian O'Shea, now is not the time to tease me," she scolded. "Tell me anything you can remember or I'll leave this room and let you deal with Orla."

"Hey," Orla interjected.

Killian ignored the older woman. "The pain is mostly gone, although I'm weak."

Brenna glanced at Dr. O'Brien. "How long before we know the results of your tests?"

The doctor never ceased changing out his blood draw tube. "Several hours, at least. All we can do is give him pain medication and monitor his vital signs. While he was unconscious, his heart rate skyrocketed for about thirty seconds, but it's back to normal now."

She continued to stroke his forehead, her feminine scent invading his nose. When she wasn't angry or irritated, her face was softer somehow. He wished she would lay beside him and lend him some strength.

He nearly frowned at that thought. She was his mate out of necessity. He shouldn't have any expectations about how she'd treat him beyond civility.

She met his gaze again. "I need to talk with Orla briefly. Are you okay with me leaving the room for a few minutes?"

No. "Why wouldn't I be?"

Her brows raised. "Happy mating day to you, too."

Before he could think of how to reply to that, Caitlin stood next to Brenna and said, "I'll watch over him."

He may not remember his mother, but Caitlin's kind eyes, full of concern, added to the calmness caused by Brenna.

Removing her fingers, Brenna turned and exited the room, with Orla on her heels. He debated what to say to the female at his side, but she soon started to sing a song that seemed familiar.

Not that he could place where he knew it from. However, with each verse, his eyes drooped a little more until he fell asleep.

⌘⌘⌘

Brenna guided Orla into the empty patient room across from Killian's and shut the door. Not wanting Orla to beat around the bush, she simply asked, "Where does Killian's true mate live?"

She raised a gray eyebrow. "First, tell me what you're planning, child. Then we'll see if I tell you."

At least Orla wasn't holding a grudge because of Brenna's remarks a few minutes ago.

39

She decided honesty would speed up the process. "Do you remember me telling you about what happened to Dr. Sid Jackson on Stonefire?"

"Yes, the female who lost and found her dragon."

"Right. Well, her dragon emerged after kissing her true mate. You mentioned once that Killian's true mate had come and gone. I was hoping we could locate her and see if a kiss might help reverse the effects of the drugs used on him."

Orla leaned on her cane. "That female will only bring trouble. She's with Clan Northcastle in Northern Ireland."

She may end up needing Bram's help after all since Clan Northcastle was in the UK. "Did she know about her and Killian's true mate connection?"

"I'm not sure. Male dragons always sense it first, but instinct and love don't always go hand-in-hand."

"True enough, but surely we can reach out to Northcastle and at least ask for a meeting along the border. Not even the DDA would consider that breaking the rules, as the border is open between the UK and Ireland anyway."

Orla harrumphed. "The DDA might not care, but Lorcan Todd would."

She frowned. "The leader of Northcastle? I know relations are tentative at best, but surely he'd be open to negotiation."

"Not in this, child. Killian's true mate is Lorcan Todd's daughter, Georgiana."

Blinking, she blurted, "What?"

"Aye, it's true. She accompanied Lorcan during a visit several years ago. Once Killian's dragon took notice, I helped my grandson to keep his distance from the female. Not even Teagan knew, although I suspect her dragon might've sensed it. However, because of it, Killian became unable to lead the negotiations and Teagan had no choice but to share her secret of being the leader with Lorcan."

While Glenlough had a history of female leaders, they had always ruled in secret, with a male to act as the public face of the clan. Otherwise, the other clans would've seen a female in charge as a weakness and attacked. Teagan's secret had only become known to the world in the last month or so.

"It couldn't hurt to ask Lorcan for help," Brenna suggested.

Orla tapped her cane. "He'll say no, the bastard. After all, in exchange for keeping Teagan's secret, he'd wanted my daughter Caitlin as his mate so that Glenlough would never attack or antagonize Northcastle again. Not to mention he'd hold dual citizenship and could come and go as he pleased between Northern Ireland and the Republic of Ireland, without DDA interference."

Brenna wondered why no one had thought to brief her more on the history between the two clans. "Since Caitlin's still here, the offer was plainly refused. And yet, Lorcan wasn't the one to reveal Teagan's secret."

The older female shook her head. "No. We ended up giving him resources and a few clan members to keep him quiet. Teagan eventually gathered evidence of Lorcan stealing sheep from local human farmers, and they came to a stalemate of sorts. The DDA would've taken Lorcan from his leadership role, if they knew of the theft."

Her frown deepened. "I think I'm missing another piece of information. Teagan's secret is out now, so she holds the cards. Why won't she put pressure on Lorcan?"

Orla sighed. "One of our clan members named Sadie ran off with a Northcastle bloke. Teagan is negotiating for Sadie and her lad to live here. Until that's done, she won't risk alienating the Northern Irish dragon clan."

"Right, then we need to do something else. While it's a big

if, I can reach out to Bram and see if he has any suggestions. Northcastle and Stonefire aren't close, but Northcastle doesn't mind the Scottish dragon clan. Perhaps something can be done through them."

"I'll talk with Teagan about it. For now, just take care of Killian. He's a little less of a bastard when you're around. Who knows, maybe you're the key to his recovery."

"I'm not his true mate, Orla. The entire clan saw us kiss, and my dragon didn't go into a frenzy."

Orla thumped her cane again. "So? Teagan and Aaron aren't true mates, but they fit quite well together. Fate and instinct might have been necessary in the days of old to keep us alive, what with all the violence and mistrust, but I'm thinking it's no longer imperative for a dragon's happiness."

"You're somewhat forward-thinking for your age."

Orla shrugged a shoulder. "Change is necessary to survive." She tapped her cane harder. "Now, go back to Killian's room and maybe chat with my daughter. Caitlin takes after my late mate and is shy. Fake mating or not, she wants to know the female paired with her son. Killian losing his memory hasn't been easy for her."

She sensed there was more to the story, but instinctively knew that it wasn't Orla's to tell.

Brenna nodded. "I will, but I have a request."

"Aye?"

"I want all the information Glenlough has on Lorcan Todd and his daughter. I don't want to throw up any red flags about my possible plans, and I'm sure you know how to covertly get the files without getting caught."

"At least you don't underestimate me. I knew there's a reason I like you."

She winked. "You just want someone to sneak in weapons on demand."

"Hmph. I've been warned that my cane is too dangerous. Otherwise, I wouldn't need your help."

"Of course not." Brenna moved to the door. "Talk with Teagan as soon as possible, Orla. I know there are many ways to help Killian, but the more options we have available at our fingertips, the better."

Her dragon spoke up. *You want to do everything in your power to get him to kiss the other female.*

Look, Killian returning to his old self will make a lot of people happy. That's all that matters.

It won't make you happy. After all, he never looked twice at us before he lost his memory.

That doesn't matter. I'm not going to be selfish in this. As it is, I have no wish to have a real mate for many years to come.

Her beast fell silent. Brenna pushed aside any worry at her usually forceful dragon, pasted on a smile, and entered Killian's room.

⌒⌒⌒⌒⌒

Caitlin O'Shea watched her son's chest rise and fall in a steady rhythm and tried not to feel guilty.

After all, if she hadn't been so afraid several years ago, she would've taken Lorcan as her mate and he could've helped protect Glenlough. The attacks may never have come, to either her daughter or her son.

Her dragon huffed. *You are assuming more blame than is necessary.*

Not true. The alliance would've kept the other Irish clans at bay. Northcastle is stronger than most.

But not Glenlough.

Cockiness won't help anything. Strong as we are, we couldn't save Kieran.

Kieran O'Shea had been her mate and father to her children. He'd been killed during a skirmish with the Northern Irish humans decades ago.

Circumstances have changed. Dragons aren't fighting humans. Rather, we're trying to get along with them. We don't need Northcastle.

Caitlin hated to give up, but when her dragon formed an opinion, it was hard to shift it.

Instead, she picked up a wet cloth and wiped Killian's forehead. Her son was handsome, but Caitlin wished at least one of her children had inherited the blond hair of her late mate, to give her one more piece of her former love to cherish.

Her dragon sighed. *Kieran is gone. We loved him, but it's time to move on. Stop ignoring every male that comes our way.*

It's more complicated than that, dragon. Teagan is clan leader. I don't want to cause any problems, and taking a male could do that.

You never *cause problems. After fifty-five years, maybe you should take a chance and live a little.*

Why do you keep trying to change me?

I'm not. I'm trying to get you to accept who you are instead of being the shadow of our mother.

Caitlin leaned back. *That's not fair.*

It is entirely fair.

She wanted to growl and toss her dragon into a mental maze, but a knock at the door garnered her attention. Brenna entered with a smile. "Any changes?"

"No. But now that you're here, I'm sure you want to spend some time with Killian. I can leave."

She made to stand, but Brenna placed a hand on her shoulder. "Stay for a bit."

Brenna sat next to her, and Caitlin looked back at her

son. Starting a conversation had never been her strong point, and it was even harder with an alpha personality such as Brenna's, even though she knew the female had a good heart and had been kind to Killian.

Used to her ways, her dragon merely curled up at the back of her mind and watched to see how things would play out.

Content to pluck at her trousers, Caitlin hummed a tune. After a few minutes, Brenna's voice interrupted the song. "I haven't heard that one before. What is it?"

Shrugging, she said, "Just a tune I made up years ago. I've always loved music, but I was never good enough to make a living with it. So, I contented myself with singing to my children and these days, to the children in my daycare."

She felt Brenna's eyes on her face. "I somehow think it's less to do with a lack of talent and more to do with singing in front of a large group of people."

Meeting Brenna's gaze, she asked, "Why would you say that?"

The female smiled warmly. "Believe it or not, my father is somewhat shy. He loves to play the guitar and sing, but standing up in front of a crowd bigger than five people sends him into a panic attack."

"So, you must take after your mother."

Brenna laughed. "Mostly. It's probably why we butted heads so many times over the years."

Longing flashed in Brenna's gaze, but promptly disappeared. The poor female was in a strange land, and dealing with her temperamental son couldn't be easy. "I know your mother can't be here right now, what with the Irish DDA's restrictions, but I'm sure we'll find a way to reunite you."

"Maybe." Brenna focused back on Killian's face. "All that matters right now is helping Killian."

As she watched Brenna's face, Caitlin's theory was all but proven. The mating may be a sham, but Brenna fancied her son, amnesia and all.

Brenna continued, "I may have a plan to help bring your son back to you."

Tamping down her initial shock, she asked slowly, "Are you sure that's what you want?"

The younger female's eyes widened as they met her gaze. "Why would you ask me that?"

"Just because I'm much quieter than my mother or offspring doesn't mean I'm not a keen observer. I've never seen Killian so consumed with a female, like he was with you on the stage in the great hall."

Brenna flicked an imaginary speck of dirt off her top. "It was a kiss, nothing more."

"I know you want to do everything you can to bring Killian's memories back, but maybe that's not what's best for him. After all, he was a reclusive workaholic before. He may be angrier now, but he's much more relaxed."

Brenna shook her head. "That doesn't matter. A dragon-shifter without a dragon is only half a person. He deserves to have his other half back."

"Dedicating yourself to a cause is noble, but don't let it get to the point of being stupid."

That's what had happened with Kieran and his noble idea to end the fighting amongst the humans in nearby Derry.

In the end, both sides had found something to work together on—ridding their city of any dragons.

Not wanting to think of her mate's death, Caitlin sang one of the songs she'd written. The gentle tones made her forget about her past and what could've been.

And as if understanding her intent, Brenna kept quiet and merely listened.

CHAPTER FOUR

The next day, Brenna sat in Killian's hospital room as he slept, leafing through the stack of information on Lorcan Todd, hoping she'd missed something about him and his daughter.

Her dragon spoke up. *There's nothing else. Lorcan's mate died in childbirth, he raised his daughter alone, and he came into the leadership position almost ten years ago.*

You forgot his time with the British Army and stint as head Protector.

Those are positive traits and not worth noting.

Brenna set down the papers. *If only Teagan would give me leave to contact Bram again. That way, Lochguard might be able to set up some kind of meeting.*

Yes, because healing the rift between Glenlough and Northcastle will be as simple as having one meeting, her beast said dryly.

Just stop. The first civil meeting between enemies is the most important.

Killian grunted and reached out a hand into the air above him. He murmured, "Stay."

Standing, she noticed that Killian's eyes were still closed.

47

He had to be dreaming again.

Since his dreams could give her clues, she resisted smoothing his brow.

However, he relaxed on the bed and went limp with sleep again.

The nurse named Ruby rushed into the room and went to the computer terminal next to Killian's bed. His vital signs must've jumped for a second, sending a notification to the nurse on duty.

The nurse said without preamble, "Anything different this time?"

They had been keeping a log of his actions and utterances since the day before, when he'd fallen asleep and had yet to wake up. "He reached for something and said 'stay.'"

Typing the answer into the computer, Ruby said, "So that makes mirror, lake, and stay he's mentioned. That's not much to go on."

"No, but I have an idea." She leaned down to Killian's ear and whispered, "Take me with you, Killian. Where are you?"

His brows furrowed, but he didn't speak. Brenna repeated her sentences a few times before giving up with a sigh. "Well, I guess we'll just have to keep trying."

"Yes, well, Dr. O'Brien should be here any second to discuss Killian's lab results. Those will hopefully tell us more about what's going on."

She scrutinized the nurse's face, but Brenna couldn't discern any emotion. "You could warn me of what's to come."

Ruby shrugged. "That's not my job."

Since one of the key traits of a good dragon-shifter nurse was to stand up to any sort of personality, especially the dominant ones, Brenna didn't push.

Killian stirred again, and Brenna had another thought.

She opened one of his eyelids to check his pupil. The upper half was entirely round, but the bottom half came to a point like the bottom half of an almond.

The nurse was already at her side. "I've never seen that before."

Killian's pupil returned to round and Brenna released his eyelid. "Do you think he's talking to his dragon in his dreams?"

"Maybe, but the shape of the pupil worries me. The closest I've seen to that in the past was when a dragon-shifter was dying."

Her dragon growled. *He's not dying.*

Maybe he is, dragon. We have no idea.

Regardless, Sid and Gregor need to hear about this.

Before Brenna could respond, Dr. O'Brien walked in. "Something happened, Ruby?"

The nurse must've hit the emergency call button. "It's better if I sketch it for you." The nurse sketched the oddly shaped pupil and continued, "When Killian stirred in his sleep, Brenna opened his eyelid and his pupil looked like this. Have you ever seen anything like this before?"

Dr. O'Brien grunted. "No, but that doesn't mean no one has." He moved his gaze to Brenna. "Your Dr. Sid and Dr. Innes have been laying the groundwork for a worldwide dragon doctor network to share information and research. How far along are they?"

"I'm not sure," Brenna answered.

"Then find out," Dr. O'Brien ordered.

She raised her brows. "Shouldn't you reach out to them, since you're the doctor?"

"I'm understaffed and still nursing the remaining few dragon-shifter visitors who came to judge the leadership trial and got injured in the process. I don't have time to make social calls."

She wanted to say such a network would benefit him professionally, but she held back. "Then how about you tell me Killian's lab results so that I have the full picture to share with the Stonefire doctors?"

He shrugged. "There's not a whole lot to tell. All of his readings are normal, with the exception of his dragon-shifter hormones. They were higher than usual."

"Wait, Killian still has dragon-shifter hormones, even without his dragon?"

Dr. O'Brien bobbed his head. "Of course. Dragon present or not, it's part of our biological functions. Much like how if a human has a hormone deficiency, they need to balance it to lead the best life. Dragon-shifter hormones are the same."

"I'm not a doctor, but would giving him a higher dosage maybe bring out his dragon?"

Dr. O'Brien didn't miss a beat. "More likely it would kill him."

"Oh."

"Any other questions? Otherwise, I have patients waiting."

Her dragon spoke up. *Is it just me or has he been grumpier as of late?*

To be honest, I have no idea. I've been too busy with everything else.

"Did you send the results to Stonefire?" Brenna asked. "Because I know Sid and Gregor will want the finer details."

"As soon as Teagan gives her approval, I will."

She nodded, and Dr. O'Brien and the nurse left the room.

Brenna had just sent a text message to Teagan, asking for a short meeting, when Killian's voice filled the room. "So, you're plotting to kill your husband already?"

50

No sooner had the rolling hills and glass-covered lake faded into nothingness when Killian heard Brenna ask, "I'm not a doctor, but would giving him a higher dosage maybe bring out his dragon?"

"More likely it would kill him."

He vaguely listened to the rest of the conversation, but he couldn't push past the fact that even Brenna wished to change him back into the man he'd been.

Rationally, he shouldn't be angry about it. She probably felt obligated to help those who had taken her in and accepted her. What better way to do it than to bring back a central figure to the clan?

And yet, he'd pieced together that the old version of himself had never looked twice in Brenna's direction.

Not that it should matter. Attraction didn't mean anything beyond possibly great sex.

Still, his former life seemed lonely and empty. He had a feeling that even if he regained his memories and/or his dragon, he couldn't go back to that existence of work and nothing else.

If only he could predict what his personality would be at the end of all this.

As the doors closed and silence fell, he pushed past his thoughts and focused on his urge to tease. "So, you're plotting to kill your husband already?"

He opened his eyelids as Brenna's warm hand touched his forehead. He tried not to read too much into the concern in her gaze as she said, "You're finally awake."

"As my eyes are open and I'm talking, that's the easiest explanation."

Sighing, she continued to stroke his skin. "You're making

it quite difficult to be nice to you."

"Nice is boring. I much prefer fire and fury."

She raised her brows. "Did you really just say fire and fury?"

"I thought females liked poetic expressions. It sounds better than angry and screaming."

"If screaming is what you want, I could easily oblige."

The corner of his mouth ticked up. "It would be a waste, though. Because when your cheeks flush with anger, I want nothing but to pin you to the wall and kiss you."

"Killian," she admonished.

"What? I thought honesty was another thing women liked."

"Well, I'm going to be honest as well—the doctors don't know what's wrong with you and that's a bit worrisome."

"But I suspect you have several plans in the works?"

"Maybe."

"And?" he prompted.

"I'm still waiting for approval before I share any of them."

"Considering they're about me, I have a right to know." He paused and added, "You've been forthright with me to date, Brenna. Don't start holding back now."

Emotions warred on her face, as she struggled with what to do. He felt a bit of an arse for questioning her loyalties, but if Brenna started tiptoeing around him, he wasn't sure what he'd do.

Without any ties, it might be easier to leave and start over somewhere else. Then he wouldn't have to worry about what would happen if his memories returned.

Of course, he could also end up unconscious in the middle of the woods and die of exposure.

Brenna sighed. "I can share some of the information, at least. You've been mumbling in your sleep and we've been trying to figure out what they mean."

He frowned. "I didn't think sleep-talking could be used as factual statements."

She rolled her eyes. "I never said that. But sometimes, people mutter useful things in their sleep. And your mutterings ended up being a clue after all. Because when I opened your eyelid, your pupil looked like this."

Flashing a piece of paper toward him, he frowned at the rounded top of the pupil and the bottom, which curved to a point. "What the hell does that mean?"

"I honestly don't know. But I'm working to find out. It's possible that it's related to your inner dragon."

"I think I'd notice if I had a second someone talking inside my head," he stated.

She shook her head. "There are other ways for a dragon to make its presence known. After all, until a dragon-shifter is about six or seven years old, the dragon lurks in the mind and doesn't always come forward."

"Wait, how is that even possible? Your mind hides something from you?"

Brenna huffed. "Look, I'm not a bloody doctor or research scientist. I'm just telling you what I know."

"Let's say you're right, and it's related to this mysterious inner dragon. Does that mean anything?"

"I'm not sure. I'm going to ask some friends of mine for help." Brenna folded the piece of paper and tucked it into a trouser pocket. After quickly checking her mobile phone, she spoke again. "I have a meeting with Teagan soon. After that, I can share more details with you."

"So in the meantime, I just lie here and stare at the ceiling?" he drawled.

Tilting her head, she said, "Instead of complaining, how about making yourself useful?"

"How, exactly? The only thing I was good at since waking up without a memory is lifting heavy objects and kissing you. Right now, I'm unable to do either."

"Are you this infuriating on purpose?"

He shrugged one shoulder. "This is just what comes naturally."

"So, bastard mode is your default. Good to know." Leaning down, she never broke her gaze. "How about you stop belittling yourself and see what you're made of? Lost memory or no, you're intelligent and can figure things out. Use that to help me and your sister."

"How? I don't exactly have top-level clearance."

"Maybe not, but not everything is classified. I have an idea." She picked up a tablet from the nearby side table, tapped it a few times, and turned it toward him. "Let's see how well your memory works for non-personal things. We're trying to figure out how to tighten security against enemies, both living and machine, from ground intrusions as well as ones from the air. See if any weak points jump out at you and we can discuss it when I get back."

He raised an eyebrow. "Aren't you afraid I'll use this information to escape?"

Studying him, she said, "I don't think you will. One, you'll never kiss me again and you want to, as you keep banging on about. And two, I don't think you'd escape without a fully thought-out plan. And in that case, showing you these schematics would make little difference as you'd probably just scout out the perimeter on your own."

Out of curiosity, he took the tablet and glanced at the image. He immediately saw a weak spot.

"So," Brenna prompted, "will you try and see what you come up with?"

"I have nothing better to do," he muttered.

"Good. That's Killian-speak for you're intrigued."

Meeting her eyes again, he frowned. "Since when can you interpret me so well?"

"I've been watching you for months, Killian. Some things about you are the same, even without your dragon or memories."

Killian should avoid the subject, as Brenna's answer could hurt him. But he blurted, "Which version of me is better, now or then?"

"Does it matter?" She moved until her face was close enough her breath danced across his lips. "I mated you as you are."

Her words stirred something inside him. Laying the tablet down, he raised a hand and cupped her cheek. Brenna's pupils changed to slits and back. "What's your dragon saying?"

"I'm not sure I want to tell you."

He stroked her skin. "Honesty, remember?"

For a second, he thought she wouldn't answer. Then she smiled and said, "She says that you may be recovering, but if we straddled you and did most of the work, it would be an easy solution."

Blood rushed to his cock at the image of Brenna's body over his, her breasts bouncing as he guided her hips up and down.

He growled. "I would say that's a brilliant idea, except I don't want our first time to be like that."

"So now you're a romantic?"

"Oh, it's not romantic so much as I want you under me and at my mercy." Brenna's breath hitched. "And I see you like that idea." He released her cheek and motioned toward the tablet. "I'll work on this. I need to keep on your good side, after all."

Moving back, Brenna rolled her eyes. "And here I thought you might be nice to me for longer than thirty seconds."

He grinned. "You mated me as I am, remember."

"I'm going to regret that statement, aren't I?"

"You'll just have to wait and see. A little mystery makes for an interesting marriage, don't you agree?"

"Mating. Marriage is the human term."

"You're changing the subject."

"Since our mating isn't traditional, I can't comment." She took another few steps toward the door. "I need to meet with Teagan. I'll check back after. See if you can stay awake, old man."

She dashed out the door before Killian could reply.

Early thirties wasn't old, but Killian had more important things to worry about than the ten-plus-year age difference between him and Brenna. All he needed was to woo her and coax her into bed. Then she'd see how virile he could be.

But he would have time for that later. For the moment, he glanced down at the schematics on the tablet. Just looking at them brought instant scenarios into his head, almost if he were running through what could happen in twenty different situations.

While he was probably imagining it, Killian sensed he'd done something similar many times in the past. Whether it would help him in the long run, with regard to his memory, he had no idea. All he thought about was Brenna smiling at him for helping and proving he still had worth to both her and the clan.

He blinked. He wasn't a fucking dog, out to please his master.

No, he'd do it for himself. Killian might need to start over at some point, and the better he understood his skills and limits, the easier it would be to pitch himself to a future employer.

CHAPTER FIVE

$\mathcal{T}$wo days later, Brenna sat across from Teagan O'Shea and waited for a response.

Glenlough's leader leaned back in her chair and sighed. "I'm not sure I like either option."

"Well, since neither Dr. Sid nor Gregor have been able to do much from afar, it'd be easier for them to help in person. Since they can't come here, because of the temporary stay for foreign dragon-shifter visitors by the Irish DDA, taking Killian to England will hopefully speed up the process."

"And if I don't agree to that, the other option is to find a way for him to kiss Lorcan's daughter?"

Brenna shrugged. "I don't know if it'll work, but there's a small chance it might."

"Let's say that it did. You'd be okay with that?"

Her dragon spoke up. *I wouldn't.*

Ignoring her beast, Brenna answered, "I promised to help bring Killian back and that's what I'm doing."

Teagan raised an eyebrow. "I think you're full of crap, but I'm not going to waste time arguing. You're a grown female. Besides, my more important question is—are you willing to give up your place as the temporary head Protector on

Glenlough? You may be English by birth, but you more than proved yourself during the clan's recent troubles and I think of you as part of my clan now."

At one time, she'd wanted acceptance more than anything. However, to be a true Protector meant putting duty above most personal desires.

Pushing past the emotion in her throat, Brenna replied, "I spent two days thinking on it. I'm not giving up my dreams forever, but I'm twenty-one years old and can afford to step back for now and work my way into a similar position in the future."

Teagan leaned forward. "Whilst it's noble to stick to your vow, I'm not about to make you give up your career to see it through. I love my brother, but as he is right now, I'm not sure he deserves your dedication."

She sat taller in the chair. "He is a duty like any other, which means I'll see it through to the end."

Teagan opened her mouth, but quickly shut it. Picking up a piece of paper, she laid it in front of Brenna. "Sign this and I'll submit it via fax to the DDA. You should have clearance to visit Stonefire in a day or two."

Staring down at the paper, Brenna hesitated. She put on a brave face and words for Teagan, but the thought of leaving Glenlough made her heart heavy. As long as she remained mated to Killian, she could return. However, if he escaped and filed for a separation, it could be months or years before she could come back, depending on the Irish DDA's whim.

Her dragon grunted. *I don't think Killian will escape. He flirts and stares at us most of the time.*

Lust is not loyalty. I wish you'd remember that.

Her beast huffed. *Regardless, you're hiding a deeper reluctance—to see our parents again.*

Not wanting her dragon to be right, Brenna picked up

a pen off Teagan's desk and signed her name. "There. I'll start making preparations and tell Killian the news. When do you plan on saying your farewells?"

Sadness filled Teagan's eyes. "I'm not sure he'd care one way or the other."

Reaching out a hand, she took Teagan's and squeezed. "He often stares at the photo album you provided and lingers on pictures of you, your mother, and grandmother more than the others. He may not know why, but somewhere deep inside, I think he recognizes you were important to him."

"Maybe. But don't worry, Aaron will make me say goodbye to my brother." Teagan's pupils flashed. "That gives me an idea. Aaron is a brilliant cook and we can have a farewell family dinner. That way, even if things turn awkward, everyone can fill their mouths with food and keep busy. Can you convince Killian to come over to our cottage later?"

"It won't be easy, but I'll find a way."

"Good." Teagan picked up the signed document. "I'll send this straight away. You'd best go since you'll need to brief Lyall O'Dwyer on Protector-related items so he can assume your position, and then tell Killian the news."

Lyall was one of the most experienced and loyal Protectors on Glenlough.

Standing, she nodded. "Thanks, Teagan, for understanding my request."

Teagan smiled. "Don't feel too much gratitude toward me. After all, sending him to Stonefire is highly preferable to him kissing Lorcan's daughter and causing a possible war."

Her dragon growled. *And it means he won't kiss anyone else.*

Seeing as he hasn't kissed us since the mating ceremony,

you seem optimistic he wants to do it at all. After our news, he might want nothing to do with us.

And whose fault is it that he hasn't kissed us again? You've been avoiding him on purpose, only seeing him when others are around.

Brenna finally voiced her concerns to her beast, or the dragon might never be quiet. *Growing attached to him is dangerous. I'll never fulfill my duty that way, as I won't want to help him.*

He's lost amongst a sea of people he doesn't remember. Friendship would do more good than you know.

Brenna had deduced the same, but didn't want to risk friendship turning into anything more. Killian's future was unpredictable and she needed to guard her heart and feelings. Especially given her history of becoming obsessed with a male and the ensuing dereliction of her duties, like with Cedric in the army.

Focusing back on Teagan, Brenna waved goodbye. "We'll be over around seven. And tell Aaron not to make fish. I can't stand it."

"Good thing you're telling me and not him, otherwise he'd make it on purpose to spite you. I swear he lives to irritate those he cares about."

At the love shining in Teagan's eyes as she spoke of her mate, a small tinge of jealousy flared. Maybe someday she'd have what Aaron and Teagan had—a love between partners, who each made the other better.

Not wanting to waste time thinking of something that would happen far in the future, Brenna murmured her parting and exited the room. She'd handle the Protectors first. That way, Killian would have less time to come up with an excuse as to why he wouldn't go to dinner.

Because even if she had to tie him up and toss him in a wheelbarrow to get him to Teagan's cottage, she'd do it.

Teagan and her family deserved the chance to say goodbye.

Her dragon spoke up. *Funny you think that now. You didn't say goodbye to Mum and Dad three years ago.*

Only because Mum would've locked us up and sent us to relatives in Italy to keep us from joining the army.

I suppose none of that matters now. However, signing the document means you're going to have to face them again.

I'll worry about that when the time comes.

⌀⌀⌀⌀

Killian eyed Teagan O'Shea's cottage in the distance with irritation. "There is no reason for them to wish me farewell. I don't remember any of them."

Brenna matched his strides toward the cottage. "That's not the point. This is for them, not us. And if you don't attend, you don't leave, end of story."

He grunted. "Maybe I don't want to leave."

She looked at him askance. "You were all but giddy earlier, when I told you we were going to England."

The news of him going somewhere new, even for a short while, would give him more time to figure things out. As much as he understood his supposed family wanting to help him, everyone walking on eggshells and pretending to be perfectly fine was driving him crazy. The grandmother was the only one who wasn't shy about voicing an opinion, but even she would often remind him of how he had been.

But he kept his excitement at bay and feigned boredom. "I don't become giddy. You mistook my happiness at finally seeing my wife again as me being excited for this bloody trip."

Brenna had spent most of the last few days away, doing things with the Protectors. He hated how much his mood depended on whether the woman was near him or not.

His only hope was for the Stonefire doctors to run their stupid tests, proclaim his case incurable, and then everyone would allow him to decide his own life.

Brenna replied, "I mated you, yes, but that doesn't mean I'm going to wait on you hand and foot."

"There's a difference between doting on me and avoiding me. You've been doing the latter."

"I've been busy. It happens."

Her tone signaled the conversation was over, but Killian wasn't about to let her avoid the topic forever. He gently gripped her wrist and they both stopped walking. "People will talk, darling. You'd better start paying me some attention."

Tilting her head, she said, "In front of your family? You sure you want that?"

Leaning down, he whispered in her ear, "And if I said yes?"

"I'd call you crazy." She tugged her wrist and he released it. "Let's just survive this dinner, okay?"

Brenna turned and marched to the cottage door.

Something had happened, but he wasn't sure of what. Maybe going to her home in England would give her the freedom to avoid him, since Stonefire would most likely protect her and no one would think of betraying their fake mating to any DDA officials.

Or, she possibly had a man she fancied back home, banishing any thoughts of kissing or more with Killian so she could try to win the nameless bloke.

Whatever it was, he didn't like the cool distance she'd put between them. Considering they'd have to be in a car, a ferry, and driving again in the car to reach Stonefire—apparently, dragons rarely rode in airplanes—it would give him a chance to learn a few of her secrets.

Not that he should care about learning any of her secrets. She was a means to an end, and nothing more. True, he'd love to fuck her once or twice and walk away, but that was it.

He reached the cottage door a second behind Brenna, and the door swung inward. Aaron Caruso's black-haired, olive-toned form looked straight at Killian. Without preamble, the male said, "Act too much of a bastard, and I'll kick you out of this cottage. Understood?"

Killian growled, but Brenna stepped between them. "You could try saying this is difficult for everyone involved instead of issuing threats, Aaron." She looked at Killian. "And remember, you promised to behave. That was the deal for leaving tomorrow instead of a few days from now."

"As long as this bloke minds his manners, I'll do the same," Killian muttered.

He expected Aaron to issue a challenge, but the male merely nodded. "That should make Teagan happy."

Brenna pushed Aaron to the side. "Then let us inside. I'm starving."

With little other choice, Killian followed Brenna's lead. He barely noted the stacks of items on tables and bookcases in the hallway as he steeled himself for the upcoming dinner. With no doctors or passersby watching, who knew what might happen.

They entered the dining room and all eyes turned toward him.

Caitlin, Orla, and Teagan sat around a table. He barely noted Brenna sliding into one of the empty chairs before Teagan spoke up. "You may as well sit down, Killian. Unless you plan to stand all evening?"

He crossed his arms over his chest. "Considering I don't want to be here, I'm tempted to do just that."

Brenna rolled her eyes. "Sit down, Killian. Knowing

Teagan, she'll postpone dinner until you sit, and you're only prolonging the evening with your defiance."

"Defiance is the only thing I seem to have left," he grumbled, sliding into the seat next to hers.

"Defiance only causes more issues in the long run, Killian," Caitlin said. "It's fine to be angry, but you shouldn't take it out on others who don't deserve it."

It was on the tip of his tongue to say he wasn't a child, but Caitlin's kind, patient eyes stopped him from doing so. Out of all of his supposed family, she had been the nicest and most understanding, and she didn't deserve his temper.

Aaron disappeared through a door and Teagan spoke again. "Look, I understand you don't want to be here. We're just people you see in pictures, part of memories you no longer have. But I signed off on you leaving the clan for a while, so all I ask is for you to behave for an hour or two and stop trying to pick a fight. I would be angry, too, if I couldn't remember who I was. But anger won't solve your problems. Hopefully the Stonefire doctors can, though."

He raised an eyebrow. "This is the most forthright you've been with me since the first day I met you, with no memory. Why act this way now?"

She shrugged. "I have nothing to lose. You'll be Stonefire's problem soon enough. And clearly the soft approach hasn't worked with you, so I'm trying something different."

Before he could reply, Orla chimed in. "I know you're a grown male, but be careful on the journey. We still don't know the particulars about who took you or why, and there's always a possibility they'll try to snatch you or even Brenna on your travels."

He looked around the room. "I would assume our transfer wasn't public knowledge."

Teagan waved a hand in dismissal. "It's not. But both the British and Irish Department of Dragon Affairs know about the transfer. Given the rocky history of the British DDA and betrayals in recent years, I wouldn't dismiss an undercover spy in one agency or the other. Preparation and caution will only go so far in such cases."

Aaron returned, carrying a roast on a platter. Placing it on the table, he grunted and said, "The bloody dragon hunters or Dragon Knights don't seem to want to give up, no matter how many times they're caught or arrested."

Teagan smiled at her male. "We managed to keep the hunters from setting up a base in the northern part of the Republic of Ireland. That's something."

No matter how much Aaron irritated him, Killian had to admit he and Teagan cared about each other. Just watching them gave him a toothache from all the sugary sweetness.

Brenna squeezed his thigh under the table and he glanced at her. She mouthed, "Be nice."

Orla's voice carried across the table. "So what are you two going to do about your mating in England? Can you trust that lot? Because I must admit, most of the time you two look as if you're trying to purposefully avoid touching the other. And then you go and make small gestures, like reassuring Killian just now. What is actually going on between you two? I want the truth."

"Mother," Caitlin admonished.

Brenna's gaze swung to Orla. "I didn't think dissecting my personal life was part of the agenda."

Orla clicked her tongue. "When it puts my granddaughter's reputation on the line, it is."

Teagan clapped her hands. "Stop it. I trust Brenna, and that should be enough, Gran."

Orla shook her head. "I still say letting him kiss the Todd girl would've been easier."

Killian frowned. "What are you talking about?" Teagan shared a glance with Aaron, and Killian noticed Brenna go unnaturally still at his side. "Someone tell me what the fuck you're hiding. I have a feeling it's to do with me, right? Then I deserve to know." Brenna pulled her hand from his leg, but he gripped her wrist. "What happened to honesty?"

She finally met his gaze, but it was unreadable. For a second, he thought she'd keep silent. Then she cleared her throat and said, "While just a theory, kissing your true mate might bring back your inner dragon."

"And you just happen to have a database of true mates on hand, to find this woman?" Killian demanded.

Brenna shook her head. "There's no such thing. But you discovered who she was years ago, and kept your distance."

He frowned. "Why? Is she a horrible person?"

Teagan jumped in. "By all accounts, Georgiana Todd is a lovely female. But she is the daughter of a current foe, the leader of Clan Northcastle in Northern Ireland. We were at odds with Northcastle back then, too. Kissing her would cause a mountain of trouble."

Killian released Brenna's wrist and stood. "And you lot decided to make this decision without me? That's a bastard move considering it could fix my situation within seconds."

Brenna stood and turned toward him. "Odd that you're upset about this now, when you've been going on about not wanting to return to whatever wanker you were before."

Leaning close, he whispered, "I'm tired of this half-life everyone is forcing upon me. Either let me kiss this woman, or let me forge a new path as I am."

"The Stonefire doctors can help you better than a kiss can. I'd rather negotiate for that," Brenna stated.

Brenna was close enough that her breath tickled his chin. Even though he was angry, his body was more aware of her scent and heat so close to him.

If she hadn't fucking betrayed him, he'd kiss her.

Caitlin's voice broke the spell. "I agree you should see the

Stonefire doctors, but I might be able to get Lorcan Todd to allow Killian to kiss his daughter once, as well as form a treaty of sorts with our clan."

"Don't, Caitlin," Orla warned.

Killian forced his gaze from Brenna to the woman who claimed to be his mother. She added, "It's the easiest solution and one I should've done years ago. I'm done hiding and allowing everyone else in my family to help the clan."

"What are you talking about?" Brenna asked.

Caitlin took a deep breath and said, "Lorcan Todd once proposed an alliance, on one condition—that I agree to be his mate. Since he's still without one, he might still be open to the proposal, especially since he secretly sends me flowers every year on my birthday."

"Mam—" Teagan began.

"No, Teagan. You've enough on your plate, what with you trying to placate the DDA by getting all the Irish clans to sign a peace treaty. Northcastle will be an important ally, and having them at our back may convince the rest of Ireland to join with us. I need to do this and mate their clan leader."

Killian jumped in. "You'd do that for me?"

Caitlin smiled warmly. "Of course I would. You're my son, Killian."

Orla growled. "How do you know Lorcan won't mistreat you? We know little about him, apart from the fact he's a thief."

Shaking her head, Caitlin replied, "He sends notes every year, accompanying the flowers, and they're always kind. If we were younger, I'd almost think I was his true mate and he was trying to woo me."

"Why did you never mention this before, Mam?" Teagan asked.

"I'm a private person, Teagan. You know that. Besides, I was afraid if I mentioned it, I might be forced away. I was nothing more than a coward."

Teagan leaned over and touched her mother's hand. "I would never force you to do anything you didn't want to, Mam. You don't have to do this."

Caitlin met Killian's gaze again. "But I do, for Killian's sake."

A woman he'd been less than courteous to was now willing to upend her life to help him.

If only he could remember her.

A boom reverberated inside his head and he clapped his hands over his ears. People were talking, but another boom sounded, and his skull felt as if it were being ripped in two.

He'd barely slid to his knees before an even louder sound echoed inside his head and the world went dark.

CHAPTER SIX

*B*renna kneeled next to Killian's body and checked his pulse. At the steady beat, she let out the breath she'd been holding. "He's alive."

Caitlin joined her, kneeling on Killian's other side. "I thought Dr. O'Brien cleared him."

"He did," Brenna answered. "But he also said Killian's condition was unpredictable. Given this has happened twice now, there might be a link concerning what caused it."

"Let me know if anything changes. I'm going to call Dr. O'Brien," Teagan said as she and Aaron went into the kitchen.

Caitlin brushed the hair off her son's forehead. "Then it's decided, I'll reach out to Lorcan and arrange the kiss. I can't stand my son suffering like this."

"And if it doesn't work?" Brenna asked softly.

"I have faith in your Stonefire doctors. The female one knows what it's like to lose a dragon, she, more than anyone, will do her best to bring his beast back," Caitlin replied.

Brenna tore her gaze from Killian's face to study Caitlin. The quiet female was proving to be stronger than she'd initially realized. "Everyone says Teagan and Killian get

69

their strength from their grandmother, but I think some of it is from you, too."

Shaking her head, Caitlin murmured, "No. Any mother would do the same for their child."

It was on the tip of Brenna's tongue to say that wasn't true, but she held back.

Killian stirred and Brenna focused back on her mate. His eyes fluttered open, his gaze meeting hers. "Why am I on the floor?"

"Tell us what happened and I might be able to work it out."

Rubbing his temples, he said, "I don't know. There was a loud booming sound inside my head. Next thing I know, I woke up here."

Brenna stilled. "What kind of booming sound?"

"I'm not sure. Almost like someone was banging a pot against a door. Why?"

Her heart rate kicked up. "I don't want to get your hopes up."

"But?" he prompted.

"But Dr. Sid endured years of banging in her head before her dragon finally broke free."

"Isn't she the one who regained her dragon by kissing her true mate?"

"Yes."

His gaze shifted to Caitlin. "Then I need your help. I don't know how I'll repay you, but if kissing one woman will end this, I will do whatever it takes to do so."

Caitlin glanced at Brenna, an apology in her eyes. "I'll contact Lorcan straight away."

Brenna's dragon spoke up. *This is a bad idea.*

No, it's the best path forward at the moment.

And if the frenzy breaks free?

Then so be it.

Her beast huffed. *Someday, you'll realize that always being noble comes at a cost.*

This is the right thing to do, dragon.

Not wanting an argument, she tossed her beast into a mental prison. "Do you think you can stand, Killian?"

"I have a headache, but I'll live."

"Are you sure?" Caitlin asked. "Maybe we should wait for the doctor."

Killian gave a derisive laugh. "No offense, but he has no idea of how to deal with my condition." Killian sat up slowly. "The best thing you can do is ask for Lorcan's help as soon as possible."

With a nod, Caitlin stood. "I'll do it now."

Before anyone else could say a word, Caitlin exited the room.

A second later, Orla banged her cane against the ground, obviously not caring about Killian's wince in response. "I have a feeling my daughter will need me shortly. Since no one seems to want to listen to me, I'm sure Brenna can handle the situation."

Before Brenna could do more than open her mouth, Orla had also left.

Since dragon-shifters had supersensitive hearing, no doubt Teagan had heard everything from the kitchen. The fact the female wasn't storming back into the dining room told Brenna she had to approve of the idea. Or, at least had accepted it.

Brenna put out a hand and helped Killian to his feet. He stumbled a second, and she grabbed his arms to steady him.

Simply touching his skin sent a rush of awareness through her body, instantly raising her body temperature. Allowing Killian to kiss another female wouldn't be easy. Maybe she could find a logical excuse as to why she didn't have to watch it.

Her dragon banged against her prison, but it held. Focusing back on the present, Brenna whispered to Killian's chest, "You might soon be a whole person again."

He placed a finger under her chin and forced her to meet his unreadable gaze. "Even if my dragon returns, I'm not sure I can forget you, Brenna."

Not wanting to entertain the impossible, she gave a strangled laugh. "Does it matter? Not five minutes ago, you were furious with me for keeping information from you."

Stroking the underside of her chin, he murmured, "And to a degree, I still am. But regardless of what happens with the Northcastle woman, I doubt it'll be anything like this."

He lowered his head and kissed her.

If Brenna were a stronger person, she'd push him away. Their futures were not meant to be together.

But as Killian wrapped an arm around her waist and pulled her up against his body, she sighed, and his tongue slid into her mouth.

Each lick, caress, and nip only made her body warmer, and she threaded the fingers of one hand through his hair and took the kiss deeper.

He lifted her leg up and ground against her core. Gasping, she broke the kiss, but Killian only took her lips again, never ceasing the motion of his hips.

The friction of her trousers against her clit only pushed her closer to orgasm. All she needed was another minute, and she'd come. True, she'd much prefer Killian naked and inside her, but since this could be her last chance to kiss him, she hugged him closer and increased the pace of her own body.

She was so close. Digging her nails into Killian's scalp, he growled and nipped her bottom lip. Just as she was about to retaliate, Teagan's voice carried across the room. "I'm not sure now is the best time for that."

Brenna ended the kiss and tried to back away, but Killian never released his grip on her waist. He whispered, "Never be ashamed for wanting a male, Brenna."

With him so close, his hard muscles pressing against her front, she couldn't think. As long as his heat and scent surrounded her, she'd be ineffective at decision making, not to mention fulfilling her duties.

And no doubt, if she were alone with him again, she'd cave and welcome his attentions once more.

She needed to get away from Killian in order to help him properly.

She pushed again and he finally let her go. After staring at Killian for a second, she looked to Teagan. "I'm sorry, but I can't be his guard any longer. You'll have to find someone else."

Turning around, she rushed out of the room and then the cottage.

Her lips were still slightly swollen from Killian's kiss and she resisted the urge to touch them with her fingers. She'd been kissed before and she should be able to forget him.

And yet, she couldn't. If anything, she craved more.

Much like what had happened when she'd been newly arrived in the army, which meant she'd do anything for Killian's touch.

No. The memory reminded her of how desire could make her do stupid things. She wasn't about to repeat her mistakes.

Pushing her body harder, she ran toward her home on Glenlough, the wind against her cheeks helping to cool her body and reinforce what had to be done.

Killian wasn't meant to be hers.

Georgiana Todd was a much better option for him. Not only could the female possibly make Killian whole again, a mate-claim frenzy would also force Brenna to keep her distance from the male. It was the best solution for all.

And yet, the idea didn't sit well in her stomach.

No. She wouldn't let a feeling derail her life once more. Killian would kiss Georgiana, and Brenna would move on, end of story.

⌒⌒⌒⌒⌒

The door had barely closed behind Brenna when Teagan's voice garnered his attention. "You're a bastard, Killian." He met her gaze and she continued. "That female has fancied you for months, and here you are about to kiss your true mate, and you give her false hope. I should knock you out cold right now for how you're treating her."

He ignored the sting of Teagan's words. "You know nothing of my motives."

Teagan raised her brows. "Then enlighten me."

Running his fingers through his hair, he growled. "Do you think I want to kiss some nameless woman and possibly enter this frenzy mess, and end up impregnating a stranger? Believe me, given the choice, that is the last thing I want."

"And what do you want?"

"Does it matter? Things have already been set in motion, and if we change them, it will only make things worse."

She waved toward the door Brenna had exited. "I'm sure what you want matters to her. You can act the bastard all you like, but you soften when Brenna is nearby."

"So what? You've been going on about how I need my memories and my dragon. I finally agree to your plans and now I'm the bastard? Ever since I woke up like this, you've put me on this path. If anyone is at fault for hurting Brenna, it's you, Teagan."

As he stared into green eyes similar to his own, Killian wondered if Teagan would be truthful with him or simply dismiss him and claim she had leader duties to attend.

Not everything was her fault, after all. But he was too upset to be rational.

When she spoke, her voice was soft. "You're right. I just miss my brother, and I might have lost sight of everything else with the goal of getting him back."

He blinked. "Well, I wasn't expecting that."

"It's true. While Aaron is now one of the pillars of my life, you should be one, too. And yet, you're not truly here and it kills me."

At the sadness in her voice, Killian's anger faded. "I'm not this way by choice."

She nodded. "I know." Teagan cleared her throat. "So, tell me, what do you want? Don't tell me what I want to hear. Tell me the truth."

He debated his next words before saying, "I think I want to try and get my memories back. However, if kissing the Todd woman doesn't work, I'll give the Stonefire doctors two weeks to help. After that, you allow me to start a new life, the best I can, which means stop meddling in my life or placing extra restrictions on what I do or say."

She crossed her arms over her chest. "So far, that seems reasonable. Anything else?"

"I think it's best if Brenna keeps her distance from me as much as possible. When she's near, I want her. And that will only lead to hurting her."

Teagan shook her head. "That will be harder to do, Killian. Brenna is the reason you can travel to the UK at all. If she doesn't go, the DDA could be finicky and say you should stay in Ireland; they would love the excuse to punish my clan after recent events. Or, if they catch you alone, you could even end up in prison."

An hour ago, he probably would've cursed and said he'd think of his own idea. However, Teagan was being honest and trying to help him. He owed her more than that. "If I have to be near her, then there's only one thing I can do."

"Which is?"

"I need to learn to control my emotions so Brenna won't know how she affects me. Can you teach me a few tricks?"

The woman studied him a second before saying, "While I'm happy you're asking for help, I'm uneasy about doing this to Brenna."

He resisted a growl. "Do you have any other suggestions?"

Aaron joined them and said, "How about just telling her the truth? Deceit usually backfires in a spectacular way. Brenna is an adult. Lay out rules and try to follow them."

Teagan rolled her eyes. "Because your rules worked so well in the beginning, what with 'this is sex for one night only' rubbish."

Aaron frowned. "If I recall, Killian's phone call is what interrupted the night. Who knows what would've happened if he hadn't done so. I might've followed our rule."

Teagan narrowed her eyes. "Right, I'm sure that's how it would've worked out." She looked at Killian again. "It couldn't hurt to give you a little training. After all, it'll be easy to keep your distance from Brenna until you leave, and Gran can give you at least one coaching session before you depart in the morning. If my mother is successful with negotiating with Lorcan, then you may only have a few hours in each other's company. I'm sure both of you can resist each other for a short while."

The thought of kissing anyone but Brenna didn't sit well with him, but he pushed aside the feeling. "And if kissing that Northcastle woman doesn't work?"

Teagan shrugged a shoulder. "Then I'm afraid you'll have to go to Stonefire and discuss what happens there with Brenna."

"So my choices are either kiss a stranger and possibly

end up with a child at the end of it, or spend weeks living with the woman I'm supposed to keep my distance from," Killian bit out.

"I'm afraid so," Teagan stated. "But if the kiss with Georgiana Todd doesn't work, then who knows what will happen. Maybe Brenna can be yours after all."

"I never said I wanted her forever," Killian grunted out.

Aaron took a few steps closer to Killian. "Don't you fucking hurt my cousin. Because if you do and you come back here, then I'm going to make your life hell."

Teagan stepped between them. "Just stop it, you two. If I ever have children, I hope they're girls. The last thing I need is more testosterone in my life."

Killian retreated to the far side of the room and paced. "So what happens now?"

Teagan leaned against Aaron's side. "You wait here until our mother contacts us. Then we can start making more concrete plans."

Unable to stand still, Killian paced the room. He couldn't wait for the day when he didn't need to rely on so many people just to live his life.

The pacing gave him time to remember his kiss with Brenna. What he wouldn't give to have that every day.

No. She deserved better than a man who could fall unconscious at any moment, and who might not ever wake up. The best thing for everyone was for Killian to fulfill Teagan's requirements and work on controlling his emotions. He doubted he'd ever be able to fully hide his longing for Brenna's touch, but he was going to do the best he could.

～○～○～○

Caitlin O'Shea sat inside one of the private conference

rooms located in the Protectors central command building and plucked at her trouser leg.

Waiting to see if Lorcan would answer her message and contact her via video conference wasn't easy. She could handle the rejection if it weren't for Killian. She'd do almost anything to ensure her son had a chance at being happy once again.

Shifting in her seat, she resisted looking at the clock again. It'd been less than half an hour since she'd called Northcastle's main contact number. The female on the other end had ensured she'd pass along the strange message.

Her dragon spoke up. *If we had my way, we would've flown and risked the DDA.*

You're not being helpful.

Caitlin went back to plucking the material of her trousers and started humming a tune.

Her mother had offered to sit in, but she'd declined. After all, this was her decision and her life. She wasn't about to let anyone else speak for her.

The video conference app chimed, displaying Northcastle's name. For a second, she froze. Accepting the call possibly meant uprooting her life and moving to a clan full of strangers.

Then she remembered Killian's cry of pain and his unconsciousness, and it fortified her resolve. Her son had spent years protecting her. She needed to do this for him.

Clicking the Receive button, she instantly recognized the face that appeared as Lorcan Todd's.

She'd only seen him a few times in recent years, but his short, light gray hair and mismatched eyes—one brown and one blue—were the same. As was his strong jaw and broad shoulders.

In other words, he was as handsome as she'd remembered.

Her dragon spoke up. *I still don't understand why you've*

spurned him for so many years.

Not now, dragon.

Lorcan raised his silver eyebrows. "I must say I was surprised to hear you wanted to talk to me, what with you ignoring my previous attempts to contact you."

Drawing on years of raising two strong-willed children, Caitlin sat tall and forced her voice to be strong. "I'm talking to you now."

"That you are. Care to tell me about what? If there's one thing I know about your family, a call from you lot never comes without a request."

She decided to get straight to the point before she lost her nerve. "You once offered a treaty between our clans, with a few conditions. I want to know if that offer still stands."

"So Teagan is having her mother speak for her now?"

"Don't disrespect my daughter. I'm sure you wouldn't stand it for yours."

He studied her a second and Caitlin wondered if she'd just lost her only chance to help her son. Unlike her mother and daughter, she had no experience with political negotiations. If that was what Lorcan was looking for, she might be in over her head.

Lorcan's deep voice filled her ears. "I always sensed there was steel behind the gentleness. I'm glad to see that I was right."

Before she could stop herself, she blurted, "Only when it comes to my children and family."

"And that, Caitlin, is not a negative. We should always look out for our children."

Her stomach churned. Maybe Lorcan wouldn't agree to her plan after all.

He continued, "If you were referring to my previous condition, about a treaty in exchange for a mating, I'm open to the idea. But I won't force it. I've learned my lesson on those grounds."

She frowned. "What do you mean?"

"Maybe someday I'll tell you, but not now. What is it you want, Caitlin? Just tell me straight."

Lorcan's eyes were gentle, as if coaxing her to tell him her secrets. She had a feeling the trait came in handy when leading his clan. "What I'm about to tell you must remain a secret. If I get wind that you've shared it, then everything I'm about to propose will be called off." He nodded and she continued. "Killian has lost his memory and his dragon. Your daughter may be the key to bringing him back."

He frowned. "What are you talking about?"

Taking a deep breath, she answered, "Killian was kidnapped for a day and drugged. He came back as I described, with no memory and no inner beast."

"I'm sorry for that, Caitlin, I am. But how does my daughter fit into it all?"

"Well, we know of one dragon-shifter who lost her dragon regained it by kissing her true mate. I don't know if Georgiana ever sensed it or not, but she and Killian are true mates. Or, at least they were. I'm not sure how things stand now, with my son changed."

"And you want Killian to kiss my daughter."

"Yes."

He paused and finally spoke again. "That's why Killian disappeared several years ago, when I came to visit your clan, with my daughter in tow. He was keeping his distance and that was why Teagan had to reveal herself."

She bobbed her head. "He didn't want to cause any trouble, so we kept Killian hidden away."

"You should've just told me the truth."

"Because I'm sure that would've worked out so well," she said dryly.

The corner of Lorcan's mouth ticked up. "My, my, there

is more to you than a pretty face, Caitlin O'Shea."

She fought a blush at Lorcan's words and the appreciation in his eyes. "We were talking about my son and your daughter."

His face instantly returned to a neutral expression. "She won't want the frenzy, that I can tell you."

"Killian doesn't, either. But it's happened before, with two dragon-shifters kissing their true mate and being held apart long enough to allow it to fade."

Granted, both parties would be in physical pain for weeks, possibly even months, and would probably have to drug their dragons into silence at first.

She stilled. *What am I doing?* How could she even ask Lorcan to put his daughter through such pain.

She opened her mouth to apologize, but Lorcan beat her to it. "And in exchange for agreeing to this, you want to offer yourself up as my mate?"

She nodded, and Lorcan fell silent.

If she were a stronger person, she would dismiss the idea and end the call. But with each second that ticked by, she thought maybe her sacrifice would help Killian after all.

It was a big ask, her request. But she didn't have any other choice.

Lorcan finally spoke again. "I need to talk with my daughter. This is her decision."

"Of course."

"Then stand by for my call. I'm going to talk with her right now and give you an answer."

The screen turned dark and Caitlin slumped in her chair. She was no closer to securing Killian's future than before. On top of that, she had to talk with Lorcan again. The next conversation might be even more difficult if his daughter said no.

Her dragon spoke up. *He's not that bad. And that's*

not true, about Killian's future. Lorcan could've said no straight away.

Maybe. I still feel awful for what his daughter could endure, if the true mate link still exists.

It may not, and then our number of solutions dwindle.

Caitlin's phone beeped, and she barely glanced at her mother's message. She wasn't about to share anything until she had an answer.

Not wanting to fret over a decision beyond her control, she needed a distraction.

She pulled up information about the area surrounding Belfast, where Northcastle was located. While there was a huge lake nearby—Lough Neagh—that she'd always wanted to swim in, being so close to Belfast and its roughly half a million humans living in or near it caused any number of dangerous situations to run through her head. After all, her mate had died at the hands of humans.

And not only that, there was a dragon hunter base not far from Clan Northcastle.

Maybe moving there would be a worse idea than she'd originally thought.

Her dragon spoke up. *Lorcan keeps his clan safe. Things will be different, but maybe we need a change of scenery.*

What are you talking about?

Well, our children are grown and soon both will hopefully lead full and happy lives. Mother is busy helping Teagan, and our mate passed away a long time ago. Living in a new place may help us find a new purpose. After all, fifty-five is young enough still to do many things.

What about the children we watch? Their parents rely on the daycare center.

Your assistants are more than capable of taking over.

You just want to stretch your wings and travel.

Maybe.

The video conference app rang again. She clicked Receive in the next beat, revealing Lorcan's unreadable face.

"Well?" Caitlin asked. "Please don't keep me waiting."

He grunted. "As long as Killian doesn't expect a frenzy and will be kept away until it fades, Georgiana has agreed to help. I'm assuming you want this done as soon as possible?" She bobbed her head. "I checked into it and know he's mated to an English dragon-shifter and can freely travel. I'll put in the request tonight with the DDA about our mating. Someone owes me a favor, so the pair of you can come the day after tomorrow."

Her heart skipped a beat. "So soon?"

Lorcan raised his brows. "Have you changed your mind?"

Even though he was giving her a choice, she didn't really have one. "No."

"Then the sooner the better." His voice softened. "And don't worry, you'll have time to acclimate. While you do that, you can help hash out the details of the treaty."

"But Teagan is the negotiator, not me."

"She will have the final approval. However, you will help draft the agreement."

She blinked. "You want me to help you? I have no experience in that kind of thing."

He smiled warmly. "Knowing your clan is an asset, Caitlin. You'll do fine. Unless there's anything else, I have much to do to set this all in motion."

She shook her head. "No, that's all for now."

"Good. Then I'll send the final details to Teagan. I look forward to talking with you under more relaxed circumstances, Caity. Good night."

The screen went blank and Caitlin tried her best to tame her thumping heart. Lorcan via video conference was all business with only a rare glimpse of the male who'd sent her flowers and notes. She only hoped the softer side of him came out more with time. Otherwise, she was in for yet another battle of wills in her life.

And she wasn't sure if she had the strength to handle another alpha personality, especially one she was supposed to spend the rest of her life with.

⌒◡⌒◡◡⌒◡

Brenna finished her hundredth crunch and lay on her back, staring at the ceiling of her bedroom on Glenlough. A few weeks ago, she'd wanted nothing more than for Killian to kiss her. And here she was, running away from him and trying to think of ways to keep her distance.

Her dragon grunted. *Part of me thinks it's because you don't want to go to Northcastle and risk seeing Cedric.*

Cedric Templeton was the male who'd manipulated Brenna during her army days. *Not true. I couldn't care less about him. Watching Killian kiss another female, however, is too much.*

Then you finally admit you want him, too?

She'd been waging this battle with her dragon for days, trying to deny the truth, but no longer. *Yes. But it doesn't mean I won't do what I've been doing, in that I have to protect my heart and my future.*

Even if Killian kisses the female, I can't see him agreeing to the frenzy.

If the old version of him returns, he might. Remember, he was nobler than we'd ever be and took duty to the extreme.

Her dragon shook her head. *And to think, that was one of the reasons he caught your eye before.*

Maybe. But after seeing the less restrained version of him...I'm not sure I can ever look at old Killian the same way again. He's so much more alive now than before.

84

Alive in a way you wish you were. You try to convince yourself that work is the answer, but sometimes, it's not.

A knock on the front door of her cottage echoed through the house. She said to her beast, *We'll finish this discussion later.*

With a sigh, Brenna stood and went to the door. If Killian were on the other side, she wasn't sure how she'd act.

Taking a deep breath, she opened it and blinked at the female standing there. "Caitlin?"

The older woman smiled. "May I come in?"

Stepping aside, Brenna motioned toward the living room. "Of course. But I can't say that I'm at my most social right now."

"I don't think any of us are," Caitlin murmured. Brenna was about to press for more details when Caitlin continued, "Lorcan's daughter has agreed to kiss Killian."

She searched the female's gaze. "I'm not sure why you're telling me this. I told Teagan I didn't want to be his guard any longer."

Caitlin tilted her head, her long, black- and gray-streaked hair falling over one shoulder. "I think you understand why I'm telling you this news."

Brenna shifted her feet. She was used to people demanding answers or giving orders. She wasn't sure how to respond to Caitlin's kind, inquisitive gaze.

Thankfully the older female spoke up again. "Teagan will give you all the details, but you will be accompanying me and Killian the day after tomorrow. Before you say you don't want to, just know that you're the only reason Killian can travel to Northern Ireland without special permission in the current climate."

Rather than think of spending time alone with Killian, let alone watching him kiss another female, she focused on Caitlin's role. "You being here and telling me this must

85

mean that you're going to mate the leader of Northcastle."

She smiled. "Yes. I don't have the skills to fight an actual battle, nor do I possess any sort of political acumen. But I can at least do this."

Brenna touched the older female's arm. "A clan needs all sorts of members, Caitlin. If it only consisted of fighters and politicians, I'm sure we'd be extinct by now."

Caitlin laughed. "You're probably right." She sobered. "I have no right to ask anything of you, but I hope you don't give up on my son. I think you care for him, and he desperately needs that right now."

It took everything she had not to look away. "He has all of you."

"It's not the same. We keep seeing who he used to be. You accept him as he is now. For a male lost in the world, that is a tremendous thing." Brenna opened her mouth to reply, but Caitlin continued, "But don't worry, you won't have to see him until the day after tomorrow."

Brenna should thank Caitlin and ask her to leave. Killian's condition shouldn't matter.

Liar, her dragon growled.

Ignoring her beast, Brenna blurted, "You'll let me know if Killian falls unconscious again?"

Or worse was left unsaid.

"Of course. Dr. O'Brien will keep the Stonefire doctors apprised of the situation as well. The more information they have, the more likely they can help him."

"So you don't think the true mate kiss will work?"

"I don't know, honestly. But I'd rather be prepared." Caitlin took her hand and squeezed. "You're a fine female, Brenna. I hope you can stay on Glenlough and help look after my family."

At the sadness in Caitlin's eyes, Brenna engulfed the female in a hug. "I will, but you'll visit and probably call more often than any of them will want."

"Maybe," Caitlin whispered.

She pulled back. "Look, agreeing to stay here initially was difficult for me. I gave up everything I knew and had no idea when I might return to Stonefire. But now Glenlough feels like home and I can't imagine staying away forever. You might one day feel the same way about Northcastle. I would hazard to guess that you never would've agreed to mate Lorcan unless you believed him to be a somewhat good male."

The older female bobbed her head. "I think he is. I've never heard anything bad or had any warning signs from my dragon when I interacted with him in the past. But at the end of the day, all we can do is wait and see what happens."

Brenna released Caitlin. "Should I put the kettle on for some tea?"

"No, no, that's unnecessary. I have much to do before my departure." She paused and added, "Thank you, Brenna, for your encouragement. I love my family, but they handle situations differently than I would in most circumstances. Sometimes, a person just needs a hug and a set of ears to listen."

Smiling, she said, "My father is the same way. Maybe someday you'll meet him and gain an ally against all of us alpha personalities."

Brenna and Caitlin said their goodbyes. The second Brenna closed the door, she leaned against it and closed her eyes. *By avoiding my mother, I'm starting to realize how much I abandoned Dad.*

We will have time to make up for it.

I hope so. I miss him.

And Mum, although you'll deny it with your last breath.

Not wanting to think of the arguments she'd had over the years with her mother, Brenna opened her eyes and headed

87

toward her bedroom. She probably wouldn't sleep a wink, but she'd at least try. Otherwise, she would spend the night thinking of what was to come.

Of course, if she did fall asleep, she might dream of Killian.

She wasn't sure which would be worse.

CHAPTER SEVEN

Two days later, Killian sat in the back seat of a car with his mother, trying his best to avoid looking at Brenna's profile in the driver's seat.

For a little over two hours, they'd all remained quiet during the journey to Clan Northcastle. Even going across the border from Ireland to Northern Ireland had been uneventful. Putting aside there was no formal border checkpoint between the two countries, the DDA and local police officers would often keep an eye out for any cars traveling from Glenveagh National Park. He'd been told that many people were pulled over and checked, as a precaution, to ensure dragon-shifters weren't trying to travel without authorization.

He should be grateful for the smoothness of the journey. However, a small part of him had wanted there to be a complication. He was not looking forward to kissing Georgiana Todd.

Studying the curves of Brenna's face, he willed for her to turn around or look at him in the rearview mirror. But she didn't. He fucking hated how she'd ignored him the last two days. True, it was for the best that she kept her distance since that made it easier for him not to hurt her, but it didn't mean he liked it.

When he'd agreed to mate her, he'd had an entirely different view of where they'd be right now. He'd barely kissed her twice, for fuck's sake.

His gaze moved to her neck, and he wanted to lean forward to kiss the soft skin. Afterward, he'd take her earlobe between his teeth and lightly tug. Her soft intake of breath would encourage him to do more.

He stilled. *No.* He had to remember the purpose behind the car ride and his mother's sacrifice. She was giving up her life so that he could have a chance at regaining his dragon and maybe his memories.

Glancing at the clock on the front media panel of the car, he guessed that they should be arriving at any moment. He could keep his thoughts from Brenna for a few more minutes and then do what needed to be done.

He forced himself to stare out the window at the passing houses, petrol stations, and occasional shop. Clan Northcastle was outside of Belfast proper, but there were still many more people here than back home near Glenlough. While far from crowded, their current location was stifling to him. He much preferred the open landscapes back home.

Yes, despite everything, he thought of Glenlough as home.

Brenna turned the car down a road and soon all the houses and shops disappeared. Nothing but trees and foliage filled the sides of the road for a good fifteen minutes. After another turn, the car stopped outside ten-foot-high walls. The stone looked older than those back on Glenlough, which made sense since Teagan had mentioned that Northcastle was tied for the oldest clan in the whole of Ireland, along with the one near Dublin in the south.

The gates swung inward and Brenna drove to just inside, where a male directed her to park the car. As soon as she turned the engine off, everyone sat in silence. Partly out of waiting for Northcastle to give them their instructions, and probably also because each of them was thinking about what was to come.

He glanced over at Caitlin, but her gaze was fixed on the window on her side of the car. Her jaw looked clenched, and the usual softness of her eyes had been replaced with strain.

Out of instinct, he reached over and took her hand. As soon as she turned her head at the touch, he whispered, "Thank you."

She smiled. "Stop saying that. I made my decision, and I'm proud I did so." Lifting a hand, she gently touched his arm. "But I want you to know that regardless of what happens here today, I will always love you. And no, not just the ghost of who you were. You will be always be my son, Killian, no matter what form you're in."

He struggled with what to say to that. Another person finally accepted him as he was, and he was going to lose her, too. Just as he might lose Brenna, if he hadn't already.

A loud rap on the driver's side window interrupted the moment. Brenna glanced back at them. "That's our cue."

They exited the car and faced a male who was just over two meters tall, with blond hair and blue eyes. The tattoo on his bicep indicated he was a dragon-shifter.

The male spoke up. "I'm Adrian Conroy, the second-in-command of the Protectors on Northcastle, and I'll be your escort today."

Killian was tempted to say he was their babysitter, but he didn't want to cause any unnecessary strife for Caitlin. After all, this was to be her new home. His temper could cause a lot of heartache for her in the future.

Adrian continued, "This way."

The tall man walked toward the nearest building to the gate, which was a two-story stone structure.

Killian expected people to stand about, gawking at them. However, there were few people he could see and the handful of males they passed on the way to the door barely paid them any attention.

The Northcastle population were either treating it as business as usual or the clan was on high alert, meaning the regular members were staying indoors until given the all clear.

Killian sensed he'd ordered something similar in the past, but he quickly pushed it aside. Any time he tried to remember something from before waking up with amnesia, it usually caused a blackout. He wasn't about to risk one on a foreign clan's lands. After all, he'd kept his deductions to himself, not wanting Glenlough to isolate him or some other extreme to keep him awake.

Adrian finally guided them into a large conference room and motioned toward the table. "Brenna and Killian, take a seat. Caitlin, you're to come with me."

Killian opened his mouth, but Brenna beat him to it. "Where are you taking her?"

Adrian raised a blond eyebrow. "She's to be our clan leader's new mate and you don't trust me to take care of her?"

Brenna didn't back down. "I don't know you, so I ask again: where are you taking her?"

"Not that it's any of your bloody business, but Lorcan wants to see her alone first. Unless you want to embarrass Caitlin by making her meet her new male in front of you two?" Adrian asked.

"There's no need to be snarky. I'm doing my job, same as you," Brenna stated.

Killian watched as the tall male studied Brenna's face. The bloke smiled with a wink and said, "Female Protectors are few and far between here, but between you and Faye MacKenzie, I'm starting to think we could use a few."

Clenching his fingers into a fist, Killian resisted the urge to punch the bastard. "That's my mate you're winking at."

Adrian swung his gaze to Killian. "And you're here to kiss another female, so I think you have little say in the matter."

Brenna stepped in front of Killian. "Just stop, you two. I understand there's a history between your two clans, but this isn't going to accomplish anything."

Caitlin spoke up. "Brenna's right." His mother stood taller. "Take me to Lorcan, Mr. Conroy. I'm ready."

The Northern Irish dragonman guided Caitlin out of the room. A beat after the door clicked closed, Brenna turned on him. "You need to be careful of your temper, Killian. You may not remember it, but these people have been at odds with Glenlough for quite a while."

"That male was flirting with you, Brenna. I couldn't let it go without comment, or I'd appear weak."

She rolled her eyes. "You're sounding more like a dragon-shifter now."

"I don't fucking care what I sound like. Until we sign any sort of separation agreement, you're my mate and I'm going to defend you."

"I can take care of myself. Or do I need to remind you of our mating day and what happened when we were alone?"

He closed the distance between them. "Just because you can take care of yourself doesn't mean you couldn't do with a little looking after."

"What are you talking about?"

"You work hard, and I have yet to see you do any sort of hobby. I think you need someone to relax with."

She narrowed her eyes. "If that's an invitation to strip off my clothes and 'relax' with your penis inside me, I think I'll resist somehow."

He growled. "You may find it hard to believe, but I think about more than sex."

She studied him. "Such as?"

If he were smart, he'd avoid answering. He was supposed to be avoiding Brenna, not opening up to her.

But it irritated him that she thought he only cared about her body and what he could do with it. "Such as how I'd like to swim with you in the lake, or maybe even teach you to ride a motorcycle."

She blinked. "You can ride?"

Information about motorcycles flooded his brain. "Yes, and fix them up, too. Although I don't think I've done it in a while."

"What else?"

"I'd like to dance with you again, and hopefully not end up unconscious."

She smiled. "I thought you hated dancing."

"It seemed ridiculous until I had you in my arms, and then it felt as if I'd done it hundreds of times before."

She counted off each thing on her fingers. "Swimming, motorcycles, dancing, and kissing. They're all things you enjoy."

It took everything he had to keep his distance from Brenna. "Yes, and more so when I'm with you."

She bit her bottom lip before saying, "Killian, you can't say things like that."

"Why not?"

"Well, for one thing, you're right—I work too much. And if you regain your memories after kissing Georgiana, then you'll probably morph back into your old workaholic state. The two of us working together wouldn't end well and we'd probably end up killing ourselves within twenty years or less."

He should keep quiet, but he asked, "And what if the kiss changes nothing?"

"Then there's still the two weeks you promised to give the Stonefire doctors."

Not wanting to be so far away from Brenna, he leaned closer and she took a step back. They continued the dance until she was up against a wall and he finally whispered, "And after that? What happens if I'm still this way?"

"I-I don't know."

He smiled slowly. "Then let me clarify—I will ask you out on a proper date and convince you to give me a chance."

As they stared into one another's eyes, a sense of rightness settled in his stomach. Keeping away from Brenna forever was simply not a viable option. At least, until she honestly told him she didn't want him. Then he knew himself well enough to know he'd honor her request.

However, just as he raised a hand to brush her cheek, Adrian's voice echoed in the room. "It's time to discuss the details of what's about to happen with Georgiana."

With a mental curse, Killian forced himself to turn away from Brenna. More than ever, he just wanted to get the blasted kiss over with so he could learn more about the female who intrigued him. After their conversation, Brenna knew more about him than he did about her. He'd still never found out who had most likely hurt her in the past.

Sitting down across from Adrian, he listened to the male's rules and directions. Never once did he look at Brenna. Because if he did, he might lose his nerve and piss off the Northcastle dragons with his rejection of Georgiana.

⁓⁓⁓⁓

Caitlin wiggled her fingers from pinky to forefinger and

back again as she followed Adrian Conroy down one corridor and then up a flight of stairs. She should be grateful that she was seeing Lorcan in private for their first meeting, but a part of her longed to have her son and Brenna in the room for support.

Her dragon spoke up. *You have me.*

I know, love, but it's not quite the same.

I'm not sure why you're nervous. If he tries anything, I will take control and protect us.

Her beast's words helped to ease her tension a fraction. *Let's hope it doesn't come to that.*

I'll give him a chance, but just one. How we interact with him now will set the tone for our future.

As her dragon's words set in, Adrian stopped in front of a door and knocked. Sending a request for her dragon to be quiet for a little while, Caitlin took a deep breath as Adrian opened the door and she followed inside.

It took everything she had to keep her gaze from looking downward to avoid eye contact. Not that finding Lorcan was difficult. He stood at the far end of the room, near a window, the light highlighting his form.

His mismatched eyes found hers and her heart rate kicked up. While she'd thought him attractive via the video conference, being in the same room as him stole her breath away. He wore the traditional dragon-shifter garb of a kilt-like outfit, complete with a dark green swath of material tossed over his shoulder and fastened with a brooch. The outfit displayed his muscled chest dusted with gray hair. Her gaze traveled up to his broad shoulders, lightly stubbled jaw, and she met his gaze once more.

More than his physical features, it was the kindness shining in his eyes that made her relax a fraction.

When he smiled at the sound, showing his white teeth, her mind went blank.

Lorcan chuckled. "You look like a deer caught in the headlights, Caitlin. I assure you that I'm not going to run you over." He waved at Adrian and they were instantly alone.

With the young man gone, Caitlin found her voice. "I wasn't prepared to see you in formal attire, is all."

"I wanted you to see what you were getting, Caity."

She tilted her head. "No one's ever called me that before."

He took a step toward her, but Caitlin didn't have the urge to move away. "It suits you, I think. Caitlin is a bit formal for such a shy lass."

"I hope you don't think shy means weak."

Amusement danced in his eyes. "Of course not. Any clan leader who thinks that clearly doesn't understand people. Especially since you've raised a clan leader yourself, and a former head Protector."

At the mention of her children, Caitlin remembered why she was in Northern Ireland. "Do you have the documents ready to sign?"

Lorcan didn't blink at the change in subject. "I'm hoping for this to be more than a mere transaction, Caity. I want you to have a chance to know me before committing your life to me."

"A more conniving person would use that to their advantage."

"I don't think you will."

The certainty in his eyes unsettled her. It seemed unfair that he could read her so much better than she could read him.

Her dragon whispered, *Give it time.*

Placing a hand on one of the plush chairs in the room, she asked, "Why me? I'm not sure I've ever understood your attentions in recent years, ever since that visit to Glenlough with your daughter."

He raised his brows. "You don't remember, do you?"

She frowned. "Remember what?"

Lorcan took a step closer, but Caitlin didn't move. For some reason, being alone with the male wasn't terrifying, as it probably would've been with another stranger.

His voice filled the room. "In the late 1970s, both the humans and dragon-shifters started to grow tired of the Troubles. There was a brief truce between Northcastle and the Irish dragon clans for a few years. Glenlough and Northcastle had a celebration of sorts, near The Giant's Causeway."

She vaguely remembered the party, as it was her first time meeting anyone from Northcastle. "In 1978."

"Yes, you were sixteen and I was nineteen. I found you lurking on the edge of the gathering, staring up at the rock formation known as the Chimney Stacks. I came up and told you the story of Finn McCool, the giant who lived on the causeway with his wife."

A memory niggled at the back of her mind. "The one who built a bridge to Scotland to challenge his rival, saw how big the rival was, fled back to Ireland, and his wife hid him by dressing up her husband as a baby."

"Right, and when the Scottish giant saw the size of the baby, he ran back home, afraid of how big the father was."

The hazy image of a tall, gangly boy with mismatched eyes and brown hair came into her mind. "You said your name was Lorry."

"Aye, well, at the time that's what everyone called me. But the bigger question is, do you remember what happened next?"

Caitlin had long suppressed the memories of that evening since Glenlough and Northcastle had become enemies again within a year.

Not that she hadn't thought about it for weeks afterward.

"You told a few more legends and then kissed me."

It had been Caitlin's first kiss, and she hadn't known what to do. Young Lorcan had patiently guided her, until she'd allowed his tongue to stroke the inside of her mouth.

"Your cheeks are pink, Caity."

Clearing her throat, she replied, "Well, first kisses tend to hold a special place in someone's heart. But you can't say that one kiss has made you wish for me all these years."

"While the kiss was brilliant, there's more to it."

She tilted her head. "Then tell me."

"Well, you were young. Too young, and couldn't possibly have known. But my dragon said you were my true mate. However, he would wait until you grew up before he did anything."

She blinked. "B-but, they say your late mate was your true mate."

He shrugged. "A dragon-shifter can have more than one. I found Rebekah more than a decade after you, Caity."

"Why did you never say anything?"

"We were enemies again soon after that party, not to mention you mated Kieran by the time you were nineteen. I had no choice but to stay away."

She prodded her dragon. *Did you know?*

No. I didn't pay attention to such things at that young of an age.

Lorcan's voice garnered her attention again. "But if you think I only want you here because of a kiss from almost forty years ago, then you're wrong."

Her heart rate jumped. "Then why?"

Closing the distance between them, Lorcan's voice was low as he said, "There are few people I feel comfortable around, and you're one of them. And not just because of the party, but you were kind to me and my daughter when we visited several years ago. I soon put together you were the same female from that gathering near the causeway in 1978. With your mate also gone, I thought maybe we should have our own go around. That's why I started sending flowers and notes on your birthday—to see if what could've been would come true or not."

His gravelly voice did something to her insides, not to mention Caitlin easily lost herself in the depths of Lorcan's eyes. There was desire there, yes, but a longing she understood, one that could only be recognized by someone else who had lost their former love and secretly wanted someone to care for again.

Raising his hand, Lorcan gently brushed a section of hair behind her ear. "So, what do you say, Caity? The time for having children and raising them is over. I want a companion by my side." He cupped her cheeks and she stopped breathing. "And I can't think of a better one than the girl I kissed all those years ago. You're sweet with a hidden strength, and I desperately need that in my life." He lowered his head until he was a hairbreadth away from her lips. "Let me kiss you again and show you we suit."

Caitlin had never been a spontaneous person by nature. She liked to plan and organize. It made life simpler that way.

But as Lorcan's lips waited so close to hers, she was curious to see if her memory lived up to the man in the flesh. After all, she was too old for a mate-claim frenzy to take hold. One kiss wouldn't determine her future.

She closed the distance between their lips, and the second they touched, electricity raced through her body.

Lorcan kissed her gently before nibbling her bottom lip. He continued his ministrations for a few seconds before seaming her lips, asking for permission. Without hesitation, she opened. As his tongue entered her mouth, she groaned at his taste. It had been a long time since she'd been kissed, but only one other male had tasted as good.

Not wanting to think of her dead mate, Caitlin focused on matching him stroke for stroke. When Lorcan growled, the vibration sent a shiver down her body.

The response stirred the dragonman into action. Wrapping his arm around her waist, he tilted her head for better access. Each slide of his tongue against hers made the years fade away, back to 1978 when she'd been a girl reveling in her first kiss.

Their encounter back then may have been sloppier, but the rush of heat and desire she'd felt then was the same as now.

As soon as she gripped the back of Lorcan's neck, he broke the kiss and laid his forehead against hers. His breath tickled her chin as he murmured, "So, do we suit, Caity?"

Her breath was as labored as his. "There's more to life than kisses, Lorcan."

"I agree. But it's a good place to start."

As they each caught their breath, she couldn't help but admit how nice it felt to be in the arms of a strong male. Maybe even one she could lean on, or an ally to have against her mother or children on occasion.

Her dragon spoke up. *Kiss him again. Just to make sure we suit.*

You're just being greedy.

Then why are you holding back?

Because it's been a long time and I'm not sure I'll do it right.

Her dragon snorted. *You'll do fine.*

Lorcan's voice prevented her from replying. "What's your dragon saying, Caity?"

"I'm not so sure I want to tell you."

Leaning his head back, she instantly missed the warmth of his forehead against hers. He said, "There are few things

I'll demand of you, but I want there to be honesty between us. Even if I don't want to hear it, tell me."

She smiled. "Even if my dragon is saying you're the worst kisser of all time?"

"And that, my dear, is a lie. Clan leaders are fairly good at detecting them."

Her dragon huffed. *Just tell him.*

"Well, she thinks we should kiss one more time, just to make sure we do indeed suit."

Lorcan chuckled, the deep sound soothing Caitlin's nerves. "Does she, now?" He closed the distance between their lips and gave her a quick, rough kiss.

He pulled away far too soon. "That will have to do, Caity. Our children are waiting for us, and I imagine we all want to get their kiss over as soon as possible."

"Of course." Caitlin stepped back and smoothed her top and trousers.

The male stared at her for a few moments before he turned toward the door. "Come. Let's see if we can fix your son."

She didn't like the idea of "fixing" Killian, but didn't think it was worth arguing over.

Her beast sighed. *You're going to have to learn how to voice your thoughts. He will want to hear them.*

Maybe with time. Right now, I'm not going to risk Killian's chance.

As her dragon went quiet, Caitlin followed Lorcan out the door. It was time to see if her sacrifice would result in anything.

Not that being around Lorcan would be much of a sacrifice, if she were honest. She only hoped he wasn't charming her for a short while before he turned into a cruel male later on, once she was mated to him.

CHAPTER EIGHT

Brenna could've opted to stay back in the conference room and not watch the kiss. Instead, she stood just outside the prison cell containing Killian, Adrian Conroy, and a doctor with a syringe filled with a sedative, just in case the kiss with Georgiana started the frenzy.

Staying behind would've been cowardly. Not only that, she wouldn't know what happened until someone thought fit to tell her.

Her dragon spoke up. *It wouldn't matter if you didn't care so much.*

Wanting him healed shouldn't be a surprise.

No, I think you don't want it to work.

Ignoring her beast, she glanced at Killian. But he had his back to her, shifting his feet as he waited for Georgiana's arrival.

For all she knew, this could be the last time she ever saw the dragon-less version of Killian O'Shea.

And a small, selfish part of her wanted to mourn that fact.

Footsteps echoed from the stone stairwell. Brenna

glanced in their direction. Lorcan led the way, with a female not much older than Brenna behind him.

The female with blonde, curly hair nearly to her elbows approached, and only when she was close enough did Brenna note she had the same eyes as her father—one brown and one blue.

If anything, the different eye colors only enhanced her beauty. Brenna had always preferred to keep her hair short out of convenience, even if most males seemed to prefer long hair. Maybe Georgiana was more "old" Killian's type. And perhaps the pair of them might want to experience the frenzy after all.

No. She wouldn't dwell on that.

Caitlin brought up the rear. Lorcan and Caitlin each stood to one side of Georgiana, who had been staring at Killian without speaking. Brenna knew the female wasn't a Protector, but she hid the emotions from her face extremely well.

Lorcan was the first one to speak. "This is your last chance to back out, Georgiana."

Brenna strained to hear the female's soft reply, "No, it's nice to be useful for once."

She sensed a story behind those words, but Killian spoke before she could think too much on it. "Thank you in advance for your help."

Georgiana bobbed her head, her curls bouncing. "I hope it helps. I can't imagine my life without my dragon."

Lorcan grunted. "Enough stalling. Let's get this over with."

Georgiana glanced at her father. "Is it necessary to keep him behind bars?"

"Yes," Lorcan stated.

Caitlin chimed in. "It's all right, Georgiana. I'm sure Killian understands the precaution."

Killian moved to the bars of his cell and pressed the center of his face between the metal bits, his nose and mouth sticking out in the free space. "Whenever you're ready."

Brenna's heart rate sped up, each second seeming as if it were weeks. *This is it*. The old version of Killian might be on the cusp of returning.

Georgiana approached the bars. Since she was shorter than Killian, the Northcastle female stood on her tiptoes before pressing her lips to Killian's. After a chaste kiss, she stepped back and all eyes zeroed in on Killian.

For a few seconds, he frowned and said nothing. Then he arched his back and roared. Adrian quickly wrapped his arms around Killian to hold him. It was then that Brenna noticed blood trailing out of one of his ears. "Something's not right. His ear."

The doctor in the cell cursed and stuck the syringe into Killian's bicep. Even after it was all dispensed, Killian's roars continued, as did the slow trickle of blood.

Were they going to lose him forever?

With a final yell, Killian slumped in Adrian's arms and the Northcastle Protector gently guided him to the ground. As the doctor did his check, both Brenna and Caitlin moved closer to the bars, waiting for the doctor to say something.

The doctor spoke without taking his focus from Killian. "He's alive, but I need to get him to my surgery straight away."

Brenna barely noticed Adrian on his mobile phone, probably calling for help. She couldn't tear her gaze away from Killian's pale, still form.

Each progressive spell of unconsciousness seemed to become more painful. It could only be a matter of time before it killed him.

Her dragon spoke up. *We don't know that. Maybe his dragon breaking free was too much. We shouldn't draw conclusions so quickly.*

I'm not about to be optimistic on this issue.

Lorcan's voice garnered her attention, but she didn't turn toward him. "Georgiana says her dragon is unaffected and there's no mate-claim frenzy pull."

"Then what happened to him?" Brenna whispered.

Caitlin answered, "I wish I knew."

She had forgotten about Killian's mother. Turning toward her, she pulled her into a hug. "Hopefully we don't have to wait too long."

Some more tall, muscled blokes who were probably Protectors hustled into the room. Brenna released Caitlin so they could move out of the way. The males soon had Killian off the ground and they carried him up the stairs, the doctor right behind him.

She moved to follow, but Lorcan stepped into her path and said, "Dr. Cahir Silver will do everything he can to help him. It's best to stay out of the way and come with me instead."

If she were on an ally's land, Brenna would've pushed him aside and followed Killian. However, she wasn't about to risk starting a war. "Why?"

"Because my clan has fulfilled our side of the bargain and it's time to start working on Glenlough's," Lorcan answered matter-of-factly.

She motioned toward Caitlin. "Her son was just in pain and is now unconscious. Have a little compassion."

Lorcan raised his brows. "I'm well aware of what happened. However, a distraction will make time pass quicker, and that means Dr. Silver's prognosis will arrive before you know it."

She opened her mouth to argue, but Caitlin stepped forward. "It's okay, Brenna. He's right. Waiting with Lorcan and working is little different from sitting in the surgery waiting room, twitting my thumbs for any news."

"Are you sure you're in the frame of mind to work?" Brenna asked.

Lorcan jumped in. "It's only a preliminary draft. We'll revisit it when everyone is in their right mind."

As much as she wanted to wait in the surgery, Brenna wasn't going to abandon Caitlin. Not just because she'd promised Teagan that she'd look after her mother, either. She knew what it was like to be a new face on a strange clan and having a familiar face close by at first, like she'd had with Aaron, could make the transition easier and less scary.

Dipping her head in agreement, she said, "Okay, but as soon as you know anything, you share it."

"Aye." Lorcan motioned toward the stairs.

As they all made their way toward a conference room on the top floor, Brenna couldn't help but replay the scene with Killian inside her mind. Blood trailing out of an ear was never a good sign; it could mean brain damage.

Her dragon spoke up. *Or, it could just be his dragon bursting free.*

I wish we understood more about how inner dragons work.

Once Killian is well, we'll go to Stonefire and Dr. Sid will figure it out.

She wanted to say *if* he got well, but kept the thought to herself. She only hoped the most recent episode wouldn't sentence Killian to a life of unconsciousness, being nothing more than a vegetable.

⁕

Killian stood at the edge of the mirror lake, the eerie stillness signaling he was back in his dream world.

Scanning the surrounding hills, he waited for the baby

dragon to appear. Minutes ticked by, and no one came.

Suddenly, a loud pounding came from under the lake's surface and Killian's eyes darted toward it. At first, the mirror reflected back the hills and sky. But soon, a shadowy outline of a dragon flashed, before disappearing. The booming happened again, but the shadow dragon never returned.

After what he guessed to be five minutes had passed, a childlike voice echoed behind him. "The shadow dragon comes to the lake's surface quite often now."

Turning slowly, he found the baby blue dragon with large patches of white standing a few meters away. "Do you know anything about him?"

"He's always angry and I'm afraid to go back into the lake."

Killian remembered his last visit, when the baby dragon had dived into the mirror, the pieces reassembling themselves almost as soon as they broke. "What's on the other side?"

"I would show you, but I'm afraid of the shadow dragon."

He had no idea why, but finding out what lay on the other side of the mirror seemed extremely important. "We don't have to go through. Just tell me what's there."

The baby dragon toddled from one back foot to the other. "It's mostly a giant cave, with lots of ledges to climb up. Then I can jump, spread my wings, and glide down."

He frowned. "Mostly a cave?"

"Yes. With tunnels and places to hide."

"Why would you need to hide?"

The dragon shook and folded his wings against his back. "It's safe and allows me to sleep without worry. Although whenever you visit this side of the lake, the ground rumbles a little, almost like a signal."

If he were indeed dreaming, this was the most coherent one he'd ever had. "Does anyone else visit you?"

The baby dragon shook its head. "No. I wish they would. It's quite boring, even with all the tunnels and ledges on the other side." The dragon studied him. "Maybe you can come back more often. Next time, I can think of some games to play."

"Am I supposed to be able to come back whenever I wish?" Killian asked slowly.

"I have no idea. But we can play now. I've always wanted a roll-down-the-hill contest. Do you want to try?"

Killian glanced toward the lake. "What about the shadow dragon? Does he come out?"

"Not yet. I'm not even sure if he can come to this side."

Before he could change his mind, Killian turned toward the lake and walked to the edge. Taking a deep breath, he gingerly placed his foot on the glass. Leaning his weight onto it, the mirror held. He took a few more steps before the shadow dragon appeared in the mirror under him.

Doing his best not to show fear, Killian studied the shadowy figure. While it appeared black at first, it was actually a dark blue. Something about the shape and size of the beast seemed familiar.

Then the dragon banged against the mirror, and the vibrations traveled up Killian's spine. Not wanting to risk dying since he had no idea if it was final in this place or not, Killian retreated to a safe distance from the lake. The baby dragon spoke up. "Do you want to play now?"

Scanning the little dragon's short snout, chubby cheeks, and glinting hide, something about the smaller version was familiar as well. "I have just one more question." The dragon tilted his head and Killian continued. "Are you related to the shadow dragon?"

"I don't know. I first woke up on the other side of the

mirror lake alone."

"And yet you know my language and can talk."

He tilted his head one way and then another. "I never thought about it. I just woke up with the knowledge."

Similar to what had happened with Killian. "What else do you know?"

The dragon sighed. "You said that was the last question. I want to play."

Not wanting to drive away the only source of information he had in this place, Killian motioned toward the nearest hill. "Then let's have our contest. If I win, I ask more questions. If you win, we try again."

The little dragon hopped from one back foot to the other, his wings spread out to keep his balance. "I'll win, you'll see. I've been practicing."

As the dragon jumped and flapped awkwardly to gain his balance, Killian smiled. "I used to compete a lot and usually won."

"Against whom?"

Frowning, Killian tried to recall, but the memory never came. "I don't know."

"Right, then let's race and see who is better."

The baby dragon flew to the top of the hill and stared at him. After taking one last glance at the mirror lake, Killian charged up the hill and readied himself by lying down. "Go!"

They both rolled, and Killian managed to reach the bottom first. Just as he was about to ask his question, the scene faded away to a bright light.

Killian's eyes popped open and he gasped. Various people he didn't know stood over him.

A female said, "He's awake and stable."

"Good," a male said, before lowering his face closer to

Killian's. He recognized him as Dr. Silver from the holding cell. "Do you remember who you are?'

"I'm Killian O'Shea. What happened?"

The doctor placed his fingers on Killian's face and opened his eye wider to study it. "Tell me the last thing you remember."

Since he didn't think his dream counted, he answered, "The kiss with Georgiana."

Dr. Silver released his eye and leaned back. "Is there another presence in your head with you?"

A childlike voice spoke inside his head. *I am. This is much better than the boring lake and hills.*

Baby dragon? Is that you?

The blue and white figure from his dream materialized inside his head and stood tall. *I'm not a baby, just young.*

He smiled at the dragon's tone. *Okay, young dragon. I wish I had a name for you.*

Why? I'm part of you, so I must be Killian, too.

A name would be easier for me.

Dr. Silver interrupted the conversation. "Your pupils were slitted just now. Tell me what happened."

Killian was afraid the doctor would call him crazy. "Where's Brenna?"

"She's with Lorcan. Now, answer my question."

He was about to tell the doctor to stuff it, but the dragon spoke again. *He's just trying to help us. Tell him.*

And then you'll give me a name?

Maybe. I need to think on it.

Killian focused back on Dr. Silver. "I've been seeing a young blue and white dragon in my dreams. However, this time he seems to be inside my head when I'm awake, too. What does that mean?"

"I don't know, but I know some people who might." Dr. Silver looked at one of the nurses. "Keep an eye on him. I need to make a call."

Before Killian could ask another question, the doctor was gone. He growled, and the baby dragon spoke up again. *Why are you always so angry?*

Because people don't tell me what's going on.

Maybe there's a reason why they wait?

Killian did his best to keep the anger from his voice when he asked, *Why are you here?*

I don't know. But I hope I don't have to go back. I don't think the shadow dragon can come here. And seeing all these new people is much more interesting. Such as that female. Her pupils are slitted like mine. Is she a dragon? Or does everyone have dragons in their head, like us?

Killian resisted a sigh. *Stop asking so many questions.*

Why? I'll never learn without them.

As the little beast continued to ramble, Killian rubbed the spot between his brows. Between little dragons and shadow dragons, he might be going mad.

Or, he might already be there.

He needed to talk with Brenna. She'd listen to the facts and make a conclusion, one that he'd trust. If she thought he needed help, he'd heed her advice.

As he tried to sit up, the nurse gently pressed against his chest until he stopped moving. The female rose a black brow. "You stay in this bed until the doctor clears you."

The dragon said, *She's scary.*

Not wanting to be distracted from his task, Killian focused on the nurse. "Then tell Brenna and my mother I'm awake and asking for them. Or is that not allowed, too?"

The dragon tsked. *Try being nice. That works better.*

And you know this how?

It just seems like the right thing to do.

Taking a deep breath, Killian forced his tone to be gentle. "Could you please call my mate and mother? They must be worried about me."

After one long second, the nurse smiled. "I suppose so." The nurse looked over to a male in the room, dressed in the same pale blue nurse's top and bottoms. "Calvin, call Lorcan and let him know what's happened. And tell him that the Glenlough male is asking for his mate and mother."

Calvin bobbed his head and exited the room.

The female nurse went back to typing something into a tablet and Killian decided to use the time to better assess the dragon in his head before Brenna arrived. *Are you going to constantly comment on everything?*

Maybe. I've been lonely. I like being useful.

I haven't said it's useful.

The nurse liked my suggestion. So, yes, I've been useful.

Killian resisted grunting, not wanting to draw the nurse's attention. *Keep it up, and I'll find a way to send you back.*

Please don't. I don't want the shadow dragon to eat me.

The fear in the dragon's voice softened his mood. *Has he tried to do so before?*

Not yet, but he appeared inside the tunnels once, and reached for me. I managed to run between his legs and out the tunnel. Being smaller worked well. And then I went through the glass lake. He wasn't able to follow.

Why would he reach for you?

I think he was hungry.

Dr. Silver returned with a tablet in his hand. The doctor said without preamble, "Killian, I have two doctors here who might be able to help. Tell them what happened."

He flipped the tablet toward Killian. The faces of Dr. Sid Jackson and Dr. Gregor Innes of Stonefire—Brenna had shown him pictures before—greeted his eyes. The female, Sid, spoke first. "Is it true? Is there a dragon presence inside your mind?"

Since Brenna trusted these doctors, he decided not

to fight it and just speak the truth. "For the time being, although it's a young one. I thought it was a baby, but he said he was young."

Sid didn't miss a beat. "So you're talking with the dragon? What did he say?"

He frowned. "You want me to rehash all of our conversations?"

Gregor jumped in. "Just how many have you had?"

"Several in my dreams. But this is the first time I've had them whilst being awake, at least since I woke up without my memories."

"You never answered my question," Sid pointed out. "What has he said to you?"

Killian sighed. "I don't know, mostly the dragon asks to play or suggests I should be nice. Or, he goes on about the shadow dragon."

Sid frowned. "What the bloody hell is a shadow dragon?"

Killian explained what he'd seen in his dream and added, "The baby dragon says he was trying to eat him."

Gregor whispered something into Sid's ear before looking back at Killian. "I think you need to come to Stonefire. Dr. Silver is a good doctor, by all accounts, but he hasn't studied the two personalities of a dragon-shifter like I have. There are things we need to discuss and possibly work on."

Dr. Silver turned the tablet back to face him. "I'm not sure I can clear Killian just yet."

Sid's voice filled the room. "I understand. But the sooner we see him, the better. Delaying his treatments could result in losing the dragon he's regained."

Not waiting for Dr. Silver to respond, Killian growled, "I have a question. If my so-called dragon is back, then where the fuck are my memories?"

Dr. Silver swung the tablet around again. Sid raised her brows. "First, your anger isn't going to make me work any faster. And second, we have some theories but need more information before sharing them." Killian opened his mouth to demand more, but Sid cut him off. "If you think bellyaching and cursing at me is going to help, then you've not worked with a proper dragon-shifter doctor before. I've dealt with far worse than you, Killian O'Shea. So save us a lot of time and stop dragging your feet."

His dragon spoke up. *She's right. Yelling and being rude only makes her mad.*

Not now, dragon.

Gregor whistled. "There *is* a dragon inside his head again. His pupils slitted."

"If you double-guess everything I say, then I'm not sure going to Stonefire is worth the effort," Killian replied.

"Enough," Dr. Silver stated. "I'll clear Killian as soon as I can, but not before. I won't risk him dying en route."

Gregor replied, "Of course, Cahir. Just send me a text as soon as you think he's ready."

Dr. Silver walked out of the room with the tablet and Killian couldn't hear any more of the conversation.

His dragon spoke up. *I'm excited to meet the funny talking doctors.*

Sid is English and Gregor is Scottish. They have accents, not speech impediments.

Still, it's different. Maybe there are other funny talking people there.

He couldn't help but smile at the young dragon's enthusiasm. *If you can understand them. Some people have trouble with thick accents.*

Before the dragon could ask for clarification, Brenna's voice filled the room. "Were you talking to your dragon?"

Slowly turning his head, he met Brenna's gaze. "A dragon. Not sure if it's mine or not."

She closed the distance to his hospital bed. "How do you

feel about it?"

Leave it to Brenna to consider his feelings over the fact he had a talking dragon inside his head. "I don't know. He's a happy, cheerful little bugger, that's for sure."

His mother appeared next to Brenna. "You were a happy child, Killian."

"What happened?" Brenna blurted.

Caitlin smiled sadly. "His father died, and Killian made it his mission to protect us all."

The dragon spoke up. *I don't like her sad.*

Me, either.

His mother brushed some hair off his forehead. "Maybe this is your second chance. A way to be the male you should've been, if your father hadn't died."

"Maybe," Killian murmured. Clearing his throat, he met Brenna's brown-eyed gaze again. "There's more." He explained about the shadow dragon and asked, "Is it normal to have dreams like that, with two dragons?"

"No, but since all of this was caused by the mysterious drug injected into your body, it doesn't surprise me that unusual things are happening to you."

"So the lake, the tunnels, and everything is a result of the drugs?"

Brenna shook her head. "No. Our inner dragons usually don't talk to us for the first five to seven years of our lives. During that time, they have a hiding space inside our minds. Usually it's a playground of sorts, with caves, tunnels, and even underground lakes."

He frowned. "Then why did I have an outdoor section, too?"

"Sid and Gregor would have a better guess than me, but it might be related to the loss of your dragon. For all we know, the shadow dragon could be a part of your former self."

The baby dragon spoke up. *I don't like that idea. The shadow dragon is scary. I never want to be scary, just strong.*

Lorcan's voice prevented Killian from replying. "As soon as Cahir clears you, you're going to Stonefire. I'll send Adrian and Calvin with you, so that you have both an extra Protector and a nurse, in case something goes wrong."

Killian looked at Lorcan. "I thought you hated the English dragon-shifters."

Shrugging one shoulder, Lorcan replied, "I vowed to Caitlin that I'd keep you safe, and I'll fulfill that promise."

As Lorcan gazed at Caitlin, a wave of protectiveness flowed through Killian. He wanted to stay and ensure his mother settled in.

His dragon huffed. *No need. He likes her. Look at the longing in his eyes.*

So now you're an expert on facial expressions?

Just because you don't look isn't my problem.

Brenna's voice cut off his reply. "Thank you, Lorcan. I know you're doing it for Caitlin, but Bram will appreciate it, too."

Lorcan grunted. "Well, I'd better set things in motion." His gaze moved to Caitlin's. "Find me when you're ready, Caity."

His mother nodded, and the Northcastle clan members left him alone with Brenna and his mother.

"Caity?" Killian prompted.

His mother's cheeks turned pink. "It's just a nickname. Now, tell me more about this wee dragon in your head."

"Yes," Brenna interjected. "He seems to make you a nicer person and I'm not sure how I feel about that."

"I'm not about to shout at a child and the easiest way to get him to hush is to give in to his suggestions."

I'm not that young, his dragon said.

Hush.

Brenna's pupils flashed and she laughed. "Be careful, or you'll end up with a spoiled dragon. And mine says that's unacceptable for a strong dragon-shifter."

He harrumphed. "It seems now even your beast wants a say in my behavior."

Rolling her eyes, she sat down on the edge of his bed. "I'd listen to her in this case. Spoiling your dragon will make your life difficult, especially if you want to do any sort of Protector-like duties in the future. You need to have a partner rather than a spoiled child."

"Is there some sort of manual I need to read?" he asked.

"They exist, but they're for children. It's probably better for you to work with Tristan MacLeod on Stonefire. He has a knack for helping people with their inner dragons. He worked with Dr. Sid when hers came back, and Sid and her beast seem to get along now."

Brenna's eyes lit up as she told him a bit more about her clan members. She had resorted to mating him in order to stay on Glenlough, but it was clear she missed her home clan.

The baby dragon spoke up. *Maybe it will be our new home, too. There are mountains near their clan. I'd like to sit atop one and look down.*

That would require flying as I've no wish to go hiking and possibly pass out en route.

I might be able to help with the flying. We can try once we get there.

Not wanting to think about changing into a dragon, he focused back on Brenna. "I'll meet with this Tristan, but I can't promise anything."

Snorting, she leaned closer. "I may need to enlist the help of Tristan's mate, Melanie, to ensure you two get along. He used to be as grumpy and angry as you. But Mel has a certain touch with him. That may prevent any sort of fighting."

"I can restrain myself."

From the corner of his eye, he noticed his mother smile. He looked at her. "What?"

Caitlin tilted her head. "You've always had trouble declining a challenge. It took two years in the army to finally tame your temper to a manageable level."

"I'm sure that discipline is somewhere inside of me, especially with my do-good dragon," he muttered.

His dragon huffed. *There's nothing wrong with being nice and doing the right thing.*

Most of the time. But sometimes it's healthy to vent. Or, punch someone.

Brenna prevented him from replying. "There might be a way for you to use up some of your excess energy, Killian. I'm sure Kai Sutherland, the head Protector of Stonefire and my former boss, will think of something. It's not every day one of Stonefire's clan members can fight an Irish dragon-shifter without starting a war."

"Are you trying to be funny?"

She grinned. "Maybe."

Between her beautiful face and teasing, he wanted nothing more than to bring her close and kiss her again.

Since he couldn't do that in the present, he wanted to keep her talking so he could watch her face and listen to her soothing voice. "Then tell me more about some of my potential opponents. A man needs to be prepared."

As Brenna continued to tell him stories of her clan members, he wished he had a moment alone with her. For some reason, he wanted to assure her that the kiss with Georgiana had meant nothing.

And if he could kiss Brenna again before they arrived at her home clan, all the better. He wasn't about to give her a chance to pull away again if he could help it. He wanted her for his mate.

Good, his young beast whispered. *I like her.*

In the meantime, he listened to both Brenna and his mother. He didn't want to leave his mother on Northcastle, but she'd made her choice.

Now it was up to Killian to make the most of the opportunities she'd given him.

CHAPTER NINE

After the long visit with Killian after he'd regained consciousness, Brenna had found excuses to stay away from him for the three days they'd remained on Northcastle. Talking and joking with Killian about her clan members had made her forget, albeit briefly, about everything that loomed over their heads. Namely, Killian could still return to his former self and she'd lose the male she was growing attached to.

The only good thing about those three days was that she'd learned about Cedric Templeton and his fate. After a string of offenses, he'd been court-martialed and sent to a DDA prison since the army didn't handle dragon-shifter internments.

His imprisonment should make her happy, but she'd rather have had the chance to confront the male who had used her in the past. Maybe she'd get the chance to do it someday.

Not that she didn't have enough on her plate already.

Stepping out onto the deck of the ferry on its way to Liverpool, England, she closed her eyes and allowed the wind to caress her face. The ferry was large enough to keep her distance from Killian. The trick would be doing so for the entire eight-hour journey from Belfast.

Yes, she was being a coward. But she suspected the shadow dragon Killian had described was his former self. She had a feeling if it escaped its current prison, it would merge with Killian, changing him.

Her dragon grunted. *There's no harm in talking with him. Especially since Adrian and Cal are his constant companions.*

He seems to get along with Calvin the nurse. I'd rather Killian enjoy himself than me sit there and create tension.

So all of this is for his benefit?

Not exactly. Besides, we'll see Mum and Dad soon and I need to prepare myself for that.

Bram had said her parents would greet her as soon as she arrived on Stonefire. Only because of the various restrictions placed on dragon-shifters in or near big cities in England kept them from greeting her near the ferry terminal.

However, Jane and Rafe Hartley—a sibling pair of humans who'd each mated a Stonefire dragon-shifter—would be waiting for them in Liverpool. Brenna hadn't interacted much with either one, but if Bram trusted them, she did, too.

A male with a Northern Irish accent appeared at her side. "It's a fine summer day to be outside."

Glancing over, the male in his twenties had dark hair and glasses. He was young, but handsome enough.

Another male's face with dark hair flashed into her mind. One of an older male who wasn't afraid to show his emotions and whose kisses made her forget about anything else.

Pushing Killian out of her mind, she smiled at the human male. "I'm surprised more people aren't out here to enjoy it, if I'm honest."

He shrugged. "People tend to love their mobile phones and tablets on journeys."

"But not you?"

He motioned toward the retreating shoreline of Northern Ireland. "How often can you see such a view?"

Her dragon yawned. *He's boring.*

Ignoring her beast, she opened her mouth to reply when a familiar Irish accent came from behind her. "There you are, darling."

Killian.

The human male's smile faltered when his gaze moved over her shoulder, and he hurried off. Brenna swung around to face Killian. She ignored the fierceness of his gaze. "You shouldn't be alone. Where are your guards?"

"I'm looking at one of them right now."

Sighing, she looked back out at the sea. "What do you want?"

"You keep avoiding me. That's not going to play well on Stonefire since we're mated."

"Not all mates are glued to each other's side. I cast adoring looks when needed."

Taking her shoulders, he gently turned her to face him. "Just talk to me and stop making things complicated."

"Me talking isn't going to make things any easier and you know it."

Leaning his face closer to hers, his hot breath danced against her cheek. "Georgiana meant nothing to me and I'm on my way to your clan. What else am I supposed to do?"

"It's not what you can or can't do, Killian. You have a dragon now, yes, but who's to say everything else won't come back, too? The male I want is the one right in front of me and if he disappears, it'll crush me."

Killian's pupils flashed before he gently murmured, "You want me."

"Of course I do. But I can't risk the pain that could follow."

"So you're going to live your life cautiously forever? Some risks are worth it, Brenna. Isn't this one of them?"

As she stared into his green eyes, she tried to think of another point to argue.

Her dragon chimed in. *Stop making excuses. Kiss him and enjoy the moment. Otherwise, you might regret it forever.*

Closing the distance between them until there was only an inch separating their lips, Killian whispered, "Kiss me, Brenna, and then tell me if you want to keep playing it safe."

She swallowed. "A kiss can't change my mind."

"Then do it and tell me that again. I'll walk away and keep my distance, as you wish."

Killian's scent surrounded her, making it hard to concentrate. Her heart pounded in her chest, as heat radiated through her body.

Staring at his warm, inviting lips, she already knew his kisses drove her crazy. The only question was whether she'd be able to stop with just a kiss or not. They may not be true mates, but desire was powerful in its own right.

Placing a hand on her lower back, Killian caressed the area in slow circles. Before she could change her mind, she closed the distance between their lips.

The instant her lips met his, lust coursed through her body. She needed to strip him, and take him over and over.

Her dragon hummed. *Yes, fuck him now. And keep on doing it until we carry his child.*

Only because of her years of military training and discipline was she able to break the kiss and push Killian away. He landed on his arse, but she barely paid attention. Instead, she squatted and curled into a ball.

Her dragon roared. *Why did you push him away? He is*

ours and will always be ours. Go to him. Take him. He is ours to claim.

Warning bells rang inside her head. The kiss with Killian had kicked off the mate-claim frenzy. *Why now?*

No talking. Stop resisting and strip him. You want him as much as I do. He should be ours, always. Don't push him away.

Killian's voice cut through her inner conversation. "What's wrong, Brenna?"

Turn around and strip him. Fuck him with the wind on our bodies.

She gripped her head tighter. "Just go."

"What? Why?"

Another blast of lust shot through her body. Through gritted teeth, she whispered, "Frenzy. Go. Get Adrian."

As she focused on staying in a hunched position so she wouldn't be tempted to give in to her dragon's demands, she tried to construct a prison for her dragon. But every time she came close to finishing the metal contraption, her dragon swung her tail and destroyed it.

Her beast shouted, *No, no, NO! I want our true mate. Kiss him. Fuck him. Claim him. He should be ours.*

Adrian cursed and said, "Brenna, come with me."

Killian asked, "Is she all right? I've kissed her before, so I don't understand."

Adrian answered, "Probably something to do with the dragon in your head. Go to Cal. I'll make sure Brenna's stowed safely in the car."

Killian growled. "Don't think of touching her, Adrian."

"I'm not a fucking idiot. Her dragon would slice me to bits in this state. Now go, Killian. You sticking around will only cause her more pain."

Her dragon expanded her wings and hissed. *Why are you letting him go? Push Adrian overboard and go to*

Killian. He is our mate and he will give us a young.

No, not with so many humans nearby.

They don't matter. If we let him go, one of the other females will claim him.

Something pricked her skin and Adrian's voice filled her ear. "A sedative. Sorry, Brenna, but it's the best I can do. Now, come. I need to get you to the car so I can give you the second dose and knock you out."

Her dragon thrashed. *NO. Our mate is close. I want him. I need him.*

Gritting her teeth, Brenna managed to stand. It took every bit of steel she possessed to resist the lust and desire her dragon continually broadcasted inside her body.

Leaning on Adrian, she put one foot in front of the other until they finally arrived at the car. Once in the back seat, Adrian gave her another shot.

As the drug took effect, her eyes grew heavy and she murmured, "Keep me out until we get to Stonefire. Let Bram know."

Adrian nodded as the world faded and she slipped into oblivion.

⁓⁓⁓⁓

Killian paced the length of the side deck, trying his best to figure out what the hell had happened.

A frenzy started when a dragon found their true mate. However, Killian had kissed her before, with no problem. Something had changed.

The young dragon was sitting toward the back of his mind, huddled into a ball. Killian coaxed, *It's okay. Come out. I need to talk with you.*

I'm scared. Why did Brenna act so strange? Is she okay?

He didn't know much about mate-claim frenzies, but he

126

decided to ask, *Do you feel any pull toward her?*

She's nice and I like her. But I'm too young to want anyone that way. I had to turn my back when you kissed her, because, well, I'd much rather play.

Running a hand through his hair, he was about to further question his dragon when Cal spoke up. "I suspected your newfound dragon might change things, but I'll admit I didn't see this coming."

He glared at the red-haired male. "That's not helping. Is there anything I can do to ease Brenna's pain?"

"Unless you're going to strip naked and take her in a car, no."

He cursed. "Then at least let me see her. After all, you said she would be unconscious."

Cal crossed his arms over his chest. "No, we can't risk it. Your dragon may not feel the pull now, but it could change at the drop of a hat."

Growling, Killian hit the top of the railing. "It's like I can't win, no matter how hard I try."

"Look, mate, this isn't something you could've controlled. The mate-claim frenzy is instinctual. No matter how much you may or may not want it, it'll hit you."

"Have you gone through it?"

"No, and I doubt I ever will. But I've seen it dozens of times back home, and it's not always for the best."

He scrutinized Cal. "What are you talking about?"

Cal looked toward the water. "My brother went through the frenzy. Not long after, his mate left him and their daughter behind, to go live with another dragon-shifter near Dublin." He met Killian's gaze again. "But there's a difference in your case since you both fancy each other."

He didn't deny it. "Things are complicated."

Cal smiled. "Seeing as I was your nurse back on Northcastle, I understand. Still, Brenna may agree to it once you're on her clan's lands."

He grunted and changed the topic. "Shouldn't you be with Brenna? I'm not sure I trust Adrian with the sedatives."

"All Protectors can handle sedative shots. After all, if they're on a mission and something goes wrong, they need to be able to calm one of their brethren." Cal shook his head. "You know, I never thought I'd be having a heart-to-heart with a bloke from Glenlough."

"Let's just say I tend to bring out the unexpected." He sighed. "I just wish it didn't involve hurting Brenna."

"You have two choices with her. One, you both agree to the frenzy and eventually have a child."

"Considering I don't know who the fuck I am, that's probably not the best idea."

"Then your second option is to keep away from Brenna and she drugs herself for weeks or months until the mate-claim frenzy pull fades."

His dragon spoke up. *I don't like Brenna in pain.*

Me, either. But I'm not sure what else to do.

Placing both hands on the railing, Killian looked out at the water. He'd grown close to Caitlin in a short period and started to think of her as his mother. If only she were there, she might have other suggestions.

His beast chimed in again. *We can try calling her when we have the chance. However, Stonefire is Brenna's home clan. They will do whatever they can to help you since it means helping her.*

I hope you're right.

Together, we'll find a way. I'm sure of it.

He gave a strangled laugh inside his head. *You're one optimistic little dragon.*

And you're one grumpy, angry male.

Since his young beast was right, he contented himself by watching the rise and fall of the water around the ferry. He yearned to see Brenna's face, but being near her would only hurt her.

So despite his best intentions, it looked like he was going to have to keep his distance from her. Maybe even for the rest of his life.

⚬⚬⚬⚬⚬

Caitlin O'Shea may never have been clan leader or a Protector, but she'd never been an idle person. First, she'd raised two children and then when they were grown, she'd run Clan Glenlough's daycare. She'd always had a purpose and took joy in taking care of others.

However, as she stared out the window of her temporary residence on Clan Northcastle, she was close to climbing the walls. Killian had left over two hours ago with Brenna and she had nothing to do until Lorcan finished his meeting and visited her.

Her dragon spoke up. *There is plenty to do. Read, watch a film, or even bake. You always go on about wanting to bake more.*

It's hard to relax when your future is unclear.

You could always call Teagan and see what's going on.

I'd rather talk to her after Lorcan's visit. She has a meeting planned with Clan Seagale later today and needs all the time she can manage to prepare for it.

Seagale, the Irish clan inside Connemara National Park, was Teagan's first target for her Ireland-wide peace treaty. If Teagan didn't get all the clans in Ireland to agree and sign, the Department of Dragon Affairs might never lift the ban on foreign dragon-shifters visiting the Republic of Ireland.

Her dragon huffed. *Humans have stupid rules. The DDA should know that a ban won't stop people from finding a way in.*

I know, love, but not angering them works to our advantage.

If only we could go back to the days when dragons ruled the island.

Right, and have humans hunt us to near-extinction again? I think not. This is how it must be.

Her dragon harrumphed and fell silent.

With nothing else to do, Caitlin studied the area in front of the terraced housing where she was staying. The attached dwellings were used for single adults. Since Caitlin had yet to mate Lorcan, she qualified.

At the word "mate," she closed her eyes and took a deep breath. Truth be told, she didn't think she'd ever have a mate again after Kieran had died. Getting to know someone had been fun in her late teens, but it was a different story in her mid-fifties.

She knew most of her friends still enjoyed their mates in all ways, including physical. The thought of a male naked and above her caused a wave of longing to crash over her.

Her dragon growled. *If you hadn't denied us for so many years, you wouldn't be yearning for him so much. He might use that against us.*

Life has been busy. Ever since Teagan became clan leader, she's needed my support. I also couldn't risk a male courting me just to get close to her.

Some might argue Lorcan is doing precisely that.

I disagree.

Regardless, don't wait too long to kiss and claim him. Enjoy life in the moment. Killian's condition should've taught you that.

Opening her eyes, she watched a young couple walking past. The female laughed at something the male said, and he promptly frowned.

Maybe someday she would act the same way with Lorcan.

As if her thoughts summoned him, Northcastle's leader turned the corner and walked up the footpath to her living quarters. The dragonman walked with a straight spine and an ease that said he knew and accepted himself.

In other words, a male with the confidence that came with age.

His gaze found hers, sending a flush to her cheeks. There was something about his confidence that appealed to her.

As he approached the door, she went and opened it. Lorcan smiled. "Waiting for me, I see."

She frowned. "What else do I have to do? My instructions were to not leave this house."

Lorcan strode past her, and she closed the door. "Now, now, Caity, you know I had no choice. Until we sign the mating documents, you're here illegally. There are some who will always see you as a foe, no matter what I say or do. You staying out of sight is for your own safety."

"And yet, I'm to live here for the rest of my life. I hope that doesn't mean I'm going to be a prisoner forever."

"You won't be a prisoner." He took a step toward her, his nearness making her heart skip a beat. "I'm sure your daughter understands, as her mate is English. As long as the majority of the clan accepts a foreign mate, everything should be fine. No one is ever liked by all, that's just a fact of life."

"Well, if there was more intermingling and inter-mating between the clans, I think there would be less bias and hatred."

"I agree." He glanced to her suitcases in the hallway. "Do those mean you're ready to move in with me?"

She allowed the change of topic. After all, she had the rest of her life to convince Lorcan to open up to her clan. "You said tonight would be the earliest we could mate, so I'm ready."

He studied her a second before reaching out a hand and lightly caressing her jaw with his finger. "Are you truly ready, Caity?"

As he continued to stroke her skin, her dragon spoke up. *Kiss him.*

Lorcan's whisper filled her ear. "For the moment, talk to me and not your dragon. I can't take care of you if you don't speak your mind."

His words made her want the mating to work even more. Her daughter might make a quip about being taken care of, even if her mate did so sometimes now, but Caitlin missed having someone look after her.

She cleared her throat and replied, "Yes, I'm ready to move in with you. Kiss me again and maybe you'll believe me."

Lorcan's pupils flashed. His voice was gravelly when he answered, "Kissing you alone, in private, is dangerous, love."

"Why?"

"Because I'm not sure I can stop at kissing your lips."

Her heart thundered in her chest. She could easily tell him they could go outside for a quick kiss and play it safe.

But that wasn't what she wanted.

It was time for Caitlin to live a little, so she leaned against him and looped her arms around his neck. She smiled at Lorcan's intake of breath. "This might be the best way to discover if we suit, I think."

Nuzzling her cheek, he murmured, "I like the way you think, woman."

Before she could do more than open her mouth, Lorcan pressed his lips to hers and slipped his tongue inside. She groaned as each stroke wiped away any lingering hesitation.

She wanted Lorcan Todd, and for once, she was going to think of her own needs over anyone else's.

He ran a hand down her back to cup her arse cheek. The second he pulled her even tighter against him, she groaned at the feel of his hardness against her.

She'd been a fool to wait so long to have sex again.

Lorcan soon had both his hands on her bum and lifted. She wrapped her legs around his waist without hesitation, almost desperate to feel his hard muscles under her thighs.

She barely noticed the wall against her back when Lorcan moved one hand around to cup the side of her face and then slid it into her hair.

Just as she was about to guide his hand to her breasts, a mobile phone rang. She'd barely noted that it wasn't hers before Lorcan ended the kiss and cursed. "That's Adrian's ringtone. I need to take it."

Since the news could be about her son, Caitlin nodded and allowed Lorcan to release her to the ground.

Pulling out his phone, Lorcan asked, "What?" He glanced at Caitlin. The worry in his eyes sent a thread of fear through her heart.

Still, she'd worked with enough clan leaders to know waiting was the quickest way to get information. As soon as he clicked off the phone, Lorcan said without preamble, "Killian's kiss stirred Brenna's dragon to a frenzy."

She blinked. "Wait, what? They've kissed before in front of all Glenlough without that happening."

"I don't know. Adrian thinks it might be because Killian wasn't a whole person without an inner dragon. And as soon as the dragon came back, Brenna's beast recognized him."

"Did Killian agree to it?"

Shaking his head, Lorcan headed toward the door. "No, she's sedated and Adrian is keeping them apart." He paused and faced her. "I need to try contacting Stonefire's leader." He leaned over and kissed her quickly. "We'll have to finish this later."

"Of course."

He put out a hand. "But you can come with me, if you like, and see how things work."

"I thought I was to stay out of sight?"

"There shouldn't be many people out and about at this time of day and my Protectors are loyal."

Placing her hand in his, she said, "Then let's go. If for some reason Stonefire won't take your call, then I can call Teagan and contact them that way."

He kissed the top of her hand. "And the grand alliance begins."

They made their way toward the Protectors' central command building. While she was disappointed about the interruption, she quickly brushed it aside. Brenna had done so much for Killian after his memory had vanished. Caitlin would do whatever it took to help her, even if it meant taking Killian back and keeping him away from Brenna forever if she didn't want the frenzy.

CHAPTER TEN

The ferry ride to Liverpool had been the longest hours of his life.

Or, so Killian believed, considering he couldn't remember anything beyond a few weeks ago.

Adrian and Cal had taken turns watching Brenna. Several times Killian had gone to the car to see her, but he'd been turned away every time. No one wanted to risk the frenzy erupting inside him, too.

Not that the baby dragon seemed in danger of doing so. He was more concerned with the boat sinking and them having to swim to England than any need to strip Brenna naked and take her.

Still, they didn't have a choice but for everyone to ride in the same car to exit the ferry and meet with the Stonefire humans. Adrian had made Killian sit in the front passenger's seat, but he still gazed over his shoulder at Brenna's unconscious form, leaning against Cal in the backseat. Killian frowned. "It should be me back there."

Adrian replied, "And risk your scent waking her beast? I think not. Besides, we're nearly to the meeting point. Then we can divide you two between this car and theirs, making the journey easier for everyone."

His dragon growled. *I don't want to leave her with strangers.*

Ignoring his beast, he looked over at Adrian in the driver's seat. "By law, I should have the final say in her care as her mate."

The Northcastle Protector grunted. "Fuck the law. You can't remember how dragon-shifters function. You could harm her without even knowing it."

Killian hated that the tall bastard was right.

Rather than admit it, he looked out the window. Maybe the Stonefire teacher Brenna had mentioned, Tristan MacLeod, would give him a quick course on dragon-shifter basics. Then he'd be able to make decisions and fulfill his duty to take care of Brenna.

His dragon spoke up again. *I know more than you, but you never ask.*

You're young.

So? I woke up with knowledge, much like you. I could've told you that your scent could wake her dragon.

What else?

That depends. Will you listen to me?

The car disembarked from the ferry. *Think of everything you can and tell me when we have a moment. I can't be distracted when sizing up the Stonefire humans.*

You need to stop thinking that everyone is the enemy.

It's a precaution. Besides, a weak first impression will probably hurt us later with the English dragon clan.

His beast flapped his wings and rearranged them on his back. *How? We aren't fighting them.*

It may come to a fight over Brenna, if they don't let us talk with her and send us away. Whether we stay or go should be Brenna's decision. Now, hush until after we meet the humans.

Whether because of Killian's tone or his dragon's curiosity at the upcoming meeting, he didn't know, but the little one fell quiet.

Adrian turned down a street and then another, until they reached a car park garage. Jane and Rafe Hartley should be waiting for them on the top floor.

Brenna stirred in the back seat, but she settled before he could even look at her again. Rationally, he'd always known she was younger than him by a good ten years, but with her face slack in unconsciousness, she looked more innocent and softer than he'd ever seen her before. She took on a lot for someone her age.

He hoped to be the one to help her slow down.

Provided they could find a way around the frenzy. He imagined maybe having a child someday, but his life was too unpredictable to add worrying about a defenseless person to the mix. Or, worse, his condition ended up killing him and Brenna would be left to raise the child on her own.

And she definitely didn't need that, as it would probably force her to give up her place as a Protector.

If only Killian could care for someone and not hurt them, he would be a happy male.

Adrian's voice filled the car. "There they are."

A dark-haired male leaned casually against an SUV while a dark-haired female stood not far from him, looking down at her phone. The male spoke and the woman looked up.

As Adrian pulled into the spot next to them, Killian could see the resemblance between the two—dark hair, taller than most humans, and similar shaped eyes, although the female's were blue and the male's green.

Killian moved to open the door when Adrian's voice rang out. "Try to behave. Remember, they're here to help you both."

Grunting, he exited the car. Jane was the first to speak,

complete with a smile. "So you're Brenna's mysterious mate."

He frowned. "How do you know it's me?"

"Tall, black hair, green eyes. You're the only one in the car who fits the description," Jane pointed out. "And the accent cinches it."

Her brother Rafe rolled his eyes. "Don't start going on about accents or I may have to mention it to Kai."

She shrugged. "Kai won't care. He knows I only have eyes and ears for him."

Ignoring his sister, Rafe sized up Killian, but Adrian joined them before the human male could say anything. "You'll have plenty of time to get cozy later on." Adrian motioned toward the car. "Brenna's in there."

Jane tilted her head. "I see the rumors I heard about you being charming are unfounded."

Shrugging, Adrian smiled. "You're mated, so why waste the effort? Especially when your mate is Kai Sutherland. I haven't met him, but he has a solid reputation."

"And then some." Jane tucked her phone into a pocket and clapped her hands. "Right, then let's get down to business. Rafe will ride with you lot and Killian will ride with me."

Killian glanced inside the car, at Brenna leaning against Cal. "I'd much rather she ride with you and your brother."

"Because my brother's mated, am I right?" Jane asked with amusement dancing in her eyes. Killian didn't have a chance to reply before she continued, "They'll be fine. A dragon in the midst of a frenzy pull is not someone you want to piss off. Her dragon wants you and will probably castrate any of them if they try something."

"Good," Killian stated.

Jane studied him a second before opening the driver's side door of the SUV. "Let's get a move on. We have a two-hour drive ahead of us. The sooner we get Brenna to Stonefire, the sooner we can figure what the hell to do next."

He looked back at Brenna's face again and his dragon spoke up. *Jane's right. The sooner we get her to Stonefire, the sooner they can help her.*

Killian spoke aloud. "But what if I fall unconscious again? That's what Cal's supposed to be here for."

Jane tapped a finger against the car door. "Too bad Holly's pregnant, or I would've had her flown down and accompany us. She could've looked after you instead of Cal. Even though she's a midwife, she's also a nurse."

He scowled. "Who? And what are you talking about?"

Shaking her head, Jane answered, "I don't want to overwhelm you with too many names, as you'll have loads to memorize on Stonefire. Cal can ride in our car, but in the back seat. I want to talk to you during the ride."

Rafe chimed in. "Be careful, Killian. She's notorious for questioning and ferreting out people's secrets."

Jane shrugged. "I'm a reporter. That's what I do."

Bloody fantastic. He was going to spend the next two hours being interrogated.

Wanting to get the ride over with, he moved to the passenger side door but paused to meet Adrian's eyes again. "Call us if anything happens."

"Of course," Adrian answered without missing a beat.

He had no reason to trust the dragonman after such a short time, but his gut said the male would follow through.

Sliding into the car, he quickly buckled his seat belt. Jane and Cal did the same, and they were soon on their way.

Jane didn't waste any time. "So you lost your dragon, but have it again, right?" He grunted. "You're going to have to start giving me more detail than that. Trust me, I can question incessantly until you eventually give in anyway. You've nowhere to run for the next two hours."

He looked at the tall female. "You're fairly demanding for a human."

"Oh, you should meet my mate. He's the head Protector and quite growly. Compared to Kai, you're easy."

Since cooperating would put him in a positive light and give him a better chance of seeing Brenna on Stonefire, he sighed. "Fine, what do you want to know?"

As Jane began her line of questioning, Killian watched the clock. It was going to be a long car ride.

⌒◦⌒◦⌒◦

Adrian Conroy was grateful he hadn't been saddled with the reporter. Her brother had studied him from time to time during the journey to Stonefire, but had said little.

Which made sense. Stonefire no doubt had already pulled every file they could find on him and Cal.

It gave him time to prepare for their arrival. While traveling from one part of the UK to the other was allowed, the DDA often sent inspectors to monitor the interactions. Particularly between two clans who had been at odds, like his and Stonefire. He needed to pull out all his charm and convince the inspector that he wasn't looking for a fight or to cause any trouble.

His dragon spoke up. *Your charm may not work. The ones back in Northern Ireland have always been resistant to our charms.*

Ah, but it should be an English female. I'm sure I can wax on poetically about our clan and she may fall for it. After all, the DDA is notorious for not sharing information between branches.

I don't know. Ever since the new DDA director was installed, things have changed slowly.

Not too long ago the former director of the DDA

had been caught in a scandal that involved murder and imprisonment. Rosalind Abbott took over his place and had made sweeping changes in policy and staff. Most of it had made it to Northern Ireland later than in England, Wales, and Scotland.

Adrian replied, *Stop being so pessimistic. We'll do fine.*

If you don't hit some of the Stonefire dragons first.

I'm not going to hit them.

So you say.

Ignoring his dragon, Adrian made the final turn. As they drove down the long, single carriageway, he had to admit the peaks and valleys were unlike those back near Northcastle. He loved his home, but the Lake District was beautiful in a different way.

Since Jane Hartley's car was ahead of his, the gates opened automatically and Adrian followed. She pulled off to the side. Rafe finally spoke up. "Park next to her."

It was on the tip of his tongue to make a quip, but Adrian resisted. His top concern was helping the female in the back seat, next to Rafe.

He didn't know Brenna Rossi that well, but no one deserved to be drugged into unconsciousness to avoid a frenzy. Adrian knew that from experience.

Not wanting to think on his past, he shut off the engine and exited the car. He moved to help Rafe, but the male was already out with Brenna in his arms.

A pregnant, somewhat short for a dragon-shifter female with black hair rushed up to Rafe. "Is she all right? Sid's just inside."

Rafe readjusted his grip on Brenna. "I don't know if fine is the right word, Nikki, but she's not in pain. Show me where Sid's waiting."

Killian went to Rafe's side, but the female named Nikki pushed him further away. "I'm sorry, but you need to stay away for now. Our head Protector, Kai, will take you three to a safe location."

Adrian was about to ask why Kai wasn't there when a familiar female voice filled his ears. "Adrian? Is that you?"

Both man and beast perked up, albeit for different reasons.

His dragon growled. *It's her.*

Hoping his beast was wrong, Adrian slowly turned around, only to find a short, curvy human female with brown hair and glasses over her brown eyes.

It was Elsie Day.

His dragon roared. *She's ours.*

Not this again. It's been years. The pull should've faded.

It's not as strong, but I still want her.

No. I won't allow it.

Not wanting to tempt his dragon, Adrian bolted in the opposite direction. He expected a reprimand and would happily take the consequences. What he couldn't risk was the mate-claim frenzy rekindling.

He made it about twenty feet before a large, muscled form tackled him from behind. With his dragon banging on about going back to Elsie, his concentration slipped and the muscled person pinned him down. A Northern English accent filled his ears. "Where do you think you're going?"

Jane's voice traveled on the wind. "Don't hurt him, Kai."

Kai. That meant Stonefire's head Protector had pinned him.

Since honesty was his best bet at this point, he turned his head and said, "That female, Elsie, stirred a mate-claim frenzy years ago. I can't risk it exploding again."

Kai moved his face further down and frowned. "The DDA inspector?"

He wanted to ask since when was Elsie a DDA inspector, but focused on what was important. "I just need to get away from her."

He swore understanding dawned in Kai's eyes. The male stood, and Adrian jumped to his feet. Kai placed one hand on Adrian's shoulder and used the other to motion for Jane to join them. The second she was at their side, Kai ordered, "Take him to our home and watch him. I'll send Zain over to help as soon as I can." Kai pinned Adrian with a stare. "Lay a finger on my mate and I won't be as understanding next time."

"I have no interest in harming anyone. Hence why I'm trying to get away from Elsie."

Kai looked like he wanted to ask something, but turned back toward Elsie and Cal. Kai tossed over his shoulder, "We'll talk more later, but I'll make sure she stays away."

Adrian chanced a glance at Elsie.

She stared right at him. Her hair was longer and she had different glasses, but she looked as if she hadn't aged at all in the intervening years.

His beast growled. *Why are you making this difficult? She clearly wants to talk with us.*

You want to do more than talk.

I can control myself. The pull to claim her is faint compared to before. I want her, but I would never force us on her.

I'm not risking it, dragon.

Although he hated to contain his beast, Adrian quickly constructed a mental prison and tossed him inside.

Turning away from Elsie, he looked to Jane. "Let's go."

He followed her lead. He hoped she would leave him alone, but she asked, "How do you know her?"

"That's a long story for another time."

"Maybe one day you'll trust me enough to tell me."

Jane picked up her pace and they walked the rest of the way in silence.

It should've given him the perfect time to come up with a plan, but the image of present-day Elsie kept flashing inside his mind.

Given what had happened between them, he never would've expected her to become a DDA inspector. He yearned to find out the reason, but knew that would be unwise.

The best thing he could do was lay low until he could go back to Northcastle and put the Irish Sea between them once more.

CHAPTER ELEVEN

Fire raced through Brenna's body and her eyes popped open as she gasped. A familiar, stern voice filled the room—Dr. Sid's. "Brenna, who's in control?"

Her dragon roared and spoke aloud. "I am. Where is he? I want Killian. He is mine to claim."

Sid cursed and Brenna tried to take control of her mind. However, her dragon must've constructed some sort of invisible prison because her hands came across a barrier that refused to budge. *Let me out.*

No. You'll let him get away.

Sid's voice cut off her reply. "Sorry about this, Brenna. But it's the only choice."

Something pricked her arm. Her dragon tried to sit up, but something restrained their body.

With each second that passed by, her dragon's strength waned a little more. When her dragon fell completely silent, Brenna tried pressing against the former barrier and her hands moved freely. After briefly checking on her snoring dragon, she took control of her body once more and looked at Sid. "Thank you."

"I prefer not to drug dragons into silence. Sorry I couldn't ask your permission beforehand."

Brenna knew that since Sid's dragon had been overdosed into silence for more than twenty years, she was always careful when it came to using drugs.

She replied, "It's okay, Sid. It had to be done." She raised a hand to her forehead. "Although I have an awful headache now."

"You're a little dehydrated, but we'll fix that. Are you well enough to tell me what happened? While I received a secondhand report, you might have details they missed."

At Sid's question, Brenna glanced about the room. "Where's Killian? They didn't send him back to Ireland, did they?"

Studying her, Sid shook her head. "No, he's with Kai and Bram right now. What happened? By all accounts, this wasn't your first kiss with him. So why did the frenzy erupt now? A few dragons can hide the pull from their human halves, but you've always been open with yours."

Her first impulse was to ask her dragon, but the sleeping form in her head reminded her it would be a day or two before her other half would be awake again.

She tried to sit up, but the leather restraints dug into her skin. Sid added, "They'll come off soon. I want to ensure your dragon is out for a while. Now, answer my question."

Sighing, Brenna looked to the ceiling. "I'm not sure. I've kissed him a few times. The only difference is the baby dragon is with him now." She met Sid's gaze. "Could that be the cause?"

"Possibly. Dragons don't place much stock in memories, but a dragon-shifter without their dragon half is an incomplete person. It's likely that your dragon only recognized him as your mate once the dragon returned."

She frowned. "But how is that possible? I never felt the pull in the months I worked with him before he had amnesia."

After jotting a few things down on the clipboard in her hand, Sid said, "Female dragons don't always notice a true mate until after a kiss. It's entirely possible the mate-claim frenzy pull would've started if he'd kissed you back then."

Dr. Gregor Innes, Sid's mate and a former Lochguard doctor, waltzed into the room and said, "Or, maybe not. Judging by Dr. Silver's notes from Killian's time on Northcastle, the wee dragon is described as blue with white patches. Killian had been a blue dragon before. Maybe a new dragon personality has emerged."

Sid jumped in. "Unless it split, as we discussed earlier."

Brenna looked at each of them. "What are you talking about?"

Gregor turned to face her. "It's just a guess, but I think the shadow dragon and the baby dragon form a whole, and together they comprise Killian's former dragon. Whatever drug was used on Killian could've split them into two. One of which holds his memories and the main thrust of his dragon's animal-like personality, and another that's more innocent and placid. Their goal might be to find a way to banish the more instinctual half and be left with the innocent side. A less angry and instinctual dragon makes for an easier catch."

"To harvest their blood," Sid added. "Although I'm not sure if it's the dragon hunters, Knights, or a new foe entirely. Dragon's blood on the black market is sold for small fortunes. An enterprising person could be trying their own hand at it. Although I suspect the person experimenting on dragons isn't fully aware of Killian's case, or they would be kidnapping more dragon-shifters to use as test subjects."

Despite everything going on, Brenna's mind put it all together. "If whoever did this finds out that it doesn't kill a dragon completely and successfully changed their personality, it won't be good. If enough dragons are kidnapped, then it could bring about one or more wars, especially if the DDA doesn't intervene as it should."

"Aye, that's possible," Gregor stated. "But let us and Kai worry about that. The question is what do you want to do about your current situation, Brenna? Repeatedly drugging your dragon into silence may end up hurting you both in the long run. Sending Killian away may be best, especially if it's to Lochguard so I can go and easily study him."

Sid crossed her arms. "Don't let Gregor's suggestion sway you one way or the other. This is your choice, Brenna. I can continue to administer drugs if you request it, but there are cases when either the dragon becomes slightly insane or gets so angry that your relationship will be rocky for years to come. Gregor's suggestion is the second option. The third is to have the frenzy. You need to make the decision soon, too. Otherwise, Bram may end up making it for you."

Going through the frenzy would be the easiest choice. She wouldn't have to give up Killian and her dragon would be pleased.

But having a child simply because it was easy for everyone else wasn't a good decision. Brenna was twenty-one and wanted to continue being a Protector. If Killian was sent away or, in a worst-case scenario, died, then she'd be on her own. A single mother would have a hard time remaining a Protector.

Unless she asked her parents for help. Her mother would enjoy that moment, she was sure.

Gregor cleared his throat. "You have a day or two to think about everything. I'll ensure Bram waits that long for an answer."

Sid drawled, "Because Bram listens to you so well."

"On medical matters, I can make him listen, Cassidy."

Shaking her head, Sid focused back on Brenna. "Now

that you have the facts, I should let your parents in."

Her stomach dropped. "They're here?"

"Of course. They've been waiting since word reached them about you being brought to the surgery."

A part of her wanted to keep them away, but with everything going on between her and Killian, not to mention the looming frenzy and the unnatural silence of her beast, she needed to sort out matters with her parents. It would be one less thing to fret over.

Besides, she could do with hearing her dad's advice. "Show them in. The sooner I get this over with, the sooner I can think about what to do regarding Killian."

Sid gestured at Gregor and he exited the room. Sid didn't waste time in removing the straps around Brenna's body as she said, "I can't fully disclose anything, but listen to what your parents have to say, Brenna. That's all I ask."

She barely resisted frowning at Sid's words when the door opened. Gregor ushered in Brenna's mum and dad.

Her mother, Sharon, came in first. While her blonde hair and brown eyes were the same, there was one major difference—she had to be eight or nine months pregnant.

Brenna opened her mouth, but her father, Gabriele, spoke up in his accented English. "We'll answer your questions in time, *cara*." Her father closed the distance to her bed and gently cupped her cheek. "Are you okay? The doctors have been vague about what's wrong with you."

She finally tore her gaze away from her pregnant mother and met her father's kind eyes. She'd never lied to her dad and she wasn't about to start now. "I kissed a male and it started the frenzy."

"And yet you look unhappy. Why?"

A small part of her wanted to fall into her father's arms and cry. But she refused to show weakness in front of her mother, so she slowly sat up and answered, "It's complicated. The short version is that the male who started it lost his memory and only recently regained his dragon." Her father's brows furrowed, but Brenna hurriedly asked her mother, "Why didn't you tell me you were pregnant?"

Sharon Rossi placed her hands over her protruding belly. "Since I wasn't supposed to be able to have any more children, it was a surprise and high-risk. I didn't want you to worry."

"I'm not a child anymore, Mum. You should've told me."

Her mother smiled sadly. "But you are barely an adult, Brenna. And I didn't want you thinking I was trying to replace you."

As she tried to think of how to reply to that, her father spoke up. "Please no fighting right now. We came back to Stonefire to be closer to you, Brenna. Your brother should know his sister."

"Brother?" she echoed.

Her father stood tall. "Yes, I will finally have an ally."

She couldn't help but smile. "You will outnumber Mum this time around, Papa. After all, I won't be there."

"But I hope you will come around often," her father said softly.

Bram must not have told her parents about wanting to stay in Ireland. Although given recent events, Brenna wasn't entirely sure what she was going to do in the future.

However, as she looked at her mother again, she decided to be nicer to her. It was almost a miracle her mother had carried a baby to term; her parents had gone through several miscarriages after Brenna was born and had eventually stopped for her mother's health. No matter their rocky past, Brenna wasn't going to be the cause of any distress.

Although the fact she was about to have a brother twenty-one years younger than her would be strange. Not only that, if she went through the frenzy, her child and their uncle would be almost the same age.

The frenzy. She'd almost forgotten about her own complicated life.

Dr. Sid peeked into the room. "I'm sorry to interrupt, but Bram wants to talk to you in about thirty minutes. Since I have some more tests to do, Sharon and Gabriele, you have about five more minutes with your daughter."

Her father bobbed his head. "Of course, Dr. Sid." He moved his gaze back to Brenna. "That should be just about enough time to tell us what is so complicated, *cara.*"

From experience, she knew that trying to deny her father an explanation was pointless. While Gabriele Rossi was the kinder, more patient of her parents, he held a hidden core of steel. He might even do something foolish such as try to bar Bram from the room until Brenna explained her situation.

Sighing, she explained events from her time on Glenlough to the present as best she could. When she finished, her father asked, "And what do you want to do, Brenna?"

"I don't know. One decision can change my life in so many ways."

Patting her hand, her father said, "Whatever you decide, we will be here to help you."

She glanced between her parents. "You're not going back to Clan LupoForesta?"

Clan LupoForesta was one of the Italian dragon clans, located in the Abruzzo, Lazio e Molise National Park not far from Rome.

Her father shook his head. "No. LupoForesta sees Stonefire in a negative light now, after what happened with Aaron Caruso and his mother." Aaron had been kicked out of the clan and his mother had followed him. "But your mother and I knew we wanted our second child born here, near his sister. So, we will stay here."

Brenna glanced at her mum. The years of reliving the

arguments with her mother, about Brenna not being strong enough to be a Protector, seemed to fade away as she took in her mother's pale face and dark circles under her eyes.

Killian's condition had taught her a few things about living in the moment and she wasn't about to waste what time she had with her family, especially over something that could be seen as a mother merely being protective of her only child.

Raising her hand, her mother came and took it. "We should talk more later."

Her mother smiled. "I'd like that. If you need to talk with someone about the frenzy, feel free to come find me."

"Thanks, but I think talking with Killian will help."

Her mother squeezed her hand. "Once I have your brother and regain my strength, I'll help you any way that I can, Brenna. I'm sorry for not believing in you earlier. I was just afraid that I'd lose my only child."

"I somehow understand that now." Dr. Sid popped her head in the doorway, signaling it was time for her parents to leave. Brenna quickly added, "Go rest. I need to talk to my mate and figure out what to do next."

As her parents said their goodbyes and left, Brenna wanted nothing more than to talk with her dragon about her parents' return. The silence inside her head reminded her of why she was lying in a hospital bed to begin with.

The only question is whether she wanted to allow her dragon to come back and go through the frenzy, or continue to drug her for months until the mate-claim frenzy faded.

Maybe talking with Killian would make the decision easier.

∽∾∾∽

Killian O'Shea followed Stonefire's head Protector into a

cottage. Neither one spoke as they moved down the corridor to an open doorway, where Stonefire's leader, Bram Moore-Llewellyn, sat at a desk. The dark-haired male motioned toward the two chairs in front of his desk. "Sit."

While he may have been able to get away with acts of defiance back in Ireland, he was completely at the English dragon-shifter's mercy. Pissing him off wasn't an option, especially since it could mean never seeing Brenna again as a result.

His dragon spoke up. *Then be nice.*

Bram prevented Killian from replying to his beast. "It seems the Glenlough dragons are out to make my life difficult through stealing my clan members."

Killian frowned. "What are you talking about?"

"Your sister took one of my Protectors, and now her brother is trying to do the same."

"I didn't—"

Bram raised a hand. "I know. It's called teasing. You'd better get used to it."

Killian's dragon spoke up. *Maybe he's not so scary.*

In my experience, the nicest ones at the beginning can turn out to be the most protective later on.

And how do you know that?

I'm not sure. I just do.

He barely had a second to wonder if some of his memories were coming back before Bram's voice filled the room again. "Look, I'll be honest—if it were solely up to me, I'd send you back home and keep you far away from Brenna. But Teagan says Brenna fancies you, so I'm going to give you a chance. However, with the Northcastle bloke fighting his own mate-claim frenzy pull with the human female, I have a lot going on and am going to place you into Tristan MacLeod's hands. You'll be staying with his family."

He frowned. "The teacher?"

"Aye, and he's going to help you. I can't risk your newfound dragon throwing a tantrum or going rogue. Tristan will ensure that you can get a grip on your inner beast. And before you think to overpower or trick Tristan and his mate, just know various Protectors are going to be watching you in shifts."

"But what about Brenna? When can I see her?" Killian asked.

Bram grunted. "I don't know. Possibly never, if she wills it."

Leaning forward, Killian ignored his instincts and growled, "I'm her mate. You can't keep me from her."

Raising his brows, Bram leaned back in his chair. "Can't I?"

His dragon whispered, *Don't make him angry. Be nice and he may let us see her again.*

Taking a deep breath, Killian let it out and tried again. "I want to see her for myself and make sure she's okay. Even if it's with a guard, it's better than nothing."

After a few beats, Bram nodded. "I might arrange that, provided your lessons with Tristan go well."

"And how am I supposed to concentrate while Brenna is suffering?"

Bram studied him a second. "Your sister may be right about you fancying Brenna."

Killian slapped a hand on the desk. "Of course I care for her. She's done more for me than anyone else. Why can't you believe that?"

"You have no idea who you really are and don't trust yourself. So, how am I supposed to trust you?"

Stonefire's leader was perceptive.

Killian wanted to deny it, but Bram's observation was correct. "Because regardless of the mess I am, Brenna is the one good thing in my life right now. Hurting her is the last thing I want to do."

Bram's pupils flashed. "I think I believe you. Still, you're going to Tristan's house and will stay there until you hear from me or one of my Protectors."

From the dominance in Bram's voice, Killian could tell the leader wouldn't budge. So he asked, "Then just tell me if Brenna is okay or is she suffering?"

Bram's gaze softened. "Sid will take care of her. Trust me on that."

That wasn't much of an answer, but Killian had a feeling that was all he was going to get.

He'd started to think he didn't care if his memories ever returned, but it seemed people would only trust him if they did.

His dragon spoke up. *We are fine the way we are. And as long as the shadow dragon stays away, we are safe.*

Wait, what are you talking about?

I don't know where that came from. But somehow I know that if he escapes the mirror lake and comes here, things will change.

Bram's voice interrupted his conversation. "Kai will take you to Tristan's right now."

Killian didn't stand. "What about my mother and sister? Can I talk to them soon? And no, I don't remember them. But Caitlin O'Shea gave up her freedom to help me. The least I can do is check up on her."

"You can have a video conference later, provided the Northcastle leader approves." Bram waved a hand in dismissal. "Take him away, Kai, and assign a guard."

Kai nodded his head and grunted. "Let's go, O'Shea."

Not wanting to risk the few privileges he'd won, Killian stood and followed Kai out of the cottage in silence.

As they walked past various clan members, they each paused to look at Killian. Some even whispered to their companions so low he couldn't make it out.

For the first time, he realized how lucky he'd been back on Glenlough. True, he may have had some restrictions but at least most people hadn't eyed him with suspicion or skepticism.

His beast chimed in. *But didn't you hate how they tried to force memories on you? You are never happy.*

I would be happy if I had Brenna by my side and we fled to some rural location where no one would bother us.

And Mum? What about her?

She has a new life to follow. An amnesiac son would only add complications and sorrow to it.

I wish you'd stop thinking we're a bother to everyone. People care about us. Why push them away?

He mentally grunted. *And how can a baby dragon be such a philosopher?*

I'm not a baby. And I'm clever. His dragon paused before adding, *If they allow it, we could try shifting.*

I think that requires knowledge and practice.

So you aren't ruling it out? his beast asked eagerly.

I suppose not. But shifting can be dangerous. I don't want to chance it.

And how do you know that? We've never tried.

I have no bloody idea. I just know.

So, you have more knowledge out of nowhere. Maybe the shadow dragon is slowly seeping into our mind.

Kai stopped at the doorstep of a cottage and Killian quickly said, *We'll talk more about this later.*

With a huff, his beast sat down and remained quiet.

Kai had barely knocked when the door opened to reveal a short, curvy female with a smile. A boy not much older than a year or so sat on her hip. The female looked at Kai and then Killian. "So this is Killian O'Shea."

The female's American accent made him blink. "You're

American."

"Well, half American. I'm Melanie Hall-MacLeod." She jostled the boy at her hip and he giggled. "This is my son, Jack. Tristan is around somewhere. Once he catches Annabel, he'll find us." She stepped back and motioned with her head. "Come in."

The fact the female trusted a stranger into her home and around her children either made her stupid or extremely kind.

He had barely stepped inside the cottage before a tall dragonman carrying a little girl about the same age as Jack strode down the hall. He growled, "You weren't supposed to let them in yet, Mel."

Melanie shrugged one shoulder. "Kai's here, and I wasn't about to let them linger on the doorstep. After all, Killian's having a hard enough day as it is."

Tristan glared at Killian. "Harm anyone in this house and you'll pay with blood."

Melanie tsked. "Tristan." She looked at her son's wide eyes. "Daddy isn't going to hurt anyone. Fighting isn't always the answer."

Annabel chanted, "Pay, pay, pay."

Rolling her eyes, Melanie sighed. "I suspect she'll be going around the house soon, saying people will pay with blood."

Before Tristan could reply, Jack pointed at Killian. "Who he?"

Jumping on the distraction, he smiled at the little boy. "My name is Killian."

"Kill!" Jack shouted.

Melanie snorted. "That is an unfortunate nickname. But Killian is quite a mouthful for someone not yet two." She turned. "Come in and make yourself comfortable. I'm sure you have a lot of questions for Tristan."

157

The human seemed an odd choice of mate for the growly, glaring dragonman. But he wasn't going to insult the female who'd been kind to him, so Killian followed her. Tristan trailed two steps behind him.

Once they all settled down into a chair or sofa in the living room, with the children playing on the floor, Melanie spoke up again. "I've heard your story and want to let you know that you can ask Tristan anything without feeling stupid. Despite his growly exterior, he's good at helping students with their inner dragons. Trust him, and you'll have a well-behaved dragon soon enough."

His beast huffed. *I'm already well-behaved.*

Don't be offended. She's just trying to help.

Still, there isn't much I need to contain.

What about shifting? I have no idea what to expect.

Then ask him.

Killian met Tristan's gaze. The warning from earlier had vanished and had been replaced with curiosity. Tristan spoke before he could. "I've never seen a grown male with a young inner dragon before. Explain what he knows or doesn't and we can formulate a strategy from there."

It was on the tip of his tongue to ask why Tristan was offering his help so easily, but he resisted. Killian explained about the young dragon, shadow dragon, and how both Killian and his new dragon half both seemed to possess knowledge with no memory of how they had gained it.

When he finished, Tristan grunted. "You're in much better shape than Sid was. I think we should start with cooperation exercises and work our way up to shifting sections of your body, such as a hand or foot, before taking the next step."

Little Annabel stood, yelled, "Pay!" and attempted to body slam her brother.

Melanie and Tristan had just managed to each take a

child in hand when Kai's voice filled the room. "That was Bram on my phone. I'm to take you back to the surgery, Killian."

He looked at the head Protector. "What? Why did he change his mind?"

Kai shrugged a shoulder. "Brenna wants to see you."

He stood and faced the head Protector. "She's awake?" Kai nodded, and Killian asked, "But won't me being near her stir the frenzy?"

"Her dragon has been drugged and will remain unconscious for a couple days."

As much as he wanted to learn more about being a dragon-shifter, Brenna was more important. "Then let's go."

Kai focused on Tristan and Melanie. "Someone will bring him back shortly. It'll give you more time to handle those two troublemakers."

Melanie grinned. "You know Annabel wants to start training as a Protector already, right? Maybe you should take her."

"Nice try, Mel. Your lively daughter is your concern." Kai motioned toward the door. "Let's go."

As they walked briskly back toward the surgery, Killian's heart rate ticked up. The upcoming conversation with Brenna wasn't going to be a light one. Somehow or another, he needed to find a way for him to stay with her. Having a child terrified him, but never seeing Brenna ever again made his heart heavy.

His dragon spoke up. *I'm sure we can find a way to stay with her.*

How? You say you have knowledge, but this seems unlikely.

Let me think on it.

By the time they reached the surgery, his beast still

hadn't said anything else.

Before he knew it, Kai opened the door to Brenna's room. Killian rushed inside and Brenna instantly met his eyes.

While she was physically the same with her lovely olive skin and short hair that brought out her cheekbones and full lips, something seemed different about her gaze. He wondered if it had to do with her missing dragon.

His own chimed in. *Where is her dragon? She seems different without it.*

It will come back.

Are you sure? I don't like it. Maybe I should try to bring it back, like the kiss with Georgiana brought me back.

Kissing her right now is a bad idea. I suspect even drugged, her dragon could sense it and maybe wake up.

His beast huffed. *I will hold back for now, but I'm going to work on solutions whilst you talk.*

Brenna's voice prevented him from replying. "It's okay, Killian. Come sit next to me."

Dr. Sid added, "But no kissing or even hugging. I can't risk the dragon fighting off the drugs early."

Grunting his acknowledgment, Killian walked over and sat on the edge of Brenna's bed. As they stared into one another's eyes, he wanted nothing more than to pull her close, nuzzle her neck, and take a few seconds to memorize her feminine scent. After all, this could be the last time he ever saw her.

No. He refused to accept that outcome until Brenna specifically rejected him.

Killian cleared his throat and decided to get the conversation over with. "Well, it seems we have quite a few decisions to make. Let's start with the most important—what do you want to do about the frenzy?"

CHAPTER TWELVE

*B*renna moved to take Killian's hand, but quickly clenched her fingers into a fist. Touching him was a bad idea, no matter how much she yearned to feel his warm skin. Some might put it down to the mate-claim frenzy, but Brenna knew better. Killian's presence had always affected her.

What she needed to do was focus on the bigger picture. However, she wasn't about to decide her life in front of an audience. Never taking her gaze from Killian, she asked, "Can you give us some time alone, Sid?"

As the doctor exited the room, she took the opportunity to memorize Killian's face. For all she knew, it might be her last chance to do so.

His firm jaw covered in dark stubble and straight nose might intimidate some, but all it did was made her ache to kiss along his jawline and take his full lips. However, when she met his green eyes again, the concern there reminded her of what was important. No matter how it might turn out, she wasn't going to put it off any longer. "Last time we made a life-changing decision, I was the one asking you for help. This time, I'm going to ask what you wish to do and I'll try my best to abide by it."

He cocked an eyebrow. "Straight to the point, I see."

"Dancing around it won't make the problem go away, Killian."

Inching his hand closer, he stopped short of touching her finger. Despite the minuscule distance between them, she could feel the heat radiating off his skin.

She glanced down at their hands, wondering if their life would always be like this moment. Close, but never together in the way she wanted.

"Look at me." She met his green-eyed gaze and drew in a breath at the fierceness there. He continued, "Wanting you isn't the problem here. The fact my former self never saw how beautiful and strong you are tells me he was an idiot. I want you with each breath I take and not being able to touch you right now is killing me."

She almost fell for his lovely words, but she leaned back and took a deep breath. "Attraction isn't enough to form a home and raise a child."

"Then talk to me, Brenna. Tell me about yourself. I promise your silliest fear or greatest weakness won't drive me away."

Searching his eyes, she blurted, "Do you even want a child?"

He paused a second before replying, "Something tells me I never thought I'd have one. And now, I'm worried that five years down the line I'll wake up a completely different person, with my memories intact. Or, worse, my condition ends up killing me. Either situation would scar a child for life."

She risked taking his hand and ignored the rightness that came at the contact. "The best I can understand, the longer your memory is gone, the less chance it'll return. But even if it did, you'd have the memories you've made since waking up with amnesia. And I guarantee Dr. Sid and her mate will do everything within their power to keep you alive and with us for a long time to come."

He studied their clasped hands. "While I appreciate you wanting to comfort me, what about you?" He met her gaze again. "What do you want, Brenna? My part in the whole thing is brief. You'll have nine months of suffering, plus the rest of your life to deal with a child if I die or go insane."

Forcing a smile, she squeezed his hand. "Let's hope it doesn't come to that."

"But it could. My mother had a difficult time when she was pregnant with me."

He may not realize it, but Killian had remembered something.

Careful to keep the surprise from her voice, Brenna asked slowly, "How so?"

For a second, she thought his temporary memory had left. But he finally spoke again. "She had extreme morning sickness the entire time and spent more days than not in bed. Once I was born, my father said they shouldn't have any more children because he couldn't stand to see her suffer."

Somehow, some way, some of Killian's memories were trickling back.

She wanted to yell for Dr. Sid and see what she had to say on the subject, but decided it was better to keep Killian talking for the moment. "What about when she carried your sister?"

"She was fine. My mother always joked that I was the troublemaker from the start. I think part of the reason I became a Protector was to prove her wrong."

Her heart beating double-time, she decided to ask him a little more. "Was that the only reason you became a Protector?"

He shook his head. "No. I wanted to protect my family after my father died." He frowned. "Why are you looking at me like that?"

"Because you just told me something about your past, something I don't think anyone has mentioned to you."

"That's impossible."

"But it's true."

An undefined emotion flashed in his eyes. "Ask me something else."

"I'm not sure what to ask. How about your earliest memory?"

He answered without missing a beat. "Something about a toy sword and shield. Maybe for my birthday?"

"And what about your adult life? What do you remember?"

"I-I don't know. It seems only specifics work."

She leaned forward a fraction. "Do you remember when you first met me, before the amnesia?"

He shook his head. "No. I can't remember anything about you before I woke up with the tattoo on my arm gone."

"I'm not sure if I should be excited or worried about some of your memories coming back. It could mean you're recovering, but there's still a lot of unknown variables. What does your dragon say?"

Killian's pupils turned to slits. Each second that passed only made her heart thump harder.

She wasn't sure if she wanted all his memories to return or not. But she wasn't a selfish person and would do whatever she could to help him test the new boundaries of his mind.

However, when Killian gripped his head and grunted, she quickly pushed the call button just in case. "What's happening? Tell me how to help."

As he said nothing and continued to hold his head, fear filled her belly. The last time Killian had fallen unconscious, blood had dripped out of his ear. She had no idea what could happen next.

After coming so far, he might still die.

And that scared her more than anything.

⁂

Inside his mind, a dark, shadowlike swirl churned around Killian's human form. Each pass of the darkness sent another shot of pain through his body.

His dragon yelled, *I can't stop it.*

Try harder.

A pause, and then, *I'm sorry. This is my fault.*

It was getting harder to concentrate as the pain coursed through his body, but he gritted out, *What do you mean?*

I kept pawing at the invisible walls, wondering if I could go back to the lake and allow you some time alone with Brenna.

His dragon was a child and lacked adult reasoning.

Before Killian could learn anything else, the shadow substance gripped around his middle and yanked him toward something.

He blacked out and regained consciousness beside the mirror lake.

With a groan, he sat up slowly and noticed the large crack in the lake's surface. What looked like black steam rose from it, and it slowly moved to gather around Killian's body.

Whether this was another dream or he was trapped in a different part of his mind, he had no idea. But something told him that he needed to find the baby dragon if he ever wanted to get back to Brenna.

Clenching his jaw, Killian slowly stood and surveyed the area. While the shadow cloud around his body continued to thicken, he could just make out the hills nearby. At the top of one sat the young blue and white dragon.

Killian needed to reach him.

Pushing against the cloud enclosure, pain instantly radiated up his arm.

As he gritted his teeth, he returned his arm to his side. If the darkness consumed him, he would never make it to that hill. That left only one option—the young dragon had to come to him. The question was how to reach him.

An idea flashed. Since speaking in his mind had always worked, he tried it now. *Can you hear me?*

The dragon's voice wavered as he answered, *Yes.*

Then come to me. I need you.

But I'm scared. The shadow dragon is coming out and wants to eat me.

Please, if you want to make Brenna smile again, I need your help. I can't get out of this alone.

The darkness continued to build around him, to the point he could no longer see his surroundings.

When the swirling blackness closed in on him and began to shrink, Killian was forced to squat to avoid coming into contact with it. Any time he chanced touching the black mist, it burned his skin. If he couldn't find a way out, he might die.

And then he'd never have the chance to hold Brenna close and make her laugh.

Because in that moment, it became clear that even if his future was uncertain, he wanted what time he had in the present with his beautiful female. He'd wasted too much time already. Time he could've wooed and gotten to know Brenna instead of being surly and acting nonchalant.

Killian would have to fight for what he wanted, even if it meant he could die in the process.

That meant he needed to escape the darkness. Just as he

was about to chance standing up, the little dragon crashed through the swirling, thick mist. Within seconds, the cloud spread out and retreated a short distance away. The baby dragon stood in front of Killian and spread his wings wide. "Don't harm him."

The blackness morphed into the shape of a dragon. A deep voice boomed out, "I can't survive without him. You and I must become one."

Something about the deep voice was familiar, but Killian pushed the feeling aside. It may only have been a short time, but he'd grown close to the little dragon. He couldn't let him die.

Killian shouted, "Leave him be and take me."

"No," the shadow dragon answered. "I can't survive without the wee one either."

Before he could say anything else, the shadow dragon rushed at them and crashed into the baby dragon's chest. The little one roared as the entire cloud entered his body before he collapsed.

Kneeling next to his beast, he instinctively checked the artery on the little one's neck. At the soft thump under his fingers, he let out a breath. "You're still alive." The base of the baby dragon's neck vibrated. "What the fuck?"

Taking a step back, Killian watched as something grew from the dragon's hide. First, in the shape of a new bud or branch of a tree, until it was nearly as long as the dragon's neck, and then another head appeared.

When the black dragon's head opened its eyes, a rush of memories came into his brain.

Killian learning of his father's death and vowing to protect his mother.

Thrashing about in a reinforced cottage to keep his distance from Georgiana.

Growling at Aaron Caruso for courting his sister.

Brenna working with him on security and drills on Glenlough.

Waking up strapped to a table as humans pumped him full of drugs.

The black dragon head growled. "Now we are one."

In the next instant, the blue and white dragon head opened his eyes. And before he could do anything, the two-headed dragon flew through the sky toward an exit point and Killian lost consciousness.

⌒◦⌒◦⌒◦⌒

Brenna stood to the side of the room as Sid and Gregor checked over Killian's limp form on the hospital bed.

She hated being useless. Brenna was a Protector for many reasons, but one of them was because she liked to act. Be it in safeguarding the clan against future attacks or participating in a search for a missing clan member, she wanted to be doing something.

And yet here she was, standing to the side and wringing her hands.

It took everything she had not to ask for an update. While Killian was pale, he was alive and wasn't bleeding from his ears or anywhere else. She only hoped that was a good sign.

In moments like these, her dragon usually helped comfort her. The unnatural silence inside her mind only made matters worse.

If not for her mother's delicate health, she would reach out to her parents. While Brenna had tried to pretend she was grown and didn't need her parents' support, she missed her father's gentle hugs.

Instead, she hugged her upper body and watched Sid and Gregor work. The pair were mates, but they were partners in all ways and worked together seamlessly.

168

After what seemed like an hour, Sid turned toward Brenna and crossed the distance to her. "He's stable, but something is certainly going on inside his mind."

Gregor joined them. "Aye, it reminds me of a video I saw, of a child patient struggling with his rogue dragon." He motioned toward Killian, who was still being watched by a nurse named Ginny. "He's suffering mini-seizures every few minutes."

She glanced at Killian. "Will they kill him?"

Gregor shook his head. "At this point, I don't think so. But we need to watch him closely and ensure they don't intensify."

Brenna watched Killian's face twitch a few times before going slack again. She looked back at the doctors. "I know little about how to help rogue dragons beyond drugs and a slow reintroduction with coaching from an expert. But do you think a kiss from his true mate might help?"

Sid searched her gaze. "Before I answer, is this what you want? Helping Killian is noble, but there will be consequences, Brenna. Ones that will probably result in a child."

Looking between Sid and Gregor, she answered, "Gregor did the same to help your dragon, Sid. Do you regret it?"

"No," she said slowly. "But the situation was different. I had wanted children but had thought I'd never have them. After all, I had been afraid of going insane. You are clearly reluctant."

"If it can help Killian, then I'll do it. Besides, I always have the choice to give the child up for adoption if Killian's condition worsens and he needs me."

Gregor chimed in. "You're willing to do a fair bit for a male you barely know."

She stood tall. "I'm his mate, which means he's my responsibility."

Sid shared a look with Gregor before turning her head back toward Brenna. "Then if you're going to kiss him and start the frenzy, I'd do it sooner rather than later. While it's unlikely, a bigger seizure could grip him and do permanent damage." She bobbed her head, and Sid added, "We'll stay initially, to ensure nothing goes wrong. But if the frenzy erupts, we'll leave you alone. However, if anything changes or becomes out of control, you need to hit the call button."

Taking a deep breath, she looked at Killian. "Okay. Is there anything you can give me to wake up my dragon?"

Gregor answered, "The kiss may do it on its own. If not, we can try a stimulant, but it's not guaranteed to work."

Brenna walked to Killian's bedside. Running her fingers through his short hair, she hoped this worked. Even if he wanted nothing to do with her after, that was fine. It meant Killian would have the chance to protect his family back home, just as he'd vowed when his father had died.

She wasn't sure why that was so important, but maybe it was just her sympathy for a male who'd endured so much in such a short time.

Her heart thundering in her chest, she leaned down and pressed her lips to Killian's firm ones. While familiar, he remained unresponsive.

After a minute had passed and nothing happened to him or to her dragon, she stood. She refused to believe that was it. She looked to the doctors and asked, "Can you give me the stimulant? My dragon isn't stirring."

Gregor quickly cleaned an area on her upper arm and injected her with something. A rush of adrenaline coursed through her body. Her heart rate increased and after a few more seconds, a sleepy voice spoke inside her head. *What happened?*

I'll explain later. I just need you awake.

Before her beast could question her further, Brenna

kissed Killian again.

She expected her dragon to demand Killian's cock and to ride him.

However, she merely yawned and stretched out her wings. *Why did you wake me? I want to go back to sleep.*

I don't understand. We kissed him earlier and you said he was our true mate.

Whoever you just kissed is different. I want to sleep.

Standing upright again, she murmured, "What's happening to you, Killian?"

Gregor's Scottish brogue filled the room. "There's no frenzy?"

"No. My dragon said he's different."

Appearing at her side, Gregor stared at Killian's face. "Maybe the shadow dragon finally embraced him. That could make him a different male."

Not wanting to dwell on the fact that might mean old Killian had returned, she asked, "Then why is he seizing as if his dragon had gone rogue?"

"For all we know, the two dragon personalities could be distinct and are fighting inside his mind."

She clenched a fist over her heart. "Then what do we do?"

Gregor's gentle voice filled the room. "I recommend trying to wake up Killian. Then Tristan can work with him on containing his dragon or dragons. The sooner we attempt to tame the rogue presence inside Killian's mind, the better chance we have at preserving his sanity."

"I'll contact Tristan straight away," Sid said as she exited the room.

Gregor placed a hand on her shoulder and squeezed. "We're going to do our best to save him, Brenna. But you need to prepare yourself for the worst. I've never heard of a male with two dragon personalities in one brain before. It may be too much. One can be quite a handful on its own.

Two would require unbelievable strength."

She took Killian's hand and threaded her fingers through his. "If anyone was strong and stubborn enough to tackle that challenge, it would be Killian O'Shea."

"That's the way to think of it, lass. Being strong under circumstances such as these isn't easy, especially for someone you care about but who may not feel the same way. Regardless, Killian has formed an attachment to you. Hopefully no matter what's happened, it's enough to entice him to fight for sanity as well as his life."

As she gripped his hand tighter, she only hoped so, too.

Chapter Thirteen

Killian couldn't see anything, but he heard two voices—those of the baby dragon and the shadow dragon.

The shadow dragon growled. "I'm older and more experienced. I'm in charge."

"No, this is my body and you're invading it. I'm in charge."

"I will hurt you."

"I'm not afraid. If you kill me, it will probably kill you, too."

The darkness faded until it was replaced by the neutral gray and brown colors of his mind. Neither the mirror lake nor the rolling hills were anywhere to be seen.

But instead of being able to open his actual eyes and see the real world, he was trapped inside his brain with a two-headed dragon.

The black dragon head looked straight at him. "You remember me now and know what I can do. Tell the baby to listen to me."

The blue and white dragon straightened his neck. "I'm young, not a baby. And I stood by him when you left."

"It wasn't by choice," the black dragon growled.

Killian closed his eyes and opened them, but the two-headed dragon was still standing not far from him. The body remained blue with white patches, which made the black neck and head stand out and almost appear ominous.

Placing a hand on his forehead, Killian murmured, "I don't know what's happening. No one is supposed to have two dragons inside their mind. Maybe I'm dead."

The black dragon head jumped in. "I don't think so. You're just unconscious."

"And how do you know that?" he asked.

The black dragon huffed. "Because I peeked while you were lying there."

Killian looked up. "Wait, what?"

"Someone opened our eye and I took control."

The baby dragon growled. "This is my body. I should always be in control."

The two dragon heads snapped at one another, each trying to grip the other's neck. When they succeeded, both holding on at the same time, Killian's entire body jerked until they released their grips.

Once he caught his breath, he stood and put on his best stern voice. "Stop it. If you keep that up, you'll kill us all."

The baby dragon muttered, "He started it."

Narrowing his eyes, the black dragon bared his teeth. Both dragons moved to attack again when something whooshed through the area and Killian opened his actual eyes to a room full of people.

Brenna's face was closest. "Killian? Can you hear me?"

He opened his mouth to reply, but the two-headed dragon tossed him to the back of his mind. The black dragon's voice answered her, "I am here."

A higher-pitched voice came from Killian's lips. "No, I am here."

Frowning, Brenna looked to the doctors and back to him. "Who is there?"

"We are all Killian," the deeper voice stated.

Gregor asked slowly, "How many of you are there?"

"Three."

Tristan MacLeod's growly voice filled the room. "That's new."

The deeper dragon voice spoke. "We wish to shift. I've been trapped for far too long and want to feel the rush of wind against my hide."

Killian could do nothing but watch from his mental prison as the black dragon maintained control, sat up, and tore off the restraints of their human form.

Everyone sprang into action in the room except for Brenna, who never moved. She asked slowly, "Can I talk to the human part of Killian?"

The deeper voice of the black dragon replied, "No. He wants to banish me." The baby dragon pushed into control and his higher-pitched voice growled, "We both want you gone. This is my body."

"I don't understand your last statement. Are you sharing a body?" Brenna asked.

"Yes," the baby dragon answered. "I can't seem to get rid of him and anytime I attack, it hurts our human part."

The black dragon won control again. "You will never be rid of me. I'm stronger and more dominant. Accept that your place is subservient to me."

The two dragon heads snapped at each other inside his mind. Once again his entire body jerked sporadically when they caught each other's throats.

Something pricked his arm and the shaking thankfully ceased. However, the world blacked out again.

⌒⌒⌒⌒⌒

As soon as Killian was unconscious once more, Brenna brushed the hair off his forehead. He may be alive, but Killian was on the verge of going insane, provided his dragons' fighting didn't kill him first. No doubt a constant barrage of seizures couldn't be good for his health.

Tristan's voice broke the silence. "I hate to say it, but we may have to lock him up and monitor him as much as possible. One dragon is hard enough to train, but two that appear to hate each other is going to be a monumental task."

Forcing her gaze away, Brenna met Tristan's gaze. "Let me know how I can help."

Tristan grunted. "I'm not sure you can. His mother may be a better help since his dragon would think twice of hurting her."

She hated to be thought of as a near-stranger, but Brenna couldn't allow her feelings to get in the way of Killian's recovery. "Has she mated the Northcastle leader yet? If she has, then she should be free to travel here, especially if the DDA inspector is still around."

"The inspector is still here," Sid stated. "As for Killian's mum, I have no idea if she's mated Lorcan Todd or not. However, someone should be arriving soon to fetch Adrian. He needs to go back to Northern Ireland if he wants to avoid the frenzy with the DDA inspector."

In all of the commotion surrounding Killian, she'd forgotten about Adrian and Elsie Day. "Maybe I should talk with Bram and see if he'll invite Killian's mum here."

The clan leader's voice came from the doorway. "I'm already here, lass."

Turning, she saw Bram enter the room, followed by his mate, Evie Marshall, and a female she didn't recognize with dark hair on top and sections of dyed blue on the bottom.

Bram spoke up again. "This here is Dr. Alice Darby. She's

Evie's friend and knows some things about dragon-shifters that I don't."

She met the female's brown-eyed gaze. "How?"

Alice raised her brows. "I'm not partial to giving out information to people I don't know. What's your name?"

Brenna gave the human credit for standing up to her. "Brenna Rossi." She looked at Bram again. "What is she doing here?"

Bram's mate, Evie, answered, "Alice might be able to help Killian." Evie moved her gaze to Dr. Sid. "However, she can't do that without knowing what's going on. You only said it was urgent."

Sid didn't hesitate. "We think he has two dragon personalities residing inside his head, and they're constantly fighting each other. Have you heard of two dragons in one mind before, Alice?"

The human female must've been on Stonefire longer than Brenna had realized if Sid was readily asking her questions.

"Only once, and it was part of a legend, so I don't know if it's true," Alice answered as she moved to the other side of Killian's bed.

As the human studied Killian's face, Brenna's dragon decided to speak once more. *She is too close to him.*

What are you going on about? I thought you didn't want him as a mate?

I never said that. Just that there's no mate-claim frenzy pull. I was also half-asleep. Killian is ours.

Not wanting to think about her dragon's statement, she answered, *Fine. But just be quiet for now. This human might be able to help.*

Brenna asked Alice, "What was the legend about?"

The human never took her eyes off Killian's face. "Soon after the Spanish conquistador Francisco Hernandez de Cordoba fought the Mayans during his ill-fated expedition in 1517, in what is present-day Mexico, a two-headed dragon appeared not far from where the battle took place. The beast went on a rampage against the human Mayans in the area. They eventually slayed him. Reliable accounts are sparse, but one carved record written in the old dragon language of the area mentions the two-headed dragon eating something he stole from the Spaniards' supplies, which caused nightmares like none had ever seen."

Brenna jumped in. "Do you know what he ate?"

Alice shook her head. "No. Since the carved tablet was broken, we don't have the whole story. But many have speculated that whatever he stole from the Spaniards might have caused his dragon to go rogue."

Brenna had to give the human credit. Alice did seem to know a lot about dragon history. Brenna had never heard anything about the event in her history classes as a student.

Sid asked, "Is there any way to narrow down what the substance might have been? Even just supplies or records from the time might give us a starting point."

Alice answered, "The best anyone's ever been able to do is to comb the ship's logs from the era. But even then, nothing unusual appeared."

"Regardless, if you can find and share those logs, maybe I can discover something useful in them that others may have overlooked," Sid said.

Alice bobbed her head. "I'll try my best. Although it may take a few days to track the information down and obtain a translation."

Brenna should keep her mouth closed, but she knew everyone else in the room well enough that she blurted, "How does a human know so much about dragon-shifters?"

Alice shrugged. "I've been fascinated since I was a child. And since I'm incompatible with dragon-shifter DNA and can't join the sacrifice program, I decided to focus my life's work on learning as much as I could."

Evie added, "And she's found loads of other people with similar interests. It's how we met, via an online message board."

"And yet you haven't shared this knowledge with the dragons?" Brenna queried.

Alice answered, "There's no central dragon authority, and few even communicate with each other. I didn't want to favor one over another and risk them using the information to start a war." She motioned toward Bram. "Although Evie's mate gives me hope that worldwide cooperation between the dragon clans could happen one day."

Bram grunted. "I think it will. In the meantime, Alice is here to observe our clan and report back to the DDA about general practices. That may be her legitimate reason for being here, but she and Evie have plans not even I'm aware of yet."

Evie smiled up at her mate. "I'll tell you soon, love. You have enough on your plate as it is."

Shaking his head, he rubbed Evie's back. "Says the female suffering from morning sickness. A pregnancy this soon after the last isn't good."

Evie leaned against Bram's side. "I'll be fine. After all, Holly's experiments on Lochguard have been going well."

Brenna didn't know what experiments were being conducted, but she wasn't interested in them right now. She brought them back on topic. "While Alice complies with Sid's request, what about Killian's mum? Do you think Northcastle will allow her to come?"

Bram frowned. "Probably not alone. I suspect Lorcan will accompany her. And as much as I hate special dinners for guests, we might have to conduct one to please Northcastle's leader."

Brenna tilted her head. "Doesn't Northcastle get along

better with Finn Stewart? Why not invite the Scottish clan leader?"

"He will only make things worse," Bram grumbled.

Evie patted his chest. "Now, now, inviting Finn can't hurt. It'd be nice for us to see Arabella and her babies, too. If he'll allow them to come."

"They're not even two months old yet, so I doubt he'll want to travel," Bram muttered.

Brenna jumped in. "Still, you should invite someone from Lochguard to help. I know one of their head Protectors is still recovering from his recent attack in Ireland, but surely they have someone else who can act as a diplomatic envoy of sorts."

Bram grunted. "I'll see what I can arrange."

Sid lightly clapped her hands. "Right, then with that all sorted, I need as many of you to clear out as possible so I can formulate a plan with Tristan."

Bram nodded. "We'll leave. And Brenna, come with us. I need your help with contacting Northcastle and talking with Adrian. You have experience with both."

Shifting her gaze to Killian's face, she struggled to leave him. But if Killian were awake and mentally sound, he'd want her to fulfill her duties. Especially if it meant bringing his mother to be at his side.

She kissed his cheek and murmured, "I'll be back," before standing and going to Bram's side.

Taking one last look at Killian, she left the room. She might be helpless when it came to controlling his dragons and stopping his seizures, but she could help in other ways. No matter if she had to go to Northcastle herself, she'd find a way to bring Caitlin to her son's side.

CHAPTER FOURTEEN

Caitlin O'Shea stood beside Lorcan on a stage in front of the entire clan and tried her best not to shift her feet.

The mating ceremony had finished a few minutes before, but Lorcan was giving a speech about several items. One of which regarded her future in the clan.

Glancing at Lorcan's strong profile, she was both nervous and excited to finish what they had started back in her temporary housing. One clan matter after the other had come up to prevent them spending much time alone together. But while some females would be cross about such matters, Caitlin understood clan leaders and their duties.

Although when news came through about Adrian fighting off a mate-claim frenzy and Killian's change in condition, all she'd cared about was finishing the mating ceremony so she could accompany Lorcan to Stonefire. They would need to consummate the mating to ensure no challenges popped up, but tomorrow morning they would make the journey across the Irish Sea.

Lorcan glanced at her and smiled. He was about to introduce her new duties, so she returned the smile and focused back on the clan in front of them.

Her mate's voice boomed in the great hall. "While having a beautiful female on my arm is a boon, she has a brain as well and will be helping out the clan's teachers. If the alliance is to work, we must start erasing the distrust and rumors surrounding Glenlough." There were a few grumbles in the crowd, but Caitlin had a feeling that any trouble toward her would come later. Lorcan continued, "Now that I've finished my announcements, enjoy the celebration. It's been a while since our last one, and we could all do with brushing up our dancing skills."

He signaled the person in charge of the music and it filled the hall a few seconds later.

Lorcan took her hand and led her down the stairs to the main floor. He wasted no time in guiding them to the dancing area and pulling her close. She was grateful for knowing the dance well, otherwise she may have stumbled at Lorcan's hard body against hers; the thin material of her dress did little to shield his heat.

Lowering his head to her ear, he murmured, "You look beautiful, Caity. I didn't get to tell you that earlier."

"Since I spent an hour on my hair, I hope I look nice or it'd be a wasted effort."

Her mate lightly brushed the back of her neck. "Just know that your hair is coming down later. I want it to fan your body on my bed."

She should feel guilty considering her son was struggling hundreds of miles away, but there was nothing she could do until she set foot on Stonefire's land. So, for once, she decided that the evening would be hers. "Patience, Lorcan. Socializing with the clan is just as important as consummating our mating."

"I want to curse you for knowing how clan leaders work so well, but I must admit it makes my job easier."

She should merely snuggle close and enjoy the dance. But she couldn't help but say, "I hope things calm down soon enough. Because if I can be honest, you work too much."

"I won't disagree with that. Although with the alliance with Glenlough and now possibly Stonefire, it should make my life easier."

Her new mate swung her out and back again. Once Lorcan completed turning her and pulling her close, Caitlin asked, "Are there still people inside Northcastle who are looking to oust me?"

Lorcan had shared that some of the more stubborn clan members who wanted nothing to do with other clans had been grumbling to sympathetic ears.

Her mate shook his head, his strong jaw lightly caressing her cheek in the process. "I think most, if not all, have been contained and questioned thoroughly. I can't risk banishing anyone right now, or they could end up either with the rogue dragon group hiding in the wilds of Scotland, or they might be kidnapped and wake up like Killian, sans memory and eventually with two dragons."

At the mention of her son, she closed her eyes, trusting Lorcan to guide her through the dance steps. "No one should be without a dragon, let alone have to deal with two. And yet, Killian's experienced both in such a short time."

"I know, Caity. And while I don't know your family well, it pains both man and beast to see you sad." He cupped her cheek and she opened her eyes to see his face. "I will help you do whatever we can to fix this."

The conviction in Lorcan's voice brought tears to her eyes. "Thank you."

He kissed her gently. "Don't thank me. It's what a stepfather is supposed to do. Although I admit gaining two grown children will be somewhat difficult."

She smiled. "Especially when one of them is a clan leader

in her own right. If ever there was a stepchild who wasn't going to make life easy for a stepparent, it would be a fierce leader like Teagan."

"It's who she is, Caity. I wouldn't want anything less."

Since this had been the most time she'd had to simply talk with her new mate in a while, she risked asking, "How does your daughter feel about it?"

He twirled her out and back. "Georgiana is a difficult female to read. She's quiet, but intelligent. She's never really had a mother since hers died so young. To be honest, she probably won't know how to act with you. Although it's not in her nature to be cruel for the sake of it."

"I already know that. After all, she risked a great deal to help Killian. For that, I will make every effort to know her better."

Strumming his thumb on her cheek, he murmured, "This is nice, dancing and talking with you. I wish we could've mated years ago."

A small part of her mourned never being able to give Lorcan a child, but she quickly pushed it away. "It never would've worked, and you know it. Regardless of how you've thought of me, Teagan needed me the past five years, as she grew into her role as clan leader. And your clan needed you, too, after the incompetence of your predecessor."

He smiled. "You already have me, Caity. No need for flattery."

She raised her brows. "It's true. The former leader nearly started a war. Northcastle desperately needed your reasonable mind."

"I won't disagree with that. However, long-term peace is on the horizon, more than ever before. Plus, all our children are grown. Once Killian is on the mend, I can think about retiring."

She searched his gaze. "Are you sure, Lorcan? You're not

yet sixty, and a hearty male at that."

"A male could get used to your compliments, Caity."

"Well, I'll be around for a while. However, know that I only give compliments that are true."

Chuckling, he rubbed her lower back. Without thinking, Caitlin melted against Lorcan's body. His breath tickled her ear as he said, "I'll remember that. But I'm serious about retiring. With all the changes, a younger male might do better."

"Or female."

"I have nothing against it, but I'm not sure if Northcastle is ready for that, love. After all, we don't have any female Protectors."

"Then you need to change that before you retire. It'll be one of my requirements."

"Requirements, aye?"

Since she didn't feel any tension in Lorcan's body, she held her ground. "Yes."

He kissed her neck and murmured, "Good, as I'm sorely in need of a few restrictions. A bachelor's life has made my life rather routine." He kissed her neck again and she sighed. "I won't retire until everything is sorted. But I look forward to taking some time for ourselves. I've always wanted to travel and frolic in a warmer ocean with a gorgeous female, both in human and dragon forms."

Lorcan's warm thumb against her cheek easily coaxed out her past. "Truth be told, when I was younger, I was afraid to travel. The UK and Ireland weren't the only ones dealing with changing times and balances of power with the human governments. I'd heard stories of foreign dragons attacking Irish ones. But I'm wiser now and know that there will always be rumors about those who live in other countries. While it's unlikely we can visit every country, I'd like to make a go of it. The trick will be in garnering the

DDA's permission."

Lorcan pressed her closer against his body, and Caitlin drew in a breath. His deep voice rolled over her. "Once I retire, we can make that our life's mission, to allow greater freedom between clans."

She laughed. "That doesn't sound much like retiring. Accomplishing that will require maybe even more work than being clan leader."

He grinned. "Perhaps, but it also means we can travel. And with you on my arm, that sounds like heaven."

Heat rushed to her cheeks. "Keep it up and you're going to run out of compliments soon."

"Never, Caity." Moving to her ear, his hot breath tickled her skin as he added, "We can do a few more dances, but then I'm whisking you to my secret room in the great hall. I've had decades to fantasize about this night."

Lorcan's rumbly voice made her stomach flip in a good way. "Just make sure it's nothing that will pull a muscle, or you could be limping onto Stonefire tomorrow."

He lightly swatted her bum, heat radiating from his touch and traveling to between her thighs. It took everything she had to focus on Lorcan's words. "I bet I can outlast many a lad in his twenties. Just make sure to tell me if you wish to stop, Caity. I sense you care more about others' needs over your own. But as I've mentioned, I plan to take care of you and I can't do that without knowing what to look for."

She nodded just as the song ended.

Her dragon spoke up. *He will be good for us. But I won't make my final decision until I see him naked.*

You would say that.

Her beast grunted. *He's boasted quite a bit. I want to see if he can live up to the hype. Because if he can, I may see if I can tire out his dragon half.*

She laughed, and Lorcan raised his brows in response.

When she caught her breath, she said, "I hope your dragon likes a challenge. Mine is ready to outlast yours."

He snorted. "Female dragons are randier..."

Lightly swatting his chest, she leaned closer. "Don't encourage her."

Grinning, he stepped back and bowed as the final notes of the song echoed in the space.

Somehow Caitlin managed to survive a few more dances without worrying about things outside her control, enjoying the light conversation and teasing from her new mate.

It was still early days, but Caitlin began to think a life with Lorcan might be good for her. He didn't try to force her to be someone she wasn't—unlike her mother. And she didn't always have to be strong—like with her children. She was simply Caitlin Todd.

And she rather liked the sound of that.

After who knew how much time had passed, the latest song ended and Lorcan pulled her to the side of the hall. He whispered, "I've done my obligations. Now it's time to escape and take some time for just the two of us. Are you ready, Caity?"

Her heart rate kicked up at his words, and even further when he lightly stroked the bare skin of her arm.

Her dragon spoke up. *Yes, I'm ready. Let's go.*

She bobbed her head. Lorcan threaded the fingers of one hand through hers and slowly guided them out of the great hall, stopping to say hello to various clan members along the way.

While she looked forward to the next part of the evening with Lorcan, she couldn't stop her palms from sweating. The last time she'd done this had been over a decade ago.

Don't worry. I can always take over and ride him hard.

No, love. I want the first time. You'll have many more times in the future, provided he lives up to his promises.

Her dragon snorted. *We'll see. Most males like to boast, but fall short in reality.*

Lorcan took her through a secret door she hadn't noticed in the wall, and up a flight of stairs. The ensuing corridor was covered in old tapestries, helping to keep out the chill of the old stone building. He finally stopped in front of a sturdy, wooden door. "Are you ready, Caity? Because once we get inside, I'm not going to waste time with pretty words."

Taking a deep breath, she answered, "I'm ready. Besides, pretty words will only make me more nervous. I'm anxious to see you naked."

"A female who knows what she wants. You keep giving me reasons to adore you."

She couldn't stop the color rushing to her cheeks. "Let's just go inside."

Before she could do more than blink, Lorcan opened the door, tugged her inside, and shut the door again. Hauling her up against his body, he murmured, "My lovely Caity. You won't regret agreeing to mate me."

"I thought there weren't going to be any pretty words?"

With a growl, Lorcan took her lips in a rough kiss. She instantly parted her own to allow him access, the stroke of his tongue against hers sending fire throughout her body.

He cupped her arse cheeks and easily lifted her, carrying her to the bed, all while never missing a beat with his exploration and dominance of her mouth.

While she could feel his hard chest against her, she wanted to feel every inch of his skin against hers. Just as she was about to wrap her legs around his waist, Lorcan broke the kiss and gently laid her down on the large bed. "I hope you aren't attached to this dress."

She'd barely shaken her head when he ripped it down the middle and tossed the material aside. His pupils flashed repeatedly as he slowly perused her body.

Caitlin may not be twenty, but she wasn't embarrassed about her body or her age. Both told her life's story, and she wouldn't have it any other way.

Lorcan lightly ran a finger down the middle of her chest, to her belly, and stopped short of going between her thighs. "My beautiful female."

"I can't yet make the same assessment about you until you're naked."

Chuckling, he removed his fingers and quickly undressed. Her eyes zeroed in on his hard cock, thick and ready for her.

Her dragon huffed. *He had better be.*

He raised his arms out to his side, preventing Caitlin from replying. "Shall I turn for the lady?"

Biting her lip, she nodded.

Lorcan turned slowly and her eyes drank in his tall, lean frame, firm muscles, and deliciously round bum. It was a miracle the male hadn't been snatched up before.

However, the instant he finished his turn, Lorcan covered her body and took her face between his hands. It took everything she had to concentrate on his words since his cock was resting between her thighs. He murmured, "I will make it up to you later with my tongue between your legs, but right now, all I can think about is being inside you."

"Then take me, Lorcan." She raised a leg and hooked it around his hip. "I'm more than ready."

She moved her hips and he groaned. "I can feel how wet you are."

"Your time is limited. Normally I'm okay with that, but for now, I want you. Let's not waste what precious time we have together."

Lorcan position his cock at her entrance. "You are mine, Caity. And after tonight, you'll understand that well."

His words sent a shiver down her spine, in a good way.

In the next second, he inched inside her until he filled

her to the hilt. She groaned and closed her eyes, savoring the fullness.

"Look at me, love."

She forced her eyes open, the tenderness and desire in Lorcan's eyes rendering her speechless.

There were a million reasons why it never would've worked between them over the decades. But now, in this moment, they were together. And Caitlin had a feeling she'd enjoy the male above her for the rest of her life.

Lorcan moved his hips and she soon lost any thought but the pleasure he brought her. Neither one of them lasted long the first time, but Lorcan easily lived up to his word. By the end of the night, Caitlin was sated, boneless, and happier than she'd been in a long time. As she listened to Lorcan's heart beat under her ear, she only hoped everyone she cared for would soon be as happy as she was in the present.

Not wanting to think about the near future, Caitlin closed her eyes and drifted off to sleep in the arms of a male who made her feel safe and treasured.

CHAPTER FIFTEEN

Killian had no idea how many hours or days had passed, but sometime later he was inside a jail cell, trying his best to construct a mental prison for his two-headed dragon before they started attacking each other again.

The trick was in creating a divider and compartment for each head. Because containing them together would only lead to more seizures and possibly his death.

After all, Dr. Sid had been blunt—if he couldn't find a way to make the dragons get along, then he needed to keep them apart until they did. Because the constant fighting would kill him sooner rather than later.

He placed the last bar and held his breath. Each dragon head banged against the compartments, but it held.

To better keep everything straight, he referred to the dragons as Black and Blue, to correspond to each color. It was also an homage to how their fighting made his mind feel black and blue as well.

Blue spoke up. *This is unfair. Why should I be placed in here? Just put a muzzle on him and we'll be fine.*

Black growled. *You are the young, untrained one. You*

191

should be muzzled. That way I can help Killian with his duties.

Tristan MacLeod's voice interrupted the conversation inside Killian's head. "Well?"

Killian sighed. "They're contained, but still arguing. I'm not sure how to make it stop."

"Keeping them apart is the first step. Getting them to work together will take some time."

Running his hand through his hair, Killian met the dragonman's gaze. "Everyone keeps saying that. But if anyone is going to tell me the truth, I think it would be you. Will I ever get out of here and live a normal life?"

Tristan grunted. "I think your chances are greater to succeed than fail. A teenage dragon-shifter in Wales suffered a much milder effect of the same drug. Her dragon returned much younger, too, afterward, but the dragon is slowly catching up to her normal age. Now that you can contain your dragons, I think we need to focus on training the younger one. When they act about the same age, they might get along better."

Each of his dragons glared at one another, but Killian ignored them. "Does that mean getting out of this prison?"

"When you're no longer a danger to others, we'll let you out. Not before." Tristan took out his mobile phone and his face softened a second before returning to its normally gruff expression. "We'll have to stop here for now. My daughter is causing havoc and my mate needs me. I'll be back tomorrow."

Tristan exited the room before Killian could say anything else.

Sitting on the bed in his jail cell, he closed his eyes and continued reinforcing his mental prison. Before all of the shit with the drugs and amnesia had happened, Killian had been skilled in keeping his dragon contained when needed.

He only hoped he could keep it up.

After all, he needed to do whatever he could to stay awake. His dreams only plagued him with what he couldn't have. Namely, his family at his side and Brenna in his bed.

Blue spoke up. *Why hasn't she visited us? I thought she liked us.*

Black replied, *We're unstable because you keep fighting me. Of course she's going to stay away.*

No, I think it's because of you. After all, you never noticed her when you were the only one here.

Killian stepped in. *Enough. She stays away because of you both. If you never work together, we'll rot in this cell for the rest of our lives. We'll never be able to help our family or Brenna if that happens.*

Both dragon heads kept quiet.

After testing and prodding every piece of his mental cage for who knew how long, a familiar voice reached his ears—his mother's. "Killian."

Looking up, he stood and went to the bars. His mother touched his face. "Do they really need to keep you in here?"

True to form, his mother was more concerned about him than anything to do with her. "I'm fine, Mam. It's just good to see you again."

She frowned at him. "Of course I'd come. And not just because your memory has returned, either. You may be grown, but you'll always be my son, Killian."

"Mam..."

A male Northern Irish accent jumped in. "Besides, it was time to meet at least one of my new children."

He tore his gaze from his mother to find Lorcan Todd not far behind her. "With all my memories back, I'm not sure how I feel about you mating my mother."

"Killian," his mother said, her voice full of warning. "Lorcan is my mate and I won't have you being disrespectful.

At least, unless it's warranted."

Lorcan snorted. "I'll behave if he does."

His mother glanced over her shoulder and shared a smile with Lorcan. Killian should feel overprotective; after all, Lorcan's clan had been the enemy of his own for a while. But for once, Killian would take his mother's happiness at face value, try not to hover, and give the male a chance. "I will do the same."

Caitlin beamed. "The two most important males in my life are getting along. It's a good day."

Killian rolled his eyes. "We're grown males. It's not that hard."

She clicked her tongue. "It's actually quite difficult. Alpha dragon males are temperamental sorts. That's why I brought another female to help even out the numbers."

He frowned. "Teagan is too busy to come to Stonefire right now."

Brenna's voice cut in. "No, it's not Teagan."

His gaze instantly shot to Brenna's. Both dragons said in unison, *It's her.*

He yearned to touch her face and take in her scent.

However, that wasn't possible at the moment, if ever. So Killian cleared his throat. "I wasn't sure if you were ever going to visit me."

Shaking her head, Brenna replied, "Of course I'd come. I've been busy, and Tristan hadn't cleared me to visit. And you may not know him very well, but you don't want to upset Tristan. He's a gentle giant with his mate and children, but he can be quite growly and intimidating if you try to interfere with his work."

He and Brenna stared at one another. There was so much he wanted to say, and yet he didn't know where to start.

Caitlin spoke up. "Now that I know my son is well and not insane, I think Lorcan and I are going to settle in and visit with Bram. I'm sure you and Brenna have quite a bit to talk about."

The honorable thing to do would be to tell his mam that he was fine and he'd spend some time with her after everything she'd done for him.

But as he stared into Brenna's brown eyes, he couldn't find the words.

His mother gave his face one last pat before going to Lorcan's side. "I'll check on you later, Killian."

Lorcan muttered, "I think he's forgotten we're here. He looks to be suffering from cockblindness."

"Lorcan," Caitlin growled.

However, they were gone before he could hear what they said next.

Once they were alone, Brenna took a step toward his cell. "I hate that they have you locked up like this."

Black grunted. *Me, too. We're perfectly fine for the moment. There's no need for a cell.*

Killian mentally sighed. *Until the divider comes down, and then you'll go back to fighting.*

Not with Brenna in the room. I want to talk with her, Black stated.

Blue spoke up. *Me, too. I miss her.*

Before he could think too much about their statements, Brenna's voice prevented his reply. "How are the dragons doing?"

"It's a complicated situation."

Closing the distance to the cell, she smiled up at him. "I'm listening."

Raising a hand, he reached to touch her face, but stopped short. Clenching his fingers, he returned his fist to his side. "Why are you here?"

"What do you mean why am I here? I'm your mate."

He shook his head. "Not in actuality. You have no

obligation to stand by me and be nice."

She frowned. "Please tell me that Killian the dutiful arsehole isn't back."

"I'm not being an arse. I'm being truthful."

Moving her face to just outside the gap between the bars, she growled, "I'm here because I want to be. There's no need to continue with the self-sacrificing bullshit."

"You say that now, but I have a double-headed dragon inside my head and anytime they start fighting, I fall into a seizure. Standing by my side isn't going to be a walk in the park."

She motioned to her side. "Easy is boring. Besides, I've stuck with you this long."

"Now who's self-sacrificing? Bloody hell, we haven't even had sex yet."

"A relationship is about more than sex, Killian O'Shea. Although what with having two male dragons in your head, that may be all you think about now."

Blue spoke up. *I'm not thinking about that yet. I just like her voice.*

Black grunted. *I wouldn't mind fucking her, but for once, I agree with the baby. I like her voice too.*

So the only thing you two can agree on is that you like Brenna's voice?

Blue looked at Black. *I'm sure there are other things we have in common. I like food. And napping.*

Killian interjected, *Can we save this conversation for later? Once Brenna's gone?*

Both beasts grunted and remained silent.

Meeting Brenna's inquisitive glance, he said, "You don't want to know what my dragons are thinking."

She reached out and took his hand. The warm softness of her skin made him want to bend the bars aside and pull her close.

Her voice was lower as she said, "But I do want to know. Stop shutting me out, Killian. I'm not about to keep chasing you. If you want a chance with me, then talk to me. Otherwise, I will leave and never come back."

The honorable thing would be to release Brenna from the mating and allow her to find a sane, stable male.

However, the thought of anyone else kissing her or caressing her naked skin made his stomach churn in anger.

For the first time in a while, Killian knew what he wanted.

He wanted Brenna.

Both dragons roared their approval.

Squeezing her hand, he leaned closer to the bars and Brenna's face. "No more hiding on my part." He leaned a fraction closer. "Because I want you, Brenna Rossi. And provided I can find a way to tame my dragons, I will show you how much one day."

She put her face a few inches more between the bars and kissed him.

As he moved his lips and nibbled hers, a sense of rightness coursed through his body. She'd tasted fantastic before, but with his two dragons humming their contentment, she was fucking unbelievable.

There wasn't enough room to take the kiss deeper, so he contented himself with licking and nibbling, memorizing every sigh and groan to use with her again later.

He eventually found the strength to pull away. "I wish these bloody bars weren't here."

Raising a hand, she cupped his cheek and slowly strummed her thumb over his skin. "Then tell me what's going on with your dragons so I can help. There has to be a way to get you out of here."

Turning his face into her hand, he took a second to revel in her warmth and scent. After kissing her palm, he moved his head to reply, "You know about the constant fighting.

I've learned how to construct a prison, but I'm not sure how long I can maintain it. However, as corny as it sounds, they calm down when you're near."

She raised her brows. "Then maybe we should test how my presence affects them further."

"How?"

Brenna extracted a key from her pocket. "As a Protector, I have access to the keys to the cells."

His heart rate ticked up at the thought of holding Brenna in his arms. "But I thought you didn't want to upset Tristan? Coming in here with me will most definitely do that."

The corner of her mouth ticked up. "I try not to, but I can hold my own with him later."

He searched her eyes. "Are you sure about this? Locking yourself in here with me could be dangerous."

"I don't think you'll hurt me, Killian. And if there's something I can do to help, finally, after twiddling my thumbs for who knows how long, then I'm going to do it. Not just out of obligation, either, so quickly banish that from your brain." The hand on his cheek moved to brush the hair off his forehead. "I'm drawn to you, Killian. And I'd like to finally see why."

Stepping back, Brenna locked the outer door to the room and faced him again. She held up the key. "Are you ready?"

He quickly said to his beasts, *Well, are you?*

Blue spoke first. *I am. I may turn my head for the kissy parts, but I promise to behave.*

He focused in on Black. *And you?*

I won't close my eyes for any of it. But yes, I'll behave. I'm curious what she tastes like.

Killian nodded. "I'm ready. Give the word, and I'll try taking down the mental prison."

~~~

Brenna's heart thundered in her ears. Not because she was afraid, but rather she was nervous about what came next. After all, if they finally did have sex, Brenna had little experience in that arena. Not to mention last time, the guy in question had used it against her, to try and manipulate her.

No. Killian wasn't Cedric and would never use her that way. Killian had all but pushed her away to protect her. He had honor, unlike Cedric the arsehole.

Taking a deep breath, she tried to calm both her heart and mind.

Her beast spoke up. *Why are you so nervous? You were ready to go through the frenzy with him. This is nothing by comparison.*

He has his memories and his dragons. So, this is a bit more final.

So? I'm looking forward to it. After all, he has two dragons for me to tame.

Brenna smiled at her dragon's comment, and Killian asked, "What now?"

"Sorry, my dragon is being a bit randy." She went to his cell and inserted the key into the lock. Never taking her eyes from his, she turned it and opened the door.

Killian instantly reached for her and hauled her up against his body. She sucked in a breath at his firm muscles against her chest.

He chuckled. "At least something's remained constant during all the changes." His hand moved down her back to her bum. "You still fit perfectly against my body."

She cocked an eyebrow. "Your original self never held me close, so how do you reckon?"

"But I did. We danced once, shortly after you arrived in Ireland."

Scanning her memories, a hazy image of Killian awkwardly holding her as far from his body as possible filled her mind. "If I recall, you were doing everything you could to put distance between us."

"That is your side of the story. Care to hear mine?"

Tilting her head, she asked, "Well?"

She did her best to focus on his words and not the slow circles he rubbed onto her bum. "At the very beginning of the dance, our bodies touched. Blood rushed to my cock, and I quickly kept you at arm's length and did everything I could to keep any feeling from showing on my face."

She frowned. "Why?"

"Because I was determined to aid and protect my sister above all else. You were intelligent, pretty, and strong. I knew if I acted upon it, I wouldn't be able to keep it casual. I'd want more."

"So from the beginning, you felt the same pull I did?"

He nodded. "Aye. But both man and beast were more concerned with duty." He stilled his hand and pressed her closer against him. "Now, however, the thought of duty and nothing else has lost its appeal. There should be a healthy balance. A certain female's loyalty has slowly won me over and taught me that."

She wanted his words to be the end of it. They could kiss, sleep together, and try for a future.

But Brenna needed the full picture. She didn't want doubt creeping into her mind. "Right now, we're on Stonefire, far away from your home and your duties. To be honest, the entire situation is unreal. What happens when we return to life as usual? Your dragon and memories are back, so won't you fall back into your old routines?"

His green eyes remained neutral, the only change the occasional flash of his pupils between round and slitted.

She couldn't begin to imagine what having two dragons

would be like. However, they were a part of him, making one whole. She wouldn't change it.

Her beast yawned. *This is boring. Why don't you just kiss and fuck him? That will be much more interesting.*

Thankfully Killian spoke up, preventing Brenna's reply to her dragon. "I don't think I can fall back into the person I used to be, Brenna. The young blue and white dragon will need attention and training, which means I have to rely more on others. I don't even know if my future is on Glenlough, to be honest."

Her heart skipped a beat. "What do you mean?"

"Everyone on Glenlough will expect me to behave one way, all while I'm coming to terms with a new personality inside my head. Here, at least, I have the freedom to become the new me, which will be an amalgamation of old and new."

Searching his gaze, she stated, "Giving up everything you know doesn't seem like the right answer to me."

He shook his head. "I wouldn't be giving it up forever. Teagan will sort out the treaties and renegotiate with the Irish DDA. And even if that takes some time, as long as we remain mated, we can travel between the two clans. Maybe not every other day, but often enough."

A happy future with Killian where she could also be a Protector and be in her soon-to-be-born brother's life was tempting.

Not that she wanted to be the only one to gain everything. She'd find a way to ensure Killian could keep in touch and protect his family back in Ireland, too. Maybe his mother living on Northcastle would work out well, as a midway point between Stonefire and Glenlough.

Ideas raced through her mind, but she put them on the back burner. Time with Killian was always short and she didn't want to waste any more.

Moving her hand to the back of his neck, she lightly

scratched his skin as she said, "Before we start making long-term plans, how about we see if I can help your dragons first?" Stepping away from Killian's body, she closed the cell door and tossed the key beyond her reach.

Killian growled behind her. "Why would you do that?"

She turned to face him once more. "I trust you, Killian. And this is the only way to truly judge if your dragons will behave in my presence. There's no escape, no out. It's just you and me in this cell." She put her arms out. "So how about we stop stalling and get to it? No one should be around for at least an hour, and I requested the CCTV cameras to be turned off for that duration too."

Killian glanced at the mounted camera on the far side of the room. "How do you know they will listen to your order?"

"Because I cleared it with Kai and no one disobeys him, apart from maybe his mate and his sister." She took a step closer. "No more excuses or stalling. It's time to release your dragons."

"And then what?"

Taking another step, she placed a hand on his chest. "Then we see what happens and let things go where they may."

He placed a hand over hers. "If things spiral out of control, promise me you'll knock me unconscious."

The corner of her mouth ticked up. "You've spent quite a lot of our recent acquaintance unconscious, but I won't pass up the chance to do it on purpose, if necessary. I'll try to avoid your bollocks this time."

She hoped for a smile, but Killian merely took a deep breath. "Then let's begin."

Chapter Sixteen

Killian still couldn't believe Brenna trusted him, but he wasn't going to keep questioning her. It was time to see how his dragons responded.

He quickly said to his beasts, *Remember, Brenna is here.*

Black growled. *I don't like your insinuation.*

Blue added, *She will be fine. I won't let anyone or thing hurt her.*

The two dragons' heads glanced at each other and Killian swore they both nodded a fraction in reassurance.

Piece by piece he dismantled the mental prison. First, the bars across the top. Followed by the ones at the rear and front.

So far, both dragons remained in place and didn't make any sudden movements. The tricky part would come next.

Taking one more deep breath, Killian removed the pieces creating the divider and then the final pieces at the side and bottom.

His two-headed dragon stood in place. Black spoke first. *Brenna is waiting.*

After one last check, Killian looked at Brenna. She raised her brows. "Are you just going to stand there?"

Not wasting any time, Killian closed the distance between them and took Brenna's face in his hands.

Black spoke up. *Kiss her. Then strip her and fuck her. We've waited long enough.*

Killian kissed Brenna gently once, twice, three times before he pulled away. It took everything he had to not think about his hardening cock or to stare at Brenna's lips. "How do you want to proceed?"

Placing her hands on his chest, she ran them up to his shoulders, each glide of soft skin over his making him want to groan.

Black chimed in. *What are you waiting for? Toss her on the bed and taste her. We've wondered long enough.*

Blue mere shut his eyes. *You can do that without me.*

"Why are you frowning?" Brenna asked.

He wanted to answer her with his lips and tongue, but his blue and white dragon's head bowing down and against his belly helped him focus. "I want you so much that my cock hurts, but I'm not sure I can go through with this with a young dragon in my head. As much as Black and I are ready, Blue is still a child."

Her expression softened. "The fact you care so much about the little one has just raised my esteem for you." She paused a second, fear growing inside his heart at her silence.

While Killian was going to do everything he could to help his blue and white dragon's head mature, he didn't know how long it would take. The wait might be too much for Brenna.

Taking his chin between her fingers, Brenna's dominance-filled voice carried to his ears. "Stop looking so worried. If you second-guess everything, this will never work, Killian. So the real question is—are you willing to trust me?"

He didn't miss a beat. "I do. But—"

"No 'buts' allowed." His blue dragon snickered as Brenna

continued, "We'll find a solution, together."

At the conviction in her voice, a weight lifted off Killian's shoulders. "Do you have one, then?"

"Yes, but I'm not sure you're going to like it. I think you need to let your dragons take control so I can talk to them."

His first instinct was to outright deny her. However, he would honor his word about trusting her. "And what if I can't wrestle back control?"

She shrugged a shoulder. "I know how to distract Black. That should be enough until someone comes to check on us."

He spoke to his beasts. *Can you behave and promise not to hurt her?*

Black answered first, *I want her to distract me, so I won't argue with you about not trusting me.*

Not wanting to have another row, he focused on Blue. *Will you be okay?* The dragon bobbed his head and Killian added, *You two need to share. She wants to talk to both of you. And if we want to keep her as our mate, we need to pass this test.*

Says who? Black demanded.

Says me. Because if things spiral out of control, I will end it with her. That means never seeing her again. Remember that.

He focused back on Brenna. "Let's try this." He kissed her slowly, tasting every inch of her mouth before pulling away. "Good luck."

Retreating to the back of his mind, Killian allowed his dragons to take control.

Since his pupils would remain slitted as long as his beasts were at the front of his mind, Brenna knew when he'd finished ceding to the dragons. She tilted her head. "Who am I talking to first?"

Black and Blue each tried to answer, but ultimately it

was Black who spoke. "I am Black, the more mature and handsome of the two dragon heads."

She smiled. "I'll hold off making any judgment until I see you shift."

Black growled. "I would do it now, if not for the reinforced steel in the walls and the chance that the baby won't be able to complete the shift, possibly killing all of us."

Blue finally pushed to the forefront. "I will be able to do it soon enough. Unlike Black, I have patience."

Stroking his bicep, she murmured, "We all need to work together, lads. Otherwise, everyone will lose out. I'll stay as long as you behave. If you give Killian trouble, then I may just leave."

Black won control again and grunted. "You sound just like Killian."

She grinned. "Then you have double incentive to get along." Her face sobered. "I know it isn't easy. I can't begin to understand how difficult it is to share a mind three ways. However, if we're to help anyone ever again, you lot need to work together, not against one another. Is there a way we can make that happen?"

Killian resisted shaking his head from his vantage point in the back of his mind. Surely it couldn't be as easy as asking them.

Black replied to Brenna's question. "If Blue will only listen to my advice about how to live as a dragon, it would help along the process."

Brenna raised her brows. "The question is whether you're genuine in wanting to help or are you just wanting to be in charge?"

"Both," Black said. "But I *can* help. If he allows me to coach him, he might mature faster. Then we'd all get along much better. Being literally one-half child and one-half adult will only continue to cause problems."

Brenna spoke again. "Right, then what does Blue have to say about it all?"

For a few beats, Black kept control. However, he finally allowed Blue to take over and the young dragon answered, "I'd like to learn, but I don't like being ordered around all the time. If Black makes suggestions and asks me, then it might work better."

Brenna nodded. "I think that sounds reasonable. Maybe we should have a trial run. What is something that you need help with, Blue?"

Killian sat slack-jawed as his dragons easily listened to Brenna. She must be a dragon-whisperer.

Black smirked at him. *She can give me what you can't, after all.*

He mentally rolled his eyes. *We're going to have to work on that. Otherwise, she'll wrap you around her little finger in no time.*

And that's a bad thing? Black queried.

Maybe, maybe not.

Blue chimed in. *Besides, she asks and tries to compromise. I like that better than being ordered about.*

Brenna's voice stymied his reply. "Blue? Are you still there?"

Blue turned his attention back to Brenna and said, "I am. It's hard to concentrate in here sometimes, because it's crowded."

Gently brushing his cheek, Brenna smiled. "I know, but it also means you have lots of company. I suspect one day you'll all be best mates." She removed her hand. "Now, what do you need help with, Blue?"

The young dragon thought a moment before answering, "I don't know much about shifting. That's a good place to start."

Tapping her hand against her thigh, Brenna said,

"Provided I can get permission, how about this: we'll all work together to help Blue with shifting basics, but I want a few hours with Killian first, free of any fighting or seizures. If you two dragons can keep up that bargain, then it'll go a long way in showing you can be trusted outside this cell. So, what do you say? Can you do that?"

As Black and Blue studied each other, Killian couldn't take his eyes off Brenna. He had no idea why she'd only initiated the true mate pull with Blue, but in his mind, she was bloody perfect for him. How he'd ever thought he could always put duty above his own wants and resist her, Killian had no idea.

When his beasts finally spoke aloud, Killian swore they did it in unison. "We can do that."

"Good. Then let me have Killian to myself for an hour or two. Keep your promise, and I'll do everything within my power to get us out of here for at least a short while."

His dragons stepped back and Killian took their place. Hoping Blue could handle it, Killian closed the distance between him and Brenna. And then he kissed her.

⌒⌐⌐◦⌐◦⌐⌐

Killian's lips on hers took Brenna by surprise, but she soon leaned against him and opened to allow him entry.

His taste was addictive, as was his hard, warm body against hers. However, when he broke the kiss and murmured, "That's about Blue's limit," Brenna fell a little bit in love with him.

She murmured, "Under this muscled, frowning exterior is a male with a heart of gold."

He grunted. "It's not entirely noble. After all, it's hard to kiss someone when part of your consciousness is trying its best to look away."

She smiled. "Yes, I imagine so."

Her dragon spoke up. *I don't mind being patient to help Blue, but I won't lie—I'm glad to be the only dragon here. I like the extra attention.*

As her dragon stood tall and spread her wings, turning this way and that, Brenna did her best not to laugh. *I'm not sure I'm strong enough to handle two of you anyway.*

Killian brushed her short hair off her forehead, garnering her attention. "Thank you. I know you're probably going to say it's nothing and brush it off as part of your mate duties, but the way you worked with my dragons was bloody brilliant."

Grunting, she lightly ran her hand up and down his back. "I helped train new recruits during my time in the army. That experience came in handy."

"You've never told me about your time with the army."

Brenna hesitated. She wanted to be honest, but she wasn't sure about wasting what precious time she had with Killian by reminiscing about one of the worst periods of her life.

He placed a rough finger under her chin and lifted until she met his gaze. "As you mentioned earlier, we've spent a lot of our mated life either apart or with me unconscious. I want to know you, Brenna. You can tell me anything."

Her dragon grunted. *Just tell him. He won't dismiss you as weak-willed or silly, even though you think you were both. We were merely young and naive.*

Staring into Killian's green eyes, she found the courage to say, "Well, me joining the army started off a bit shaky. My mum didn't want me to go, moaning about how she didn't want to lose her only child in some foreign war zone. My father was supportive, but it was after a talk given by Nikki Gray on what to expect when it came to living a Protector's life that cinched my decision. She laid out all the challenges, but also the rewards. My biggest concern was being female, but Nikki told us that while there will always be physical differences between male and female dragon-shifters—we're smaller in dragon form, for example—a person can find advantages in the differences and use them to make life on Stonefire a better place for all."

"And so you ran away to join the army," Killian murmured.

She nodded. "Yes. While my mother refused to speak to me until recently, I could've handled that. It's what happened after I finished basic training and went to my first official posting that I soon learned not all dragon-shifters are noble."

Killian growled. "Someone hurt you, didn't they? I sensed it back on Glenlough."

She blinked. "How did you know that?"

"Even without my memories, I still had most of my skills, which included reading people." He rubbed her bicep. "But let's get back to the story. What happened?"

After years of blocking out the memories, she let them flow. "I was stationed with the human 42 Brigade at the Fulwood Barracks in Lancashire. I had excelled in my training, so I was rewarded with extra responsibilities. I was given the task of selecting and forming a team from a pool of dragon-shifters staying in one section of Fulwood.

"I enjoyed setting tasks and facilitating team exercises. Unlike what I had heard during Nikki's lecture, there wasn't a lot of pushback from the mostly male candidates. One even fancied me, praising me until I eventually started dating and sleeping with him."

The early days with Cedric had been like a dream, what with him taking her orders without question when on duty, but teasing her when they were alone.

Too bad it'd all been a lie.

"He was the bastard who hurt you."

At the anger in Killian's voice, she met his gaze again. "Yes. After the initial lust phase, I started to notice a few things. Such as how he always mentioned how difficult it must be for a female to be in charge, or how the males had told him that if they ever were stationed overseas with me in charge, they would form their own plans and initiate them, not caring about my orders."

She barely heard Killian's growl as Cedric's voice replayed all the warnings. *They're only listening to you now because the humans are watching. They won't take orders from a female in the heat of battle. Most clans don't have many female Protectors, after all.*

Pushing the words aside, she continued, "I didn't know it at the time, but he was planting doubts into my head, taking every opportunity to nurture them to the point I clung to him harder. Without realizing it, I'd shifted my entire life and point of view for him, simply because I believed he loved me."

Her dragon huffed. *I still want to find and castrate him. Even if we could get away with it, he's in prison.*

Killian's voice interrupted her thoughts. "What became of the bastard? Because I may need to find and teach him a lesson in supporting your female and not hurting her."

She shook her head. "Don't worry, someone else eventually recognized his character and he was caught illegally selling army gear. He's serving time in jail."

"He deserves a far worse punishment, but at least he's not harming anyone else. However, you still haven't finished your story."

She sighed. "It's not a happy ending. I eventually doubted myself after a while, to the point I handed more and more tasks over to Cedric. When he reported my actions to our superiors, they ruled that I had been neglecting my duties.

I tried to fight it, but Cedric blackmailed me with naked pictures he'd taken without my consent. I had no choice but to accept the ruling and Cedric took over my position. They sent me to another location, to mostly endure grunt work for six months."

Her dragon sniffed. *A dragon shouldn't be used as a crane for builders.*

I agree, but at least it made us physically stronger, which came in handy later on.

Killian took her face between his hands. "We all do stupid things when we're young. And before you protest that you're not young, twenty-one isn't exactly pensioner age. You're mature, brilliant, and strong, but believe me, I have my own mistakes to account for from over the years. All we can do is learn from them."

She tilted her head. "When has the great Killian O'Shea made a mistake?"

"The day I was kidnapped and drugged is the latest one."

Studying his face, she asked, "What do you mean? You were scouting the surrounding area, just like the other Protectors."

"Aye, but I required everyone else to go in pairs. I went alone, thinking I didn't need any help. I was concerned about my sister. Rather than trust her, I followed her secretly during the trials. The attackers must've watched the leadership trial planners place all the clues and knew Glenveagh Castle would be one of the stops. When I followed Teagan there, someone surprised me and that's the last thing I remember before waking up strapped to a table and being pumped full of drugs."

Brenna frowned. "But why would you do that? You knew Teagan could take care of herself."

"Aye, rationally, I did. But she's my sister and I didn't want a repeat of what had happened with my father. I wanted to ensure my mother didn't lose another person she loved."

"Killian," she said softly.

"So you see, we can only learn from the mistakes. I think part of the reason I was so angry when I woke up without a dragon and my memories is that deep down, I knew I'd fucked up."

"And now? Are you still angry?"

He smiled. "No, quite the opposite. Because from that mistake came something good." He leaned a fraction closer. "You, Brenna."

Her heart skipped a beat. "Don't be silly."

He growled. "I'm not. You've stayed by my side the entire time, fighting tooth and nail not only to protect me, but to also try and find a way to bring back my memories. Even when you knew it could result in me never wanting you again, you fought for me. I now have another person I'm going to try to protect with my life."

She searched his gaze. "But you barely know me."

He moved a hand into her hair. "I know enough about you to realize that anyone who doesn't fight for you is a fool."

Not giving her a chance to protest, Killian pressed his lips to hers.

At the contact, she forgot every reason and excuse as to why they wouldn't work and simply kissed him back. Each nibble, lick, and caress sent fire racing through her body. Attraction had never been an issue between them, but for the first time, Brenna was starting to think there was more than mere lust involved.

There might be feelings, too.

Not wanting to bog down the moment, she jumped and wrapped her legs around his body. Killian's hands instantly went to her bum, lightly slapping one cheek.

Her dragon hissed. *I want to feel his hands on our skin.*

As she wiggled against Killian's chest, the friction made her wetter.

With a groan, Killian moved his lips to her neck, making his way down to where her neck met her shoulder.

One of his hands moved to the hem of her shirt and slid it up to expose one cup of her bra. Her nipple ached at his gaze.

Killian's pupils flashed and he growled, "Black is going to distract Blue for a few minutes."

At the reminder of the young dragon, guilt filled her body. However, Killian pulled down the cup of her bra and took her hard nipple into his mouth, banishing everything but the feel of his warm, wet tongue as it licked and swirled around her tight bud.

Threading her fingers through his hair, she moaned and tugged lightly. As if reading her cues were second nature, he lightly bit her nipple, sending more wetness between her thighs.

What she wouldn't give to have his talented tongue move further south.

He released her and leaned back to stare at her jutting nipple and small breast. For a second, she held her breath. Maybe his dragon had had enough and they would have to stop. She understood needing to be patient.

However, as he lightly traced the sensitive skin on the underside of her breast, he murmured, "I would worship this breast for hours if I had the time." He met her gaze again. "But I don't. I want to taste you, Brenna. Will you let me?"

She didn't miss a beat. "Yes."

Killian gave an animalistic growl, and he maneuvered her to the bed and laid her down. His hands went instantly to her trousers. As he fumbled to undo them, she wished for the first time in her life she favored skirts over trousers.

But Killian was determined and soon the trousers were down around her ankles. Instead of ripping off her panties, he lightly caressed her slit through the thin material. She should restrain herself, but Brenna couldn't help but squirm, trying to get his finger to brush her clit.

Killian ran his finger up, to the hem of her underwear. He inched them down slowly. Once they joined her trousers, he ran his rough, warm hands up her legs to her inner thighs.

Just watching Killian touch her made her heart pound and her pussy pulse. Maybe it was because she wanted an orgasm, but she had a feeling it was more watching Killian take his time and truly treasure her body that made her hot.

His eyes met hers, and the desire there made her breath hitch. "This is going to be about you and not me, Brenna. It's time you learn what a real male is like."

Her dragon hummed. *Yessssss. About time.*

As Killian lightly teased her opening, all thoughts fled from her brain.

His voice was rough as he said, "I knew you'd be nice and wet for me."

He pushed his finger into her slowly, and retreated far too soon. He put the finger in his mouth and groaned. "So fucking sweet."

Before she could do more than blush, Killian leaned forward and licked her slit, stopping at her clit to lightly flick her sensitive bundle of nerves.

Her legs dropped open in invitation. She wanted, no needed, Killian's touch.

He gently spread her core open. He murmured, "So beautiful," before moving his face and plunging his tongue into her pussy.

Brenna arched her back at the sensation. Cedric had never bothered tasting her with his tongue.

No. She wouldn't let her time with Killian be tainted by that arsehole.

Gripping his hair with her fingers, she couldn't look away from the strong man as he licked, thrust, and twirled her most sensitive spots. She wondered if he would feel the same when she took his cock into her mouth.

Killian lightly bit her clit and murmured, "Stop thinking or you'll never come."

He zeroed in his attention to her clit, lightly nibbling and swirling the tight bud. Heat built in her body, but when he added a finger and then two to her pussy, her breath quickened.

She couldn't help but push his face closer. She knew she was close to something she'd only ever felt by her own hand. Maybe she would finally have her first orgasm from a male.

Killian increased the rhythm of his fingers, each thrust building the pressure inside her.

She might be breathing hard and moaning, but Brenna didn't care. Nothing had ever felt as good as Killian's strong fingers moving inside her in tandem with his tongue and teeth on her sensitive clit.

He finally sucked the little bud between his teeth and spots danced before Brenna's eyes before pleasure crashed through her body. The combination of Killian's fingers still moving and her inner spasms made her forget about everything but the sensations coursing through her body.

When she finally slumped to the bed, Killian removed his fingers and gently kissed each inner thigh before moving to her belly.

She must've closed her eyes, but she felt his rumbling voice against her abdomen. "Look at me, Brenna."

Unable to resist, she blinked open her eyes to find Killian's heated gaze. As she idly ran her fingers through his hair, he stated, "If there's ever anything you wish for me to do differently, say it. One of the foundations of a stable mating is open communication, no matter what it's about."

"Our mating isn't—"

"Don't say it." He crawled up her body until his face hovered over hers. "It's real to me." He nuzzled her cheek. "I want to give it a chance, Brenna. Tell me honestly you don't, and I'll back away. But I'm eager to know you, love. Will you give me the opportunity?"

This was it, the point in her relationship with Killian where she either committed or retreated.

He was a good male. However, her greatest fear was that she would slowly morph to fit his needs and would lose herself again.

Her dragon growled. *Stop it. He just gave us carte blanche to make suggestions with sex. How many males would do that?*

It's not him I'm worried about, but me.

Killian whispered into her ear, "Tell me why you're hesitating, Brenna."

A coward would make excuses and not answer. However, Brenna wasn't a coward. "I don't want the same thing to happen to me as it did with Cedric."

Killian met her gaze again, his expression fierce. "The last thing I want is a sycophant, following me around with big eyes. Mates make compromises, but you will always be your own person, Brenna. Even if I have to leave for a few weeks or months at your request for a break, I can do that. But I will always come back. If there's one thing you need to know about the O'Sheas, it's that we're a loyal lot."

Some males would say anything just to keep a female close. Yet, with Killian, she didn't think he was spouting rubbish to keep her in his bed.

Raising her arms, she wrapped them around his neck. "Let's give it a go, then."

Just as Killian lowered his head to kiss her, Dr. Sid's voice echoed in the room. "I'll give you a moment to right yourselves, but we need to talk."

Chapter Seventeen

Killian's joy at Brenna agreeing to give him a chance was short-lived. He'd barely tasted her lips when the blasted Stonefire doctor gave her order.

Black and Blue had ended whatever game they'd been playing at the back of his mind, and Blue spoke up. *Dr. Sid has been helping us. Be nice to her.*

Not replying to his beast, Killian helped Brenna pull up her underwear and trousers. He gave one last lingering kiss before sitting beside Brenna on the bed and asking, "What's so bloody important, Dr. Sid?"

Sid turned around, her brows raised. "If you don't want my help, I can leave."

Brenna placed a hand on Killian's thigh. "No, no, we want you to stay, Sid. Did you find something new?"

The doctor glanced between them. "First, tell me what's happened with your dragons, Killian."

He shrugged a shoulder. "They mostly behave when Brenna's around. We've been testing boundaries."

"And?"

He gave the doctor credit—she didn't scold him for his experiment, but rather just wanted to know the results.

"Brenna has worked miracles with them. I'm hoping we can chance shifting soon, to prove they can be trusted outside this cell."

"And that's why I'm here," Sid replied. She walked up to the bars, only stopping to pick up the key Brenna had thrown earlier. "Bram had to tell the DDA Inspector what's going on, and she wants to interview you."

Being angry at Bram for doing his job would accomplish nothing. His sister would've done the same if the situations were reversed. "Do you know what for?"

Sid unlocked the door. "To probably determine if you're stable, and to make a note of your situation. Ms. Day won't say whether there are other cases like yours or not. However, I almost guarantee that if you lash out at her, you'll be carried away to a DDA research facility somewhere and may never be released."

Wrapping an arm around Brenna's shoulders, he hugged her close. "I'm not going anywhere."

Sid rolled her eyes. "You can growl and protest as much as you like, but if you truly want to stay at Brenna's side, then you'd bloody well better cooperate and prove that you're not a threat. You can practice with me and allow me to talk with your dragons."

Brenna jumped in. "Before you do that, can you tell us if you've learned anything about similar cases from Alice?"

"No, she's still tracking down the ship's logs and trying to discover what the 16th-century dragon may have eaten."

Not wanting to dwell on the disappointment in his belly, Killian spoke to his beasts. *Can you handle talking with Dr. Sid alone?*

Black growled. *I'm more than capable. It's the other one you have to worry about.*

Blue grunted. *I'm the good one, but I have a feeling he won't share and allow me to talk with the doctor.*

Nodding, Black replied, *Bloody right I don't want to share. You're young and immature. We have a better chance of passing any sort of test if I take charge.*

If being young and immature is such a bad thing, then why were you playing with me just a few minutes ago?

Killian cut in. *You two need to put aside your differences. If we fuck up with the DDA Inspector, we may never see Brenna again. Do you want that?*

No, they both murmured.

He continued, *Good. Then start working together. That's our only chance for the future we want.*

Sid's voice interrupted his conversation. "I see you talking with your dragons, Killian. What do they say?"

Taking a deep breath, he removed his arm from Brenna's shoulders and stood. "They're up for trying to talk with you."

"Right, then it's probably best if Brenna leaves." He opened his mouth, but Sid cut him off. "You're not always going to have your mate by your side. This is the only way to see if you can be trusted with the DDA Inspector."

Brenna chimed in. "But what about you, Sid?"

Sid never took her gaze from his. "I doubt even his dragons would hurt a pregnant female since they don't appear to be rogue. Besides, I have a few tricks to protect myself, if need be."

Blue spoke up. *Of course I wouldn't hurt her. I want to play with her baby when it's old enough.*

Hopefully by then, you'll be mature enough not to want to do that, Black said. *But she's right, I'd never hurt a pregnant female.*

Killian asked, "Since pregnancy is a sort of protection, shouldn't we try it with your mate instead? After all, the DDA Inspector isn't pregnant and won't have that to protect her."

Sid shook her head. "No, let's start with me first. If you

do well, then we'll try it with Gregor or even one of the Protectors." She moved to the side and motioned toward the exit. "To test this, I need you to leave, Brenna."

Brenna stood at his side. "Tell me as soon as you're done, Sid, so I can come back."

"You can work that out with Bram and Kai. They have a job for you and you're to report to Bram's cottage straight away."

He could sense Brenna's hesitation. Placing a hand on her lower back, he murmured, "Go. Your work is important to you. Besides, how are you supposed to charm Bram into letting me out of here if you don't see him?"

She smiled. "It will be easier to charm him without you growling all the time..."

Lightly swatting her bum, he said, "I like this cheeky side. She should come out more."

Brenna grinned and everything vanished but her smile.

With hard work and a little luck, he hoped to see that smile every day for the rest of his life.

Rather than think on how right that future sounded, he kissed her gently and stepped away. "Go, love. I'm sure that Sid will take care of me."

Before the doctor could open her mouth, Brenna winked and exited the room.

Sid turned her stare on him. "All right then, let's not waste any more time. I want to talk with your dragons."

He warned, *Remember, behave. If you attack each other and make me go into another seizure, we'll never get out of here.*

Once both his beasts grunted their agreement, Killian slowly retreated to the back of his mind. As seemed to be the norm, Black spoke first. "This is Black. I'm perfectly in control and stable."

Sid crossed her arms over her chest. "Is that so? What if

you were in midflight, and something came up? Would you work together or simply make the decision?"

"Make the decision. I have more experience."

Sid didn't miss a beat. "Let me talk to Blue."

Mentally muttering, Black allowed Blue to say, "Hello, Dr. Sid. I don't think you're that scary."

Sid smiled. "I'm not, really, as long as people follow orders. But charm won't work with me, Blue. Same question: would you work with Black to make a split-second decision? Or, would you make it on your own?"

"I don't know. It depends. I know some things better, and so does he."

"You're the more level-headed one, then." Sid uncrossed her arms and took a step closer. "Being civil in a controlled environment is all well and good. However, we need to purposefully test you. I'll see what I can arrange."

Killian took control again. "And what do I do until then?"

"You stay here and train your dragons." She motioned toward a stack of books. "Tristan gave you those volumes for a reason."

"I know most of that information already," he grumbled.

"If I were you, I wouldn't take all this help for granted, Killian O'Shea. Read them. I guarantee there are things inside those books that you don't remember. Take in as much information as you can. After all, cockiness will only cause trouble for you later on."

With that, Sid exited the cell, locked it, and left the room.

Sighing, Killian picked up one of the books and glanced at the title: *Learning to Live with your Inner Dragon: A Beginner's Guide.*

Opening it, he began to read. Assuming he knew everything wouldn't do him any good with the Department of Dragon Affairs. After all, if they deemed him a threat, Killian would be locked away, possibly for life. He doubted

Bram could stall the interview with the DDA inspector for more than a few days, so he'd have to make the most of the time he had.

Blue piped up. *Remember, this is all for Brenna.*

Yes, Black added. *So don't fuck it up.*

He resisted a sigh. *I'm not the problem. You two maybe killing each other is.*

Black huffed. *We'll see. Maybe I can learn to live with him. Not because you asked me, but for Brenna.*

Yes, for Brenna, Blue stated. *The rest is up to you.*

Rather than think on how his dragons had turned the situation around to him being the problem and not them, he blocked their muttering and began to study.

∽∽∽∽∽

On her way to Bram's cottage, Brenna tried her best to pack away her worries. Sid would never willingly put herself and her unborn child in danger, meaning she never would have suggested being alone with Killian unless her gut said it would be all right.

Her dragon spoke up. *Stop fussing. I think Killian's dragons hated each other for simply existing. But after the recent episode, I think they're learning to work together.*

I hope so.

Besides, you should be happy. Killian is everything Cedric wasn't. He actually cares and thinks about us, without a secondary agenda.

She agreed, but rather than allowing hope to bloom, Brenna slowly forced all emotion from her face and mind. If her future ended up being on Stonefire, she needed to show she was still levelheaded and capable to Bram and Kai. Otherwise, she may spend the rest of her life behind a desk.

Just the thought of spending ten hours a day sitting inside made her shudder. She'd much rather stand watch in five feet of snow each day than endure that existence for forty-plus years.

She arrived at Bram's cottage, but she'd barely rapped a few times before Nikki Gray's smiling face greeted her. "Brenna!" The black-haired, brown-eyed female engulfed her in a hug. "It's good to see you home. There are so few of us female Protectors and I could use you at my side."

Nikki released her and Brenna answered, "More females are in training and should return home from the army before you know it. Much like with me, you're to thank for that."

Shaking her head, Nikki motioned inside. "Don't thank me. If not for Charlie, I never would have thought of signing up. She's the one we owe for the slowly growing female Protector numbers on Stonefire."

Charlie Wells had been Stonefire's first female Protector in decades. She'd died at the hands of dragon hunters, during her assignment to protect Evie Marshall.

Brenna bobbed her head. "She was a fantastic role model, and we need to keep her memory alive. Maybe the Protectors should host an annual seminar in her name, to encourage more females to join up in the future?"

Nikki guided her down the hall. "That's a brilliant idea. If there's ever enough of a lull in attacks or threats to the clan, maybe we can plan the event together. After all, as second-in-command of the Protectors, I have some sway with Kai."

The other dragonwoman winked and Brenna grinned. "And if you get Kai's mate on board, he won't stand a chance."

The door to Bram's office was open, and Kai spoke up from across the room. "I wish people would stop bloody planning things with my mate behind my back. I'm an open-minded bloke after all."

Nikki smiled at her boss. "You are, but it's fun to irritate you now and then. Also, it keeps Jane in the loop."

"Which then leads to trouble," Kai muttered, albeit with love in his eyes.

Bram sat at his desk and raised a hand. "Enough teasing. We have more important things to discuss right now."

Brenna looked at each of the three other people in the room in turn. "Dr. Sid mentioned an assignment, although she didn't elaborate on what. Has something happened that I'm unaware of?"

"As you know, Nikki has taken over the second-in-command role, leaving her old position vacant," Bram stated. "I know your future is uncertain right now, lass, but for the time being, I'd like you to take over daily sweeps and monitoring security disturbances."

She frowned. "I'd be honored, but aren't there other, more qualified Protectors?"

Nikki snorted. "You're more than qualified, Brenna. After all, you pretty much ran Glenlough's Protectors for a short while. If anything, this is almost a demotion."

To Brenna, it didn't feel like a demotion, but rather a great opportunity considering she'd been at the bottom of the ladder when she'd last lived on Stonefire.

Her heart skipped a beat in anticipation, but she had to be honest with her clan. "Are you sure about this? Until things are settled with Killian and we're sure there won't be any more episodes, I may not be as focused as usual."

Kai spoke up. "I understand the concern for your mate. After all, Jane is still healing from being stabbed in the shoulder. But as she always tells me, hovering only makes her crankier. Sometimes a little distance can do wonders for a relationship."

"Considering Killian has been unconscious quite often

lately, distance isn't exactly high on my list," she drawled.

Bram chimed in. "I think what Kai is trying to say is that Tristan, Sid, and some of the others will need time alone with Killian, to work on controlling his dragons and to prove he's stable and not a threat. I've known you your whole life, Brenna, and you've never liked to sit idly by. Working whilst Killian is with the others will help use up some of your excess energy."

Nikki placed a hand on her shoulder. "Besides, you'll mostly deal with rebellious teenagers trying to sneak off the clan's lands. And giving them a lecture or two will help calm some of your stress. I'll miss that part, although scolding adult Protectors has its benefits, too."

Kai raised a brow. "Just make sure your mate stays away, Nikki. The others are holding back because he's human, but if Rafe goes too far, it won't end well."

Nikki rolled her eyes. "I can't help it." She placed a hand on her slightly swollen belly. "Until this baby is out, I think he'll only get worse."

Brenna should hold her tongue, but she blurted, "Isn't it an inconvenience to your career, being pregnant?"

Nikki smiled as she rubbed her abdomen. "I used to think it would ruin everything I'd worked for. Not trusting Bram and Kai's faith in me was one of the biggest mistakes I've made in a while. Will it be easy balancing parenthood with my job? No. But with the clan's help, I'll manage. My parents are especially looking forward to babysitting as much as possible."

At the mention of parents, Brenna remembered her own. Given how her mum was pregnant herself, Brenna didn't think that would be an option.

Her dragon spoke up. *Killian isn't demanding a young. We have plenty of time.*

Focusing back on Nikki, Brenna said, "I'll keep that in

mind."

Bram grunted. "Well, will you be accepting the assignment, then?"

She nodded. "For now. But before I agree to any long-term commitment, I need to talk with Killian about the future. And I want to be able to contact Teagan, to give her a more personal update about her brother."

"Of course, as long as you don't mention any sensitive information without Kai's consent," Bram stated. "Now that's settled, you can begin straight away."

She blinked. "What if I had said no?"

Grinning, Bram shuffled through stacks of paper on his desk. "I knew you'd say yes."

Her dragon chimed in. *As much as I admire Teagan, I've missed Bram's good nature.*

The male in question held out a document and she took it. She read the heading, "Safe Zone Construction," and then the summary:

A neutral meeting location is needed on Stonefire's lands, but beyond the gates. An easily monitored and controlled location needs to be found and proposed. Once done, security protocols also need to be designed and tested.

Looking back up, she asked, "What is this for?"

Bram answered, "Clan Skyhunter is having their leadership trials anytime now. Once they have their new leader, I want to make contact and possibly form an alliance. But given how things have been functioning on that clan over the last few decades, I want to be cautious. If there is any malicious intent, I want to ensure it's away from the regular clan members."

Skyhunter was the dragon-shifter clan located in the

south of England, and had been ruled by fear and an iron-fist until their leader had been arrested. They currently were without a leader and being held together by a variety of watchdogs.

Kai added, "The new safe zone space will also be used for meeting with other clan leaders and officials. If there's tighter security, more people may be willing to come and talk with our clan."

Brenna closed the folder. "It's a brilliant idea. One I'm sure Lochguard will emulate."

Bram muttered something, but Nikki spoke up. "Getting back to your assignment, finding the best location is your main concern. Once that's done, you'll be working with Nathan, Lucien, and Blake here on Stonefire to design all aspects of the security, from physical to technological."

Nathan was the Protectors' head IT person and someone Brenna had worked with before. The other two she knew only by name and appearance. "So Lucien was made the permanent IT head replacement for non-Protector matters?"

Bram grunted. "Aye. And Blake has a knack for inventing or coming up with solutions to tricky technological problems. He's a bit shy, but extremely clever."

Beyond Blake's intelligence, she'd only heard that he mostly stayed indoors or in remote locations in his dragon form.

Her beast spoke up. *I don't blame him for wanting to stay away from people. Everyone makes such a fuss over him being a white dragon with a black spot.*

Even you were curious when we were children.

Yes, but adults should know better.

She focused on Kai. "Can you spare me two or three Protectors you trust to help with the initial scouting?"

"That should be fine for now," Kai answered. "Although

if an emergency pops up, all of you will report back immediately, no questions asked."

A hum of excitement coursed through her body. "Sounds good to me." She paused and asked, "Can I tell Killian about this?"

Bram and Kai shared a look before Bram spoke again. "Not just yet. I want to trust him. He's your mate after all. However, until he's stable, I don't want to risk anything." Her excitement tamped down a fraction. It must've shown on her face because Bram added, "As soon as Sid and Gregor clear him and deem him stable, you can share the assignment with him. I should also add that I don't want to share this with any other clan, apart from a select few on Lochguard."

"Teagan is worth your trust, Bram," Brenna pointed out.

"Aaron selecting her as his mate tells me that, but given the number of leaks and disgruntled clan members the world over, I can't risk it right now. Otherwise, we'll never be a step ahead of the dragon hunter or Knights. I don't want them getting information about our security plans ahead of time, or the whole project will be for nothing."

Brenna frowned. "Can't they just monitor us with video drones?"

"Blake's already worked on a temporary fix for that, creating a sort of moveable field to block out feeds and networks. He can explain it better than I."

Nikki chimed in. "It does mean that you'll have to rely on older forms of communication, such as runners and the emergency landline telephones posted around the clan's lands, to regularly check in."

Brenna sensed she was about to be dismissed. And as anxious as she was to get back to work, she needed to ask something and spit out, "Before I start, I have a request, Bram." He raised his brows in question and she continued,

"I want to test Killian's ability to shift in a controlled situation. However, it'll obviously have to be out of the jail cell since the small space is fortified against shifting dragons. Will you allow him out to try?"

"I will think on it." Bram leaned back in his chair. "Now, take the rest of the day off to spend with your mate. Report to the Protectors tomorrow morning, as soon as Tristan arrives to help Killian with his studies."

Some might push for a more concrete answer about Killian shifting, but Brenna knew Bram well enough to know that he wouldn't budge until everything was in place and safe for everyone.

She looked at each person in turn. "Thank you for this. I wasn't sure if you'd trust me again, after all that's happened."

Nikki waved a hand. "What happened to Killian wasn't your fault. And yes, you spent some time with Glenlough, but I think fostering is useful. It's why I keep pestering Bram about finally taking a foster from Lochguard, as he promised Finn ages ago."

Bram sighed. "It's on my list of things to do, but it's not a priority."

Nikki whispered loudly, "He just doesn't want to chance the foster candidate being someone like Finn or his cousins."

Kai grunted. "Regardless, it's necessary and overdue."

Not wanting to get in the middle of it, Brenna took a step back. "I should probably go check on Killian. I'll report tomorrow morning for work."

As soon as Nikki motioned with her head for Brenna to leave, the three dragon-shifters in the room started to argue.

Brenna exited the cottage and breathed a sigh of relief. She'd never understood Bram's hesitance regarding a Lochguard foster, but if anyone could persuade him, it would be Kai Sutherland.

Her dragon spoke up. *I'm excited about our new job.*

Me, too, although I wish Killian could be a part of it. He's brilliant with security.

Give it time. He's not ready to return to duty yet. Besides, you'll never be able to concentrate fully if you're always worrying about Killian falling unconscious at your side.

I know. Brenna picked up her pace. *But I'm anxious to see him again.*

And to think you wasted so much time avoiding him in recent weeks. You should listen to me. I have great instincts.

Not wanting to argue with her dragon, Brenna jogged the rest of the way to where Killian should be waiting for her.

CHAPTER EIGHTEEN

Ivy Passmore sat huddled on the soggy ground, hoping the summer rain would stop soon. She'd never been much of a rambler, and yet here she was, who the hell knew where in the Lake District, trying her best to reach the gates of Clan Stonefire.

Pulling the hood of her jacket further over her head, she remembered why she was lost in the wilderness, risking everything to reach a group of dragon-shifters.

For retribution.

Not against the dragon-shifters, but rather the human bastards who'd forced her into working for them. As soon as she'd learned that they'd killed her brother and his partner, she'd made her escape.

Her eyes watered thinking of her brother, Richard. He was her only sibling and she'd never hear his jokes again, let alone tease him about his dream of doing stand-up comedy one day at the Edinburgh Festival Fringe.

In retrospect, she should've supported him more and maybe he would've reached that dream before his death.

If that weren't enough to tear her heart in two, she'd loved her brother's partner, David, of ten years like a second brother.

She'd never see her brother or David ever again.

And it was all her fault.

No. She wasn't going down that road of thinking. The thumb drive in her pocket, protected in several plastic bags, was her only chance at getting back at the bastards for what they'd done. And to do that, she needed Stonefire's help.

If she could ever find their blasted gates. How could a fully enclosed settlement with nothing surrounding it but nature be so difficult to find?

Glancing at the sky, the amount of light peeking through the clouds told her it would be evening soon. Rain or no rain, Ivy needed to keep going because she wasn't sure if she could survive another night in the wilderness with no shelter and no food.

Standing up, she ignored the gnawing ache in her belly and her protesting muscles. Putting one foot in front of the other, she tried her best to use the mountains as a guide. Before her mobile phone's battery had died early in the morning, she'd had sat-nav and had been paying close attention to where the hills and mountains were in relation to her position. It was the only clue she had to ensure she wasn't traveling in circles. Not exactly precise, but she'd take it.

Ivy had no idea how long she'd trekked before she came to a clearing nestled between two large copses of trees. Not that she took in the landscape. Her eyes focused on the three dragons swooping and hovering in the sky. They had to be with Stonefire. She couldn't imagine other dragons venturing this close to another clan.

With her head pounding and how difficult it was to put one foot in front of the other, Ivy knew this could be her last chance at redemption. The last chance to make up for everything she'd done.

So gathering up the last of her energy, she yelled, "Help me!" several times before her vision swam and she fainted.

◦◦◦◦◦

Brenna had spent most of her first few days back at work flying over every inch of Stonefire's land and had narrowed down her list of possible locations for the safe meeting place to three.

She'd saved the most promising area for last, and she currently hovered in place over the large clearing nestled between two copses of trees. While placing the building in the open might seem a poor choice, she thought the thick trees to either side would provide ample opportunities for escape routes and even hidden tunnels. Besides, the building in the open would act as a decoy of sorts, with the real meeting place hidden further inside the woods or possibly underground.

Just as she was about to signal the two Protectors with her that they should head back, she heard a female's voice shout, "Help me!"

Even with the wind and rain, Brenna easily pinpointed the source. She watched as the female promptly fell to the ground and didn't get up again.

The female could be a trick, so Brenna signaled to her compatriots to stay in the air and keep an eye out. She'd investigate the stranger alone.

Diving down, she landed gently next to the female. She listened for any unusual rumbling in the underbrush or talking nearby, but heard none. If the female were part of a trap that involved others, the danger from the stranger's companions wasn't immediate. Especially since Blake had rigged a safety zone near her three sites, to prevent any sort of drone from flying and attacking.

Brenna imagined her wings shrinking to her back, her snout shrinking back into her nose, and her arms and legs morphing into human ones. As soon as she finished, Brenna barely paid attention to the rain as she knelt next to the female.

Her red hair was matted, her face smudged with dirt, and her clothes were soaked with rain and mud. Brenna had no idea who the female was, although she could tell she was human from her scent and shorter stature.

Her dragon spoke up. *We should take her back to the clan. If she dies, we'll never learn why she's here.*

I'm not sure we can risk that, but I won't let her die. Brenna motioned for the red dragon to land and ordered, "Zain, bring one of the doctors to the abandoned cottage near the lake. I'll take the human there and wait for you."

The red dragon bobbed his head, jumped into the sky, and sped away.

After Brenna signaled again, the remaining dragon, a black one, came to land next to her. Brenna stood. "Sebastian, I need you to carry me and the female to the abandoned cottage near the lake. I want to remain in human form in case she wakes up en route, to try and explain what's going on."

Sebastian lightly jumped up and hovered a few feet from the ground. Brenna scooped up the small female and helped place her into Sebastian's left talons. He then gently wrapped his other set of talons around Brenna's middle.

As he ascended, she barely noticed the change in altitude or the wind. While chilly, she was more concerned with the mysterious female. Humans sometimes showed up at a dragon clan's gates, but the only question was whether the woman was friend or foe. After the recent betrayals back in Ireland, Brenna was wary of trusting anyone she didn't know.

In a matter of minutes, Sebastian had placed Brenna down next to the cottage. Once on the ground again, Brenna took the woman into her arms.

The cottage was surrounded by overgrown brush and broken furniture on purpose, to appear abandoned. But there was always a cot set up inside, as well as supplies hidden within a secret cache in the floor.

As soon as she had the female on the cot, Brenna turned toward the fireplace. Grateful to find wood and kindling to the side even though it was summer, Brenna quickly had a fire roaring.

Staring down at the human, she wondered where she'd come from. Unlike dragon lovers or the media, she was disheveled and dirty. Brenna guessed she'd been walking around the surroundings for quite some time.

She searched the human and found a thumb drive wrapped in several layers of plastic, as well as a purse. Her driver's license said her name was Ivy Passmore and that she lived in Brighton.

What Brenna didn't understand was if Ivy had a driver's license, why hadn't she driven to Stonefire. The only explanation was that the female hadn't wanted to be followed, but why?

So many questions and so few answers.

Her dragon spoke up. *And I have another question: why is she here? Brighton is quite far from the Lake District. Even dismissing Skyhunter since the clan is unstable, Snowridge in Wales is closer.*

Brighton was a city along the southern coast of England. *I don't know, but she went to great lengths to protect this thumb drive. I bet it will tell us more.*

Brenna heard a dragon return outside and shortly after, Dr. Gregor Innes walked into the cottage with a medical bag in his hand. Since he was fully clothed and drenched, he must've opted to be carried.

Kneeling next to the cot, he asked, "Has she woken up?"

"No. If I knew how she'd react, I would've stripped her and wrapped her in blankets. But given how humans are overly concerned with nudity and I didn't want her to go mental, the best I could do was start a fire."

Gregor did a quick examination and reached into his medical bag. "My initial diagnosis is that she's exhausted and dehydrated. I would say take her to a human hospital, but given her state and where you found her, I'd say she doesn't want to be found."

"I agree. Can you treat her here?"

"It's not the best situation, but until we can question her, I'm wary of bringing her inside the clan's gates. For all we know, it could be a dragon hunter or Knight trying to trick us."

She nodded. "I'll leave Zain and Sebastian here to watch over her whilst I report back to Kai. If she wakes up, Zain can interrogate her."

Gregor glanced at her. "Gently, I hope. She's weak and might be ill. I don't want him to make it worse."

"Zain knows what he's doing and has never pushed to the point of endangering someone's health." Brenna stepped closer and held up the thumb drive. "I'm most concerned with what's on this."

"Explain the situation to Cassidy and mention that I need fluids for a dehydrated patient. She'll know what to assemble and send to me. Just make sure she doesn't try to come here herself."

"Her pregnancy's not that far along, Gregor."

"I know, but she was a target once, and until we know who this lass is, I'm not risking my mate again."

Since every second she argued with Gregor was time she could be spending finding out the details of the thumb drive, she went to the door. "I'll talk with Kai, contact Sid, and be back as soon as possible."

After giving Zain and Sebastian her instructions, Brenna tucked the thumb drive into the weather resistant bag she carried in her dragon form and shifted. Within seconds she was in the sky and flying back to Stonefire.

Her dragon grunted. *That human had better be friend and not foe. As it is, she's making us wait to see Killian.*

Killian has plenty going on. His interview with the DDA inspector is tomorrow.

Still, he has to take a break to eat. We can cuddle a little. Maybe even finally have sex, which he keeps putting off for some reason.

If Brenna were in human form, she would've smiled. *Someone's not only impatient, but getting attached.*

And you're not?

The landing area came into view, giving her an excuse to avoid answering the question.

As soon as she touched down, she noticed Bram and Kai off to the side, waiting for her. Quickly shifting back into her human form, Brenna rushed over to them.

Bram raised his brows. "What's going on?"

"I'm not sure, but this may tell us." She took out the thumb drive still encased in plastic bags and held it up.

Bram took it. "The human was carrying this?"

"Yes. Given her state, she went to great lengths to ensure it remained dry. I think it's important."

Kai jumped in. "Then let's take it to Nathan."

Nathan was in charge of the Protectors' technology-related matters.

All three of them jogged to the Protectors' central command, which was only about three minutes away from the landing area.

Kai wasted no time pushing his way inside. A foot past

the door, Brenna plucked one of the spare robes they left there for those who had to shift quickly and tossed it on. She'd just tied the knot as they reached the main tech center.

Nathan sat at a series of computer screens. Kai spoke up. "I need to know what's on this."

Turning toward them, Nathan's brown eyes met Kai's before glancing at the thumb drive in Bram's fingers. "Where did that come from?"

Bram handed it over. "From a human that Brenna found in the outer perimeter."

Nathan turned back to his computer terminals. "Let me quickly check for viruses first."

Since Nathan had been in charge of the Protectors' technology for years, no one questioned his decision or barked for him to hurry up.

Brenna tapped her hand against her thigh as Nathan's long fingers danced across the keyboard. After what seemed like years, he murmured, "Bloody hell."

Bram leaned forward. "What is it?"

"I'll have to confirm some of the data with Dr. Sid, but I'm fairly certain this is a stolen cache of files from the Dragon Knights."

Brenna tried to make out what was on the screen, but the text moved too quickly. "Are you sure?"

Nathan stopped scrolling and motioned toward a blueprint. "This is one of their meeting houses." He exited the screen and brought up another. "And this is some sort of chemical formula."

"Maybe it's related to what was used on my sister," Kai said.

"Or even Killian," Brenna added.

Bram took out his mobile, pressed someone's number, and put it to his ear. "Sid? I need you at central command."

Since Brenna had supersensitive hearing, she heard Sid's

reply, "What about Gregor? What happened?"

"Brenna's here and can pass on any of Gregor's messages. Come to central command and we'll fill you in on everything." Bram ended the call. "Nathan, make sure you copy all of this data somewhere safe. I want you to comb through it and create a summary of what you find. If anything important sticks out, then let me know."

Nathan bobbed his blond head. "I'm already backing it up, but it may take a while to sort through it all."

"Aye, I know. You can bring in Lucien to help you." Bram looked at Brenna. "Until we know more about this human and what she's doing here, I'm going to put your current project on hold."

"I suspected as much," Brenna replied. "I can fly back straight away and share what we know with the others. That way, once Ivy is awake, Zain knows what to ask her."

Kai jumped in. "I'm going to increase patrols as well. I'm not going to let down my guard until we know exactly what's going on."

Brenna remembered something. "What about the DDA inspector? She's here a few more days and will probably notice the extra patrols."

"She's only here until Killian passes his interview and Lorcan either leaves or agrees to a treaty. Do you think Killian's ready to do his interview with the inspector this evening?"

Shrugging, she answered, "While having more time to prepare is better, I think he should be fine. After all, his dragons have been behaving the majority of the time." She glanced at the clock on the wall. "He should be attempting his first full shift right about now."

Bram raised his mobile phone again. "Then I'm going to see what I can do about Lorcan. With any luck, Ms. Day will be leaving tomorrow morning, allowing us to discover who this Ivy Passmore is and what she's up to without the DDA's interference. If the human is the key to destroying the Dragon Knights in the UK, then I'll do whatever it takes to make that happen." Bram looked at Kai. "Deliver the news to Zain and Sebastian yourself, freeing up Brenna to tell Killian of the change and provide the necessary support."

Some might take offense at the change in duties, but Brenna considered helping Killian as important as any other duty on Stonefire.

They all split up to do their respective tasks. As Brenna rushed out of central command, she only hoped Killian had already completed his first full shift. It was the one thing that had been rocky with his inner beasts, and yet it was the most important. An out-of-control two-headed dragon would cause a panic like no other.

⌑⌑⌑⌑

Killian watched his talons return to fingers for the fifth time as Black tried to console Blue. *I know you want to be in control for this, but trust me. I can guide you through it.*

Blue huffed. *I think I know what I'm doing.*

Not enough. If we don't get the shift right, it could end badly.

Tristan MacLeod approached him. "What happened this time?"

"They're still arguing."

"If you don't sort it out, you'll never be cleared by the DDA."

"You think I don't know that?" Killian bit out.

"Look, I know it usually takes months if not years to get a young dragon comfortable and informed enough to shift. But we have hours left, a day at most. So, sort it out."

Taking a deep breath, Killian spoke to his dragons.

Enough. At the dominance in his tone, they quieted. Only then did he continue, *Blue, I know you want to prove you're as skilled as Black. And one day, I'm confident that you'll take the lead. However, for now, your main focus is working with him and ensuring your own head grows as it should.*

The young dragon hesitated. *I don't know. Giving in to Black only convinces him he should always be in charge.*

Killian spoke up before Black could. *I am ultimately in charge, at least until you two learn to work together. I promise you'll have your turn once you're ready. With more practice, I'm sure you can master it. Don't you think so, too, Black?*

For a few seconds, Black remained quiet. But he eventually sighed. *I think Blue has promise, yes. Even if he is incessantly optimistic about everything. And far too nice.*

Ignoring the insults, Killian focused on the blue dragon head. *So, let's try one more time, okay?*

Okay, Blue mumbled.

Killian blanked his mind and was about to step back to allow his beasts to take control when Brenna's voice stopped him. "Killian, I need to talk with you."

Tristan spoke up. "We're busy, Brenna, Come back later."

Brenna rushed to Killian side. "I can't. Something's happened, and Killian's interview should be happening any time now."

He wrapped an arm around Brenna's waist. "Tell me what's going on."

As she explained about the human and the initial findings on the thumb drive, Killian's frowned deepened. When she finished, he asked, "So it's possible the information on that thumb drive is related to what was used on me?"

Brenna nodded. "Yes, although we won't know for certain

until Sid and the other doctors take a closer look."

"However, if it is related..."

She finished, "Then we might be able to return you to normal." Placing a hand on his cheek, she asked, "But is that what you want?'

He should scream yes, he'd love to go back to only having one dragon inside his head.

But as Black and Blue waited to see what he'd say, he couldn't imagine picking between the two of them, let alone banishing one of them from existence.

Brenna's voice garnered his attention again. "I thought so. You're attached to both of them, aren't you?"

"I have no bloody idea why, but yes."

"Then you need to pass the interview with the DDA inspector. Please tell me that you're ready."

He spoke to his beasts. *What do you think? In order to keep both of you, we need to pass the test. Can you work together to shift?*

Black rose his head taller. *I'm ready to try.*

Blue nodded his head a few times. *Me, too.*

Then let's try quickly before the real test.

Killian quickly kissed Brenna. "Step back. I'm going to attempt my first full shift."

She gave him a quick kiss and moved to stand next to Tristan, at the edge of the space.

Retreating to the back of his mind, he watched his dragons. Black said, *I'm going to start. Once we start changing forms, focus on bringing out your head. That part I can't do.*

Black imagined their wings sprouting from their back, arms and legs changing into limbs with talons, and their nose elongating into a black snout. Probably because Black was in control, their main dragon hide color was also black.

Even though Black had finished his shift, Blue struggled.

Only a tiny, blue bud emerged from their neck.

Killian had never had to deal with this before, but he murmured, *Grow long before imagining your head as it is now.*

Blue growled, and slowly, a long, blue column emerged from their neck. It took another minute for a snout, ears, and eyes to take shape from the top.

As soon as Killian stood in his dragon form, complete with two dragon heads, Brenna rushed up to them. Both beasts lowered their heads so she could scratch behind an ear each.

Brenna grinned. "You did it!"

Killian spoke to his dragons. *Great job, both of you.*

Both beasts merely hummed in contentment, leaning more into Brenna's scratches.

Blue was the first to lightly butt his head against Brenna's shoulder. She kissed the dragon's snout. "Nice to meet you, too." She then turned to Black and repeated the gesture. "And it's a been a while since we've last seen each other."

The two heads moved to gently wrap around Brenna and hold her close. She laughed and returned the embrace.

If Killian hadn't been in love with her before, he was now. Not only had she never given up on him, but she also accepted him as he was. He'd never find another female with the same kindness, bravery, and cleverness. It was high time to make their mating a true mating.

Blue spoke up. *Then make sure she stays.*

Yes, Black said. *We love her too.*

Right, then let's make sure to pass the interview with the DDA. Then I'll ask Brenna on our first proper date.

Black grunted. *And sex. I want sex.*

As long as she wants it, too, and Blue can find a way to distract himself, we'll see.

Blue paused a second before saying, *It might not be that*

bad. I love Brenna. That should include kisses and such too.

Killian had had suspicions that Blue was slowly becoming more mature with each accomplishment. *Okay, then prove you can shift back without a problem. I have a few things to say to Brenna before our interview.*

Someone gasped, and an unknown female voice stated, "It's true, then."

Both of his dragons moved their gazes to the source. The short, curvy form of Elsie Day stood next to Tristan.

Blue spoke up. *Why is she here? I'm not ready yet. I might make a mistake trying to change back.*

We can do it, Black said softly. *We have to. Just follow my lead.*

The dragons released Brenna and Elsie walked toward them. "You're magnificent," Elsie murmured, staring up at both Black and Blue.

Brenna placed a protective hand on his chest. "Yes, they are."

Elsie cleared her throat and adjusted her glasses. "I struck a deal with Bram to conduct this trial and test now rather than later. I can see Killian's tame and successfully shifted in his dragon form. But can he fly safely that way as well?"

Tristan answered, "He will soon enough."

Elsie reached out a hand and waited. Blue slowly bumped his snout against her palm.

Killian snorted. *Always the charmer.*

It'll help us, you'll see.

Lowering her hand, Elsie looked at each person in turn. "Technically, he should be able to perform well on all dragon-related duties in order to receive approval from me."

"However...?" Brenna prompted.

"However, provided he can shift back safely and you do me a favor, I'll clear him until the follow-up tests a few weeks from now."

"What favor?" Brenna asked slowly.

"Let's see if he can shift back first, and then I'll make my request."

Elsie retreated. Brenna turned and whispered low enough that the human wouldn't be able to hear it. "You can do it. I have faith in all three of you."

She hugged the dragon's chest as much as she could with her human arms and went to stand next to the DDA inspector.

Black spoke up. *Follow my lead again. Can you do that, Blue?*

I'll try. Blue paused and added, *Thanks for asking first.*

As much as Killian wanted to tell his dragons to hurry up, the trial was too important to risk distracting them. So, he merely watched to see if they could manage it or not.

Black grunted. *I think it's best if you go first, Blue. I think bringing one dragon head in and then changing our whole form to human will be the best way.*

Blue attempted to shift back the same way he'd grown out, but only one ear and eye melded into the rest of his face. He couldn't get the remaining set to budge.

Take your time and do the other side, Black instructed.

After a few deep breaths, Blue tried again. The second ear retreated and then the eye. His snout came next and everything looked to be going fine until the end, when he couldn't put the last blue bump back into the main dragon body.

Blue growled. *It's too hard.*

Brenna's voice came from the side of the room. "Do it for me, Black and Blue. Do it for me."

I can't upset Brenna. She should think we're strong,

Blue said.

Black replied, *Then just a bit further and I can do the rest. Imagine hugging me and becoming one.*

For a few beats, nothing changed. Then the last bit of blue melded into the main, black dragon body.

With the hardest part done, Black shifted back as he had done thousands of times over the years. Slowly he shrank back into their human form.

The second he finished, Brenna raced over and kissed him. "You're all bloody brilliant."

Both of his dragons preened inside his head.

Before he could say anything in response, Elsie approached. To her credit, the human kept her gaze on his face and ignored his nudity. "Right, while the shift was a bit slower than normal, you've passed for the time being."

"So what's your favor?" Killian probed.

"Here's what I want." Elsie extracted a sealed envelope and held it out. "Deliver this to Adrian Conroy."

Brenna took it slowly. "Is that all?"

She pushed her glasses up the bridge of her nose. "Yes. But remember, when I return in several weeks, you need to pass all aspects with full marks, including flight maneuvers. If you fail, I'll have to report it back to the DDA, which I'd rather not do since I'd hate to see you locked up."

It seemed the DDA inspector had a soft spot for dragons. Given how she wanted to contact Adrian so badly, it made sense.

Killian had barely said, "Thank you," before Elsie waved and left the area.

Tristan growled. "Right, then we're done for the day. Let me know when you're ready for more training."

The dragonman left without another word.

Once they were finally alone, Killian nuzzled Brenna's cheek. "I think it's about time I took you on a proper date to celebrate."

She ran her hands over his chest and around to his back. "I hope we're going to do this date backward because I want you naked and in my bed first, and then we can eat later." Turning his head to meet her gaze, she added, "As long as Blue can handle it."

"He's starting to take an interest." Killian nipped her jaw. "So let's go before he changes his mind."

Not caring about his nudity, Killian picked Brenna up and cradled her in his arms. With her heat and scent surrounding him, it was difficult to keep his cock soft. But he mustered every trick he knew to do so and ran like he was being chased by dragon hunters.

CHAPTER NINETEEN

With each step Killian took as he carried her, Brenna's heart rate ticked up a little more. She was finally going to be able to claim her male.

Her dragon huffed. *He's been ours for a while.*

But not in all ways. After today, I will fight anyone who tries to take him from us.

I sensed as much with the DDA inspector. You may as well have said, "Stay away from my male, bitch."

I didn't do it on purpose. Other females can look, but not touch.

Someone's sounding like a dragon-shifter.

That's because I am one.

Killian reached the cottage they'd been sharing since Bram had allowed him to leave the jail cell. He adjusted his grip to open the door, closed it with a kick, and jogged up the stairs. Brenna smiled. "Someone's in a hurry. I'm surprised you didn't break down the door."

"And risk someone hearing your moans? I think not. Because then I might have to challenge them to a fight."

She rolled her eyes. "Stonefire dragons don't linger outside open doorways because it could end up being their own one day and they'd hope for the same courtesy."

He reached their bedroom and gently laid her on the bed. Threading his fingers through hers, he raised her arms over her head and held them there. "Let's not talk of other people right now." He nuzzled her cheek, his soft whiskers sending a rush of heat through her body. "In this moment, I want to be the only one you're thinking of."

She looped a leg around his waist. "Is that so? Then try harder, because right now, I can easily bring up other males I've thought handsome."

With a growl, he lowered his body on top of hers, his delicious weight making it harder to think of anything but his lean, muscled body. "No one belongs in this room but you and me." He thrust against her and Brenna sucked in a breath. "Understood?"

If they were anywhere but in the bedroom, she would raise an eyebrow and tell him to watch his tone. However, the dominance in his voice made her wet and eager to see what else he could do. After all, she knew he had a talented tongue. Maybe he had even more talent with his cock.

Her dragon growled. *Why do you play these games? Rip his clothes off, flip him over, and take him.*

He has us pinned, remember.

Killian lightly nipped her neck. "Tell me what your dragon is saying."

As he soothed the slight sting with his tongue, Brenna tilted her head to the side to give him better access. "She just wants to hurry things along."

Killian squeezed her hands with his. "She can have a quick dragon fuck later. Right now, I want to make love to my female and treasure her how she will always be treasured, provided she wishes to stay with me."

"Killian," she murmured.

When she'd first met Killian, Brenna never would've

imagined him saying those words to her.

He worried her earlobe a second, chasing away her thoughts. Releasing her tender skin, he spoke again. "It's true. Very few females would stand by a male who regularly blacked out and was teetering on the edge of insanity." He moved to look her in the eyes again. "You did all that and never lost faith in me. Even when you fought what was between us, you did everything you could to help me."

"Any honorable person would do the same."

"There's no need for modesty, even if that's one of the many things I love about you."

Brenna stopped breathing. "What?"

He released one of her hands to caress her cheek. "I love you, Brenna Rossi. Not just because you're intelligent and beautiful, but I might not be here if it weren't for your faith in me. Add in your humor and acceptance of both my dragons, and I'd be a fool not to love you."

Searching his eyes, Brenna didn't hesitate to answer, "I love you, too."

With a growl, Killian moved his face closer but never took her lips. "Don't feel pressured to say it back. I know I'm probably only going to be more trouble in the future. But in case something happens to me, I wanted to ensure you knew what I felt because you mean everything to me."

At the vulnerability in his eyes, she decided that she needed to make him understand she wasn't placating him for the sake of it. She loved Killian O'Shea and couldn't imagine her life without him.

Taking his chin between her fingers, Brenna leaned up a fraction. "I'm not saying it because of pressure, you fool. And nothing is going to happen to you, if I can help it. You're my male and I expect for us to have a long, eventful future ahead of us."

Not wanting to give Killian a chance to make up more excuses, she kissed him.

⁂

As Brenna kissed him, Killian still couldn't believe she loved him back.

Black growled. *Don't fight it. She is ours.*

Yes, Blue added. *And stop thinking. I like her kisses. But I'm curious for more.*

Not wanting to think how Blue was probably at his randy teenager stage, Killian released Brenna's other hand and threaded his fingers through her hair. She parted her lips and he took his time licking, nibbling, and tasting the only female he wanted for the rest of his life.

But as she moved her lower body against cock, he hissed and broke the kiss. "For that, I'm tempted to tear off your clothes."

Amusement danced in her eyes and she tilted her head. "Well, what are you waiting for?"

Not wasting any time, he leaned back and quickly reduced her top and trousers to shreds. He left her bra and panties intact. Once he had her socks and shoes off, he lightly traced shapes on her stomach. "I hope that was fast enough for one of Stonefire's best Protectors."

"I hope not everything is that fast."

Leaning down, he kissed the top of her breast, just above her bra. "Not this time, love." Pulling down her bra cup, he blew against her skin. "I want to make sure you realize how special you are."

To prevent her from arguing, Killian took her nipple into his mouth and suckled.

Brenna arched her back, which only prodded him to lightly bite her tight bud.

"Yes, more," she ended with a moan.

He took his time tracing the puckered flesh with his tongue, nibbling, and sucking it deep. When Brenna was nearly panting, he moved to her other breast and did the same.

Black growled. *Hurry up. I want to see all of her.*

Ignoring his beast, Killian kissed his way to her breastbone. One flick of his talon, and her bra fell to the sides of her ribcage.

He took a nipple between each thumb and forefinger and squeezed. At his female's squirms, he continued the action as he slowly kissed his way down her belly.

Only when he reached the top of her panties did he remove his hands and glance upwards.

As much as he loved Brenna's small, pert breasts, he zeroed on her half-lidded gaze and flushed cheeks. His voice was husky to his own ears as he asked, "Was that too fast?"

Smiling slowly, she answered, "No."

"Good." He sliced the sides of her underwear and the scraps fell away. "It's time to see how wet and swollen you are for me, love."

Spreading her legs wide, he moved until his chin rested on the mattress between her legs. His female open and vulnerable to him only made Killian want to please her all the more.

Then taste her, Black ordered.

Blue was silent, but Killian sensed he wanted the same.

Still, Killian took a second to blow into her core. Brenna moved her hips as she grabbed the sheets on the bed. "Stop teasing me, Killian."

With a smile, he leaned forward and licked up her slit to her clit and back again. As tempted as he was to thrust his tongue into her pussy, he pulled back.

Brenna growled. "There's such a thing as moving too

slowly, Killian. Get a move on or I'll take matters into my own hands."

The image of Brenna naked and playing with herself sent more blood to his cock. "I look forward to that later. But right now, you're mine."

Parting her folds, he licked, sipped, and twirled, increasing in time to Brenna's cues. She even started to move against his tongue.

Fuck. He'd never get enough of his female's taste or her boldness in letting him know what she wanted.

At Brenna's impatient noises, he moved his mouth to her clit. Stroking the sensitive bud made her cry out, and he knew she was close.

Wanting to give her the most intense orgasm he could manage, Killian inserted two fingers into her core and thrust them in a steady rhythm, all the while brushing and teasing her clit.

Brenna moaned. "Just a little faster."

He increased his pace and Brenna fell apart, her pussy grabbing his fingers as he continued to swirl and caress her clit.

When the spasms stopped, Brenna relaxed against the mattress. Killian took one last lick before slowly kissing his way up her body, stopping to nip each nipple, and finally taking her lips in a long, slow kiss.

He was about to roll onto his back and hold Brenna close when she wrapped her legs around his waist, murmured, "Your turn," and flipped them over so that his back was on the bed.

༄༄༄

Maybe another female would've let Killian be completely in control and let him do what he wished, but that wasn't

Brenna. Twice he'd given her an orgasm and he had yet to receive one. It was time to fix that.

After flipping him over, she sat straddled across his waist for a moment, taking in Killian's loving gaze and flashing pupils. "Is Blue still okay?"

Killian ran a hand up her chest to massage one of her breasts. "Does that answer your question?"

"So, no?" she teased.

He lightly pinched her nipple. "Cheeky female."

Reaching for her other nipple, Brenna pinched and rolled the tight bud. Killian's gaze zeroed in on her, but she didn't stop. "You haven't seen cheeky yet."

He growled. "I have half a mind to flip you over and take you from behind."

She stopped playing with her nipple and rested both of her hands on Killian's hard chest. "And later, I'll let you." She wriggled her hips against his hard cock and he sucked in a breath. "But for right now, you're mine."

Her dragon spoke up. *Stop teasing him and ride him. I want to make him ours.*

At hearing the strain in her beast's voice, Brenna knew that if she didn't do as her dragon asked, she might try and take control. And Brenna wanted the first time with the male she loved for herself.

Raising her hips, she reached between them and gripped Killian's cock. She squeezed lightly and Killian closed his eyes.

She let go.

"What the fuck, Brenna?"

"I want you to watch."

The irritation faded from his eyes and turned heated. "Then I should try my best to please the lady."

His gaze made her feel like the most beautiful female in the world. A woman could get used to such a look.

Her dragon roared. *Stop wasting time. I want him and if you won't do it, I will.*

Her beast's words snapped her into action. Taking Killian's long, hard cock, she positioned herself just above him.

"Wait, Brenna."

She frowned as Killian reached for something under the pillow. He presented a condom package.

Even in the heat of the moment when he was inches away from being inside her, Killian thought of her future. "I love you," she murmured as she took the package, ripped it open, and slowly rolled it down his erection. Maybe once they'd had more time together, she could take him into her mouth and make him come that way.

Her dragon snapped out her wings, and Brenna knew her control was close to snapping. So she pushed aside the image of taking Killian into her mouth and positioned herself again. This time Killian didn't say a word as he watched her take him bit by bit until he was seated to the hilt.

Placing her hands on his chest, she began to move. First slowly, but then building up intensity and adding a swirl of her hips every once in a while.

Killian ran his hands up her sides until he could massage and play with her breasts. His attentions made it hard to concentrate, so she decided to distract him by reaching one hand behind and fondling his bollocks.

Hissing, Killian increased his torture.

Putting her hand back on his chest to join her other, Brenna slowed down, rising until Killian was nearly out of her and then slamming back in.

"Fuck, yes," Killian groaned.

Stopping with him inside her, she squeezed her inner muscles and leaned down to kiss her male. She finally pulled away to whisper, "Just wait until I can torture you with my mouth and tongue."

"You're killing me, Brenna."

With a smile, she leaned back and moved her hips again, this time increasing her pace beyond what she'd done before.

He reached up and lightly brushed her clit, making her miss a beat. "Let's work together, love. I want to feel you come around me."

Yes, yes, we should receive the same as we give, her dragon growled.

Deciding that she'd strung Killian out long enough, she moved as quickly as she could, careful to grip his cock as she did so. Despite Killian's heavy breathing, he rubbed and pinched her clit.

Pressure built, but Brenna bit her lip. She wouldn't leave Killian hanging again. He needed—no deserved—to come.

"Let go, love. And I'll follow," Killian ordered.

Not caring about following his demand, Brenna allowed the pleasure to crash over her, making it hard to keep moving. Only when Killian roared and stilled her hips did she stop.

When her orgasm finally ended, Brenna collapsed on Killian's chest and snuggled against him.

For a few long minutes, she simply laid in his arms, content to listen to Killian's beating heart. More than once she'd come close to losing him. And yet, here she was, laying with the man she loved.

While she was fairly sure that Killian's dragons wouldn't be a problem, she hoped that whatever was on that thumb drive would have a formula they could use to protect and ensure nothing else bad happened to Killian or any other dragon-shifter she cared for.

Running his fingers up and down her spine, Killian

murmured, "You tensed right there. What're you thinking about?"

She looked up and propped her chin on his chest. "Just that I want more of this, and that maybe we'll soon have the information we need to make sure nothing else happens to you as a result of the drugs forced on you. For all we know, your dragons are stable. But there could be any other number of aftereffects from that drug."

"As long as I have you, I'm not going anywhere. That includes maintaining my sanity and consciousness."

She rolled her eyes. "Willing it doesn't make it so."

He stilled his hand on her back. "Dr. Sid has already mentioned that she and the other doctors have several good starts at preventive formulas. With skill and a wee bit of luck, we hopefully won't have to worry about dragon-shifters being drugged anymore."

Brenna opened her mouth to argue, but her mobile phone rang. The ringtone was the one assigned to the surgery. "That might be Dr. Sid. I should answer it."

Killian leaned up to kiss her, and then rolled her to the side. Leaning down, he fished out her phone from the remnants of her trousers.

Brenna took it and answered, "Hello?"

Gregor's voice came on the line. "Brenna, lass, you need to come to the surgery. Your mother's in labor and wants to see you."

A bad feeling gathered in the pit of her stomach. "Why now? My father should be there."

"He is, but your mother's not doing so well. Sid is doing everything she can to ensure she pulls through, but I suggest you get here as soon as you can."

She managed to croak, "I'll be there."

Clicking off her phone, she stared at the screen. Gregor had to be exaggerating.

Killian asked, "What's wrong?"

She met his gaze. "I think Gregor just hinted that my mother might be dying."

"Brenna."

He pulled her close and she took a brief moment to drink in Killian's heat. Then taking a deep breath, she moved away and off the bed. "But I'm not going to bloody let her."

As she got dressed in a new set of clothes, Killian did the same.

Brenna needed to see her mother, and quickly. Maybe she merely needed extra encouragement.

If at all possible, Brenna wasn't going to allow her brother to grow up without a mother. She and her mum might've had a tough time over the years, but Brenna loved her. And blast it, she hadn't just secured Killian to lose someone else she loved.

CHAPTER TWENTY

Zain Kinsella stared down at the ginger-haired female and wondered how such a delicate human could be such an evil person.

His dragon spoke up. *Just because she has information about the Knights doesn't mean she's evil.*

Right now, I don't care. Even though the dragon hunters were the ones to kill Charlie, the Knights aren't any different. I suspect they work together quite often. And anyone who associates with those bastards is evil.

Charlie Wells had served in the British Army at the same time as Zain. While there'd been nothing romantic between them, Charlie had been one of his best mates.

And the fucking hunters had drained her without a thought, only caring about how much money they'd make selling her blood on the black market.

The female shifted in her sleep, garnering his attention once more. While she was attractive with a round face and full lips, he didn't care about that. All he wanted was for the blasted human to wake up so he could interrogate her.

A knock on the front door sounded, quickly followed by Dr. Gregor Innes entering with his medical bag. He asked,

"Any change?"

"No. I understand she's exhausted, but shouldn't she have woken up by now?"

Gregor stopped next to him. "I'm not sure if she'll ever wake up."

Zain frowned. "Why not?"

"The other doctors are still working out the finer details, but I think she's been poisoned and put into a coma."

"How? She may have worked with the Dragon Knights, but I don't think anyone on Stonefire would do it. Especially no one who's been allowed inside this cottage."

"Given the amounts of chemical in her body, I suspect it happened long before she arrived."

He grunted. "It seems convenient that she fell unconscious here."

Gregor bobbed his head. "I agree. It's possible that she was given a poison on purpose by those she worked for, and they administered an antidote of sorts each day to keep her conscious and alive."

"Which makes it the perfect way to keep traitors from getting away."

"Aye. However, our best guess is that she won't die but merely remain in a coma. I'm hoping that if we find the correct antidote, we can wake her up."

Crossing his arms over his broad chest, Zain replied, "You can't be suggesting that we keep her around until you find the antidote."

"Aye, and Bram has cleared it. As long as we keep her hidden from the DDA, it should be possible. I don't think she wants to be found, so no one should be looking for her. Especially since a quick records search told Kai that her only family, a brother, was killed recently."

Zain suspected it was related to the Dragon Knights, but the female's life choices and ensuing consequences weren't his concern. He glanced at the female's pale face. "I don't know if she's worth it. If the DDA discovers we're keeping her secret, it could reverse all the progress Melanie, Bram, and the others have made with the agency."

"I know you're a bit biased given your history, but if she is a turncoat, it would be a rare opportunity for Stonefire to finally get the upper hand and maybe dismantle one of our major enemies, possibly even both the Knights and the hunters. Bram and Kai think it's worth the risk."

His dragon spoke up. *He's right. And until we know for sure that she was responsible for any dragon injuries or deaths, you should give her the benefit of the doubt.*

He ignored his beast. "I suppose that means she's to be kept inside the clan walls."

"Aye. You and Kai are going to devise the security and guard rotation. And while he can give you more information in person, he mentioned you being her main guard. That way, if she wakes up for even a short while, you can do your magic and whittle information out of her."

Gregor knelt next to the bed and went through his routine of examining the female, checking her vitals and fluids.

As Zain watched, he said to his dragon, *I can't believe she is going to be our new assignment.*

It's an important one, though. She could be the key to protecting Stonefire in a way we've never been able to do in recent years.

All I'll say is that she'd better be worth all the effort. And if I discover she's even tangentially responsible for hurting one of our clan members, then I'm going to do everything within my power to ensure she gets the punishment she deserves.

I wouldn't get yourself worked up too much. After all, we have no idea how long she'll be out.

Maybe if he were lucky, she'd never wake up and

whatever was on the thumb drive would be enough to take care of some or even all their enemies.

~~~~~~

It took every bit of training Brenna possessed not to dash down the hallway and push everyone and everything out of the way. For all she knew, the people could be on their way to help her mother.

When she finally reached the correct room, she gently opened the door. Sid sat between her mother's raised legs and Ginny—Stonefire's most trusted nurse—stood near some beeping machines. Another nurse rushed past Brenna.

She blocked out everything but her mum, who lay pale and nearly lifeless on the bed. Her eyes were open and she was breathing, but even to her, it was plain that Mum's fight to live was slipping.

Her dad looked up, but never stopped wiping his mate's brow. "Brenna, come."

Somehow she made her feet work and stopped next to her father. "Papa, what's going on?"

Her mother's weak voice garnered her attention. "Brenna."

Clasping her hand over her dad's already holding her mum's, Brenna leaned down. "Mum, you need to keep fighting. I'm sorry for the things I've said over the years. I was angry and didn't mean them. You need to live. I love you."

Her mum gave a weak smile. "Fighting was always our way, and our own brand of love."

"Mum," she murmured as tears formed in her eyes.

"Shh, Brenna. No matter what happens, I know you'll be the best big sister in the world to your little brother."

"Don't talk like that. You'll be around to raise him and

force me to babysit."

"I would like that."

Her mum's eyes closed and one of the monitors went to a flat line. Her dad cried out the same time Sid barked, "Out," and then listed off a series of orders to Ginny and the other nurse.

Brenna and her dad were pushed out of the way. Ginny pointed toward the door. "Leave so we can try to save her."

After another second of staring at her mother's still face, Brenna took a deep breath and guided her dad out the door.

The instant they were in the hallway, she hugged her dad and a strangled sob escaped his throat. Hugging him even tighter, she willed for her mother to be okay.

She had no idea how long they stood there, but at some point, Killian's voice filled her ear. "Come, love. Let's wait in the private waiting room. Sid and Ginny will tell us as soon as possible what's going on."

Her dad slowly handed her over to Killian and she clung to her mate. Her dad murmured, "I'll wait here. You two go."

She glanced at her dad. "But Papa..."

"No, Brenna. All of us can't stay or we'll congest the hallway, but I want to be here in case your mother needs me." He touched her cheek. "I'll let you know if anything changes."

Opening her mouth to protest, Killian murmured, "Come, love."

Emotionally exhausted, Brenna allowed Killian to guide her away. Once they reached the private waiting room, they sat and she snuggled into his side. She fought her tears, but when Killian whispered, "Let them out, love. I'm here," she let go and cried.

Suddenly, all the years of petty arguments and resentments melted away. Brenna would trade anything to keep her mother around so that she could actually get to know her better.

꿏꿏꿏

As Killian soothed his mate, he kept a tight rein on his emotions. From what he'd gleaned from a nurse, Brenna's mother's heart had stopped beating and the doctors had to make a choice—the mother or the baby.

However, if Brenna's mum had given the order to save the baby above all else, the doctors would have to follow it.

Dragon-shifters didn't handle anesthetics well, which made C-sections difficult. Occasionally a dragonman or woman could survive the drugs, but the chances were slim. If Brenna's mother had indeed wanted the child saved, Sid would use anesthesia to deliver her child.

That almost certainly rang the death knell for Brenna's mother, given how fragile she was.

Blue spoke up. *I don't like this. After everything, Brenna deserves a happy ending.*

Killian replied, *I wish that, too. But life doesn't always work out that way.* Black remained silent, so Killian probed, *Are you okay?*

Black grunted. *I don't like this situation. It only reminds me of what could happen if we ever have a young with Brenna.*

Killian quickly pushed away any visions of Brenna dying on a hospital bed. *We'll cross that bridge when we come to it. For now, we merely need to be here for Brenna. And I do mean all of us. She'll know if something's bothering one of you two.*

Both mumbled their assent.

He had no idea how long he sat on the sofa with Brenna, holding her close and rubbing her back in slow movements.

But eventually the nurse named Ginny knocked and entered with an unreadable expression.

Sitting up, Brenna asked, "Well?"

"You have a lovely little brother."

Killian held his breath as Brenna asked, "And my mother?"

Ginny's eyes turned sympathetic. "I'm sorry, Brenna. Sid and Gregor did everything they could, but she didn't make it."

He glanced at his mate, who sat unnaturally still beside him. Killian cupped her cheek. "Brenna?"

As the seconds ticked by, he started to worry.

Then she stood and turned toward Ginny. "I want to see my brother. He needs to know I'll protect him."

He stood. "I'll go with you."

"No, I need to do this alone, Killian. I'll find you afterward."

As Brenna left the room with the nurse, Killian clenched a fist. Maybe his love for Brenna wasn't enough. With her mother gone, her brother needed her, which meant she might not have time for a messed up male like himself.

His dragons protested, but he quickly constructed a mental cage to keep them contained.

All he could do was wait and see if Brenna came back.

He needed to think of a way to convince her he could help and wouldn't be a burden. The trick would be in proving it.

Taking out his mobile phone, he contacted the third doctor working on his case, Dr. Trahern Lewis. Trahern was originally from Clan Snowridge in Wales, but had transferred to Stonefire.

He also spoke the truth without any cushions or platitudes.

After dialing the number, Trahern's voice came over the line, "Hello?"

"Dr. Lewis, this is Killian O'Shea. I'm currently at the surgery and want to talk with you. Where are you?"

"What did you want to talk about? I'm a bit busy."

"About the formulas. I want to know what you've found and if they can help."

"I don't know why I have to meet in person for that. I can discuss this over the phone. Emily and I have made progress. And if you're willing, we'll have a test serum ready by tomorrow."

Dr. Emily Davies was a human scientist who was currently working with the Stonefire Dragons.

"Just to be clear—it won't affect my dragons, correct?"

"As far as we know, it won't. But I can't guarantee it."

His beasts thrashed in their cages, protesting the best they could. "Can you give me a few hours to think about it?"

"Of course."

Trahern ended the call and Killian stared at his phone. He could either take the serum and maybe have a stable, sane future, but possibly lose one or both of his dragons. Or, he could refuse it and risk another episode down the line that could take his life.

Neither was the future Brenna deserved, but the question was which one would he choose?

⚬⚬⚬

Ginny led Brenna to a small room used for newly born infants. Stopping outside the door, she thanked the nurse and watched her father through the small window in the door.

His eyes were red and puffy, but he held his new son in his arms, singing some tune she couldn't make out due to the soundproofed walls.

Tears formed in her eyes at the scene. She needed to be

strong for her father and brother, but all she wanted to do was crawl back into Killian's arms and cry.

Her dragon spoke up. *It's okay to show weakness in front of family.*

But Papa needs us.

I'm sure he'll understand.

Her father noticed her through the window and motioned for her to come inside with his head.

Taking a deep breath, she turned the knob and entered.

As soon as she reached his side, her father whispered, "Brenna, say hello to your brother, Ethan."

Looking down at the small bundle in her father's arms, she smiled at the tiny slack face lost in sleep. "Mum always loved that name. She often told me that if I'd been a boy, that's what she would've called me."

Her dad croaked, "Yes."

Never taking her gaze from her brother, she hugged one arm around her father's side and leaned against him. "I'll help you any way I can, Papa. I hope you know that."

His reply was so low she nearly didn't hear it. "I know, *cara.*" He cleared his throat and continued, "When your mother and I left Clan LupoForesta, one of your cousins, Serafina, offered to come with us. At the time, we thought it best for her to stay in Italy. But she's continually asked us to invite her here, so I may do so. She can help when you can't, since you must continue your Protector duties."

In all the rush of events, Brenna hadn't even thought of that. "I can take some time off to help you settle Ethan, though. Bram would understand."

Her dad shook his head. "No, work will help you just as taking care of Ethan will help me. Your mother would've wanted you to keep doing your job. She was against it at first, but she admired you because you did something she never would've had the fortitude to do."

"She said that?"

"Yes, she did. She was proud of you, Brenna. Always remember that."

"I—" She paused and continued, "I wish she were here."

"Me too, love, me too."

Unable to restrain herself, Brenna turned her head into her dad's shoulder and let the tears fall.

She'd been an idiot, plain and simple. All those years she could've reached out to her mother, she hadn't. And now, she would never have the chance.

Her dragon spoke up. *STOP. We made up in the end, and she knew we loved her. We have Killian and Ethan, now. And we can't overlook them to wonder what if.*

Sometimes, you're too pragmatic. We just lost our mother. I want to cry.

Then cry. But Mum always focused on what needed to be done. We must do the same.

Her father started singing an original tune he'd composed for her as a child. As she listened to his deep voice, Brenna laid a hand on the top of Ethan's head and vowed to protect her brother with her life.

⌒⌒⌒⌒⌒

Caitlin Todd nearly ran down the surgery's corridor, to the third room on the right. She trusted that Lorcan would be on her heels. All she could think about was getting to her son and daughter-in-law's side.

Reaching the correct room, Caitlin peeked through the small window in the door and willed herself not to cry.

Brenna, Killian, and Brenna's father—Gabriele Rossi—stood next to a bed containing the still form of Sharon Rossi.

Sharon had been almost fifteen years younger than her, with a new baby to boot, and yet she lay in the stillness of death.

It seemed unfair.

Her dragon said softly, *We can't bring her back to life. All we can do is love Brenna as if she were our own and help her any way we can.*

Lorcan stopped behind her and wrapped an arm around her waist. He said nothing, but she leaned against him for support.

They stood there watching the family in the room when Bram's voice said from behind her, "I think it's time we enter and console them."

Stonefire's leader hadn't blinked twice at postponing negotiations with Lorcan. He truly cared for his clan.

Lorcan pulled her to the side to allow Bram to enter first, and then they followed.

Bram placed a hand on Gabriele's shoulder. "If there's anything I can do, Gabriele, tell me. You're clan and we look out for each other."

Gabriele nodded. "Thank you, Bram."

Bram spoke again. "Evie and I insist you stay with us for at least a few days. We can help take care of wee Ethan while you handle the mourning arrangements."

Gabriele swallowed, but didn't cry. Brenna, on the other hand, was pale as a sheet, the poor dear.

Caitlin lightly touched Lorcan's side and he released her. She went to Brenna. "My condolences, Brenna. I know that means little, but you will always have me, if you need a motherlike figure to talk to."

Turning, Brenna gave a small smile. "Thanks, Caitlin."

She hugged her and Caitlin held her tight. Brenna was at least grown, but glancing at her baby brother, it reminded her too much of her own children losing their father early in life.

Once Brenna released her, Bram took his turn hugging

the female.

Killian touched her shoulder and Caitlin embraced her son for a few moments. More than ever, she was determined to make the most of the time she had left on earth, never taking it for granted. It would be her goal to get her children, their mates, and their families all together in one place again. Even if she had to reach out to the various dragon clans in Ireland, she would do it to help make her goal a reality.

Her dragon spoke up. *Let Teagan handle it.*

Killian's voice prevented her from replying, "I hope you understand that we're going to have to cancel our dinner plans for tonight."

She touched his cheek. "Of course I understand. Your mate and her family need you. And you are always there for those who need it." Uncertainty flashed in his eyes. She stood on her tiptoes and whispered into his ear. "You are still reliable, Killian O'Shea. There may be a few obstacles coming, but you love hard and deep. You won't fail any of us."

"She's right," Brenna interjected.

Killian glanced at his mate with guilt. "I can't guarantee it, Brenna. You know that. But I'm thinking of taking up Trahern's offer to act as a test subject."

Anger flashed in Brenna's eyes. "Don't even think about it. I'm not about to lose you as well."

"But—"

"No buts. I love you, Killian O'Shea, and that means any and everything that entails. The question is whether you love me enough to try for a future together, rather than deciding one on your own."

Caitlin had no idea what had transpired recently between her son and Brenna, but she held her breath awaiting his answer. She only hoped he wasn't a fool to be noble and throw his chance at happiness away.

He finally answered, "Together, then."

Brenna nodded. "Good." She sighed and some of the fight ebbed out of her posture. "Then the first thing is for us all to go home and take care of Ethan. We can return to the real world tomorrow." She glanced at Bram. "I hope it's okay we stay with you too?"

He nodded. "Aye, of course." He moved his gaze to Caitlin. "You can come as well, as long as your mate promises not to kill me in my sleep."

Lorcan grunted, but Caitlin beat him to the reply. "I'll hold onto him all night. I'll even lock the door and hide the key, if it helps."

"Right, then let's give Gabriele a little bit more time alone and I'll help Evie get everything prepared." Bram said to Brenna, "Bring the others when they're ready."

Brenna bobbed her head and Bram squeezed Gabriele's shoulder one more time before exiting.

Threading her arm through Killian's, Caitlin turned him toward the door. "I'll take your mate for a short while, Brenna. Take your time and find us when you're ready. We'll be in the private waiting room."

Killian kissed Brenna and Caitlin led her son out the door, Lorcan fast on her heels.

Once in the waiting room, she sat and gestured for Killian and Lorcan to take a seat on either side of her.

Taking a hand of each, she squeezed them and sang a tune, one that spoke to the loss each of them had endured over the years.

However, from that loss, she wanted to forge a better future. Together, she was confident they could.

CHAPTER TWENTY-ONE

*A*drian Conroy sat on the bed of his temporary residence on Stonefire, staring at the letter Caitlin Todd had passed on to him from her son.

The letter from Elsie Day.

If his dragon wasn't still groggy from being drugged quiet, his beast would've demanded that he open the blasted letter and see what the human had to say.

Flicking his thumbnail against one corner of the envelope, he debated what to do. If the female wanted to see him, it would only encourage his dragon to pursue the human.

And for many reasons, Adrian couldn't do that. The least of which was the history between his family and hers. They might live in separate countries in the present—his family in Northern Ireland and hers in England—but the Days and Conroys had been neighbors before the Second World War.

His grandfather had even considered mating one of them before the betrayal.

No, Adrian needed to sever ties, which meant never reading the letter. Going to the kitchen, he lit the gas burner on the cooker and put the envelope to the fire. Once it caught, he tossed it into the sink and watched the flames consume the paper.

Whatever Elsie Day had wanted to tell him wouldn't change his mind.

Or, so he told himself.

Lorcan and Caitlin would be returning to Northcastle the next day. Adrian would join them, return to Northern Ireland, and never have to see the female again.

Because if he was alone with her pretty eyes and curves made to be held close, his fortitude might slip and he'd probably end up kissing her. That meant a mate-claim frenzy.

Which could never happen.

As soon as the flames died, he turned on the tap and washed away the ashes. As the last of them disappeared down the drain, he felt a sense of closure. Elsie Day wasn't to be his. Ever.

⚜

Brenna stood next to her father and brother, with Killian on her other side, and stared at the shroud-clad form of her mother on top of the pyre.

Some said that dragon-shifters had begun cremating their own since the eighteenth century to prevent humans from digging up the bodies for research. But no matter how it had started, the tradition was ingrained into the way of life. Cremating a loved one signaled the end of one chapter and the beginning of another.

Caitlin and Lorcan had asked to stay for the ceremony, and Caitlin had been given the task of singing the traditional dirge since Brenna's father couldn't do it, being the mourner. As Caitlin's soprano tones warbled the final notes, Brenna squeezed Killian's hand in hers. It was time.

As the eldest child, she had a duty to fulfill. Brenna

released her mate's hand and marched over to Bram, who held an unlit torch. He held it up and said the traditional words, "Sharon Rossi may be departing the earth, but she will forever be a part of our clan, helping to nourish the trees watching over us all."

He flicked on a lighter and the torch soon blazed with life. As Brenna took it, she replied, "I shall also carry on her legacy, through blood and memory."

Since she had cried herself out over the last two days, Brenna took a deep breath and turned toward the pyre with a neutral expression.

She took a second to memorize the moment. The white shroud was embroidered with a large image of the Stonefire crest, which was a dragon clutching a shield and the two pieces of a broken sword. Surrounding the crest were roses, her mother's favorite flower. Every member of the clan had contributed at least one stitch to the design; appearance wasn't the most important. No, sending off a fallen clan member with haphazard designs meant little compared to the sense of clan and togetherness. It didn't matter that her mother had spent time away in Italy. She was Stonefire, always and forever.

Her dragon said softly, *It's time.*

Aware that the entire clan was watching her, Brenna kept her head high and shoulders back. Reaching the pyre, she sent one final silent *I love you* to her mother before lowering the torch to the wood stacked underneath the shrouded figure. Leaving the torch in the open space left for it, she stepped back to join her father. Caitlin began another song about how the fallen member wouldn't be forgotten as the flames licked and then consumed her mother's body.

Her father wrapped an arm around her shoulders and they stood for who knew how long, watching the dancing flames. They wouldn't stay the entire time since it would take hours for the pyre to fully burn and extinguish. But once the blaze roared, concealing her mother, Brenna looked up at her dad. "She has been honored."

Bram took the cue and raised his voice. "The commemoration continues in the great hall. We have mourned Sharon Rossi's passage and now will honor her memory with a celebration."

As members left, Caitlin sang one final song about fostering the next generation and taking care of one another when times turned tough.

Only when everyone but Brenna's family and Bram had left did she take her little brother from her father and say, "We should go, too."

Her father stared at the flames. "I'll be along shortly. I want to sing one final song to Sharon alone."

Pushing past the emotion in her throat, Brenna nodded. "Find me when you're ready. I'll watch over Ethan until then."

Her father kissed her cheek, shook Bram's hand, and moved closer to the pyre.

At her father's silhouetted figure, tears threatened to fall again.

Her dragon spoke up. *We must be strong for Ethan.*

She glanced down at her brother and adjusted his blanket. *I know, but sometimes sadness can't be contained that easily, no matter how much I wish I could do so.*

Killian placed a hand on her back. "You did brilliantly, love."

Adjusting her brother in her arms, she leaned against Killian's side. "It's easier when you're older. I can only imagine how difficult it must've been for you and Teagan when you were children, at your father's mourning ceremony."

He grunted. "Yes and no. I promised myself that I

wouldn't cry because I needed to be strong for my family."

"You weren't even ten at the time."

"That didn't matter to me. Without my dad or either of my grandfathers alive, it was up to me as the only male in the family to be strong and take care of my mother and sister."

She smiled. "Even at that age, I'm sure Teagan didn't take that well."

"No. I suspect that if it had been any other circumstance, she would've challenged me and won. However, she took dad's death even harder than me. It took years for her to smile again." He lightly caressed her cheek. "But this circumstance is different. You have me. And even if it means allowing Blue to take charge to charm you, I want to make our lives from here on out happier. That doesn't mean forgetting your mother, but there are other ways to honor someone than with tears."

Her dragon spoke up again. *He's right. Protecting Stonefire means protecting everyone we love. Mum would've approved of that, I think.*

If what Dad said is correct, about her being proud, then I think so, too.

Glancing down at her brother's sleeping face, she wished she could just kiss Killian and enjoy the celebration being held in her mother's memory.

However, that would be the coward's way of handling things. There was one remaining thing she needed to tell Killian before making any sort of plans with him.

The hard part was that it might drive him away.

No. She'd put it off long enough.

So, she mustered the courage to say what she'd been trying to say for the last two days. "I know that previously I wanted to return to Glenlough, but I can't do that anymore." She looked up at Killian. "My brother and father need me here. I understand if that's too much to ask, giving up your family and everything you've known, and that you'd rather go back to Ireland."

He frowned. "Why would I go back to Glenlough without you? You're my future, Brenna. I thought we were supposed to decide it together?"

"You may regret staying here."

He stopped and gently took hold of her shoulders. "Why? Because I can be treated as I am now, with two dragon personalities and no past to tie me down? If anything, it's a sort of blessing. I'll miss my sister and I hope we can visit her often, but Glenlough is her home and future. Stonefire is mine."

She held her breath and tried to spot if he were putting on a show for her.

But there was only truth and love in his eyes.

Releasing her breath, she whispered, "Oh, Killian."

He cupped her cheek. "It's the truth. And if being with you wasn't enough of a reason, then know that Black and Blue have grown fond of Tristan and Dr. Sid, too. Even without a cure of sorts to ensure I don't have any more episodes, I think I have the best chance at being the male you deserve here, on Stonefire."

"You are the male I deserve, and maybe more than that."

He smiled. "I'm not going to argue about who is more deserving than whom. How about we just agree to talk about any decisions related to our lives, so that we can forge a stronger future together?"

"I like the sound of that."

"Right, then open communication, no matter the topic. And let me start by saying how much I love you, Brenna Rossi."

"At least you didn't start a contest about loving me more than vice versa."

"Brenna," he growled.

At his tone and grumpy expression, she did something she hadn't done in days—she laughed.

His frown vanished at the sound. "I've missed that laugh. I hope it's the first in a long string of them to come."

"Maybe. It depends if you're amusing or not."

"You don't want to issue a challenge with me, Brenna."

"Don't I? Dragon-shifter males like challenges. It's even better when I best them at said challenges."

He moved his face closer to hers. "Then you'll like this challenge—let's see how we can help make our future the happiest it can be from here on out."

"That's one I can get on board with."

"Well, after everything we've both gone through, I think a happy future is well deserved."

Her brother squirmed a little, telling her he would wake up in the next few minutes. "Then kiss me quickly to start it because Ethan is going to need to be fed soon."

Her mate complied, slowly taking her lips and lingering as long as possible. Only when Ethan gave his first cry did he pull away.

Brenna and Killian picked up their pace and reached the great hall as soon as they could. She had a bottle warmed for her brother in short order and sat at the side of the room, with Killian next to her.

As she leaned against her mate, watching her brother eat heartily and taking comfort from the sounds of her clan members all around them, Brenna was optimistic. She may not have thought Stonefire was where she belonged, but now she couldn't imagine being anywhere else. She'd always treasure her time in Ireland, especially as she'd learned so much from Teagan and had met Killian there, but Stonefire was her future. And she was going to do whatever it took to protect her clan, her mate, and her family to give everyone the happy ending they deserved.

Epilogue One

A Few Months Later

Killian sat in one of the exam rooms inside Stonefire's surgery and resisted the urge to get up and pace the room.

Black spoke up. *It's only been five minutes. And to think you say I'm impatient.*

Blue nodded. *He's right. Good things come to those with patience. The wait only means that Dr. Sid is being thorough.*

Black grunted. *I thought we talked about your optimism and toning it down a bit?*

Blue raised his head. *This is who I am. And I know you've grown fond of me, which means your threats no longer frighten me.*

Black muttered a few choice words, but Killian jumped in. *I'm not sure why I bother, but will you two ever stop arguing?*

Both dragons shook their heads.

Black said, *Besides, why are you so worried? We passed the DDA's second interview and display of skills with flying colors.*

Blue snorted. Flying *colors. That's funny.*

Not when you comment on it, it's not.

If you don't like compliments, then I won't give them.

As his beasts continued to squabble, he sighed. He may have grumbled about not being able to help Brenna with her Protector duties and her secret project, but he'd gladly wait for several more weeks to receive clearance if it meant his dragons would stop arguing for a day or two.

He quickly constructed a mental prison, making sure to reinforce the wall between the two dragon heads. He'd barely finished before Sid and Gregor entered the room.

Killian raised his brows and barked, "Well?"

Gregor scowled. "Be nice. Cassidy is growing another dragon-shifter inside her."

Rolling her eyes, Sid handed Killian a sheet of paper. "I vomited once in the last month. I'm fine." She gestured toward the paper with one hand and placed the other on her swollen belly. "As far as we can tell, the anomalies we pinpointed months ago are no longer there. We think it means that the serum worked."

The thumb drive Brenna had found on the human had indeed contained various formulas for the drugs that had harmed dragon-shifters in the UK and Ireland. Which was good since Alice's quest to find the old ship's logs had failed. It had taken months, but the doctors had tinkered with a counteragent. The results he held in his hand were the first to come back clean.

Gregor spoke up. "However, we need to test it more thoroughly to be sure before we clear you for duty again."

He looked up at the male doctor. "You mean you need my dragons to attack each other and see if I fall into a seizure."

"Aye. I know it's not the easiest thing to ask for, but if they do it and nothing happens, we can finally recommend you to active Protector duty once more."

Which meant Killian could finally join the Stonefire Protectors and help his mate. Nikki Gray was growing closer to term, which meant Brenna would soon temporarily take over as second-in-command of the Protectors until Nikki had her baby and was cleared for duty again.

Laying down the paper, Killian said, "No worries. Let me try it."

He quickly dismantled the mental prison. Both dragons gave him the stink eye, but he quickly spoke before they could. *You can scold me later. For now, we need to test if we're truly cured or not. I need you two to fight with each other.*

Black snorted. *So now you want us to fight? You need to make up your mind, human.*

Don't test me, Black. Unless you don't want to help Brenna protect our new home?

Black huffed. *I was teasing. You need to work on your sense of humor.*

Blue had rubbed off on Black, it seemed.

However, before Killian could reply, Black quickly moved his head to Blue's neck and bit him. With a roar, Blue did the same.

Despite the pain from sharp teeth flooding his body, Killian didn't sense anything else. After who knew how long, Sid's voice finally filled the room again. "That should be enough. Behave, dragons."

Black and Blue instantly removed their teeth and went back to their respective positions.

Except for Brenna, his bloody beasts listened to Dr. Sid above anyone else. Even him.

Thankfully Sid spoke up before his dragons could say why they did it. "I think we need to keep an eye on you for another twenty-four hours just to be certain, but I'm 98 percent sure that you're stable and will remain so. I'll talk with Bram after this, but as long as nothing happens, you should be officially working with the Protectors within the week."

Both his dragons roared inside his head, but Killian pushed past the noise to reply, "Thank you, Sid, Gregor. I know you've sacrificed a lot of your free time to help me and the others, and I'll forever be in your debt."

The corner of Gregor's mouth ticked up. "We'll call you on it once the bairn is born. We could always use a good babysitter."

Sid shook her head, but Killian spoke up. "Consider it done." He stood. "Unless there's anything else, I want to tell Brenna the news."

"No, go ahead and share it with your lass. I'm sure she'll reward the news," Gregor said, winking.

Killian murmured his thanks again before racing out to the waiting room. However, he scanned the area, but Brenna was nowhere in sight.

The male working reception, Leo, motioned him over. When Killian reached him, Leo said, "Brenna wanted you to meet her near Stonefire's back entrance."

He frowned. "Is something wrong? Another attack?"

Leo shook his head. "Just something about a surprise for you that she can't give you here and that you shouldn't worry."

She could've waited a few minutes for him, but Killian pushed aside that thought. "Thanks, Leo."

With a wave, Killian raced out of the surgery and jogged toward the rear entrance. At one time, he'd hated surprises. And while sometimes Brenna went too far—such as when she'd organized a traditional Irish dance party in the great hall—he'd grown to like most of them.

Especially when it involves her naked, Black said.

Let's hope she's not naked if she's standing at the rear entrance, Killian drawled.

It didn't take long to reach the final walkway to his destination. He spotted Brenna plucking at a large, sheet-covered, rectangular object. Since it didn't even reach her shoulders, it couldn't be a car.

Once he was within a few meters from her, she smiled at him. "Well? What did they say?"

Closing the distance between them, he pulled her close. "Everything came back clean. I have to wait twenty-four more hours before they sign off, but if the next day goes without incident, I'm cured."

She squealed before bringing his head down for a kiss.

He took his time sipping and tasting his female before ending it. "So, what's the surprise?"

"Oh, just something to celebrate your recovery."

"I only just found out about it. Did Dr. Sid leak the results to you early?"

She shook her head. "No, but I had a feeling it would go well this time, and I wanted to be prepared. Kai even gave me the afternoon off."

"Does that mean you're going to tease me all afternoon about what's under there?"

"Of course not. What's under there is what we're going to do for the afternoon." She stepped back and motioned toward it. "Open it and take a look."

The rectangular shape told him little of what it could be. Quickly tearing off the sheet, he sighed. "You put a box over it too?"

She grinned. "A little suspense can sweeten the reward later, as you often remind me."

A naked image of Brenna in his bed, moaning as he slowly licked between her thighs, flashed into his head. "And I'll be reminding you of that later as well. I plan to make good use of our afternoon."

She gestured toward the box. "Let's take things one step at a time. Hurry up and open it."

He went to slice the tape, but the box moved. There wasn't a bottom, so he lifted it off and gasped.

It was a motorcycle. A Kawasaki Ninja ZX-6R, to be exact.

Brenna spoke up. "I couldn't afford a new one, but I asked Blake to go with me to check it out. Apparently, he loves motorcycles, too. You should ride with him sometime."

He ran his hand over one of the handlebars and then the other. "I love it." He glanced at his mate. "And my first ride will be with you, once we have helmets."

She kissed him quickly before dashing behind a bush and producing two helmets. "I thought of that. I've never ridden one. Maybe one day you can teach me, but for now, I just want to ride on the back."

"I might be able to do that. For a price."

"Killian O'Shea—"

He shut her up with a long, slow kiss before finally laying his forehead against hers. "If you think I'm going to ride this with you on the back and not find a spot to make love to you along the way, then you don't know me well enough."

"One day, you'll tire of so much sex," she teased.

"With you, never." He kissed her nose. "I love you, Brenna, and will never let you forget it."

She tilted her head. "A female could get used to that."

He lightly smacked her bum. "Good, because having you in my life is a treasure I'm never going to take for granted." Plucking one of the helmets out of her hands, he situated it on Brenna's head and fastened it. "Now, there's a sexy sight."

Rolling her eyes, she held out the second helmet. "I draw the line at wearing helmets during sex, Killian."

He fastened his own. "Why would I ask you to do that? Undressing you is the fun part." Straddling the motorcycle, he patted behind him. "Let's go for a ride. I promise you it's the closest thing to flying you'll feel while still being on the ground."

Brenna climbed up behind him and wrapped her arms around his torso. He took a second to memorize her heat, scent, and toned body against his back before starting the bike. As it revved to life, a sense of peace came over him. It'd been too long since he'd ridden and having his mate at his back made it perfect.

Black growled. *Yes, yes, it's nice. Now, get going. I love riding and want to feel the wind again.*

Killian slowly pulled up to the gate and glanced at the hidden security camera. A few seconds later the gate opened and he said, "Hold on tight," before taking off.

At first Brenna held him tighter as he took the turns and guided the machine in graceful movements. When she shouted, "Go faster," he only loved her more.

Increasing his speed, Killian took off, the vibration of the bike between his thighs making his heart rate tick up.

Biking through the Lake District with the female he loved at his back was almost too good to be true. He'd come a long way from waking up with amnesia and always wondering if he had a future. He may not know everything it held, but with Brenna at his side, it would be a bloody good one. And a male couldn't wish for anything more.

EPILOGUE TWO

Many Months Later

At the edge of Glenlough's main landing area, Caitlin Todd waited for Lorcan to finish dressing after his shift. She should feel guilty since Georgiana hadn't felt well enough to come with them. However, even though her stepdaughter was ill, it had been a few weeks since Caitlin had visited her family and she was anxious to see her children and mother again.

Her dragon spoke up. *Would you rather have Lorcan waltz in naked?*

No. He's mine.

Exactly. So have a little patience.

Once Lorcan made the final adjustment to his formal kilt-like attire, he strode to her side. "You can stop tapping your fingers, Caity."

"I can't help it. This is the first celebration after Teagan's pregnancy announcement. I want to make sure she's all right and no one tries to organize some sort of revolt."

Slipping his arm through hers, he guided them out of the landing area's exit. "Killian and Brenna should be here

289

already. Although I think Teagan is more than capable of taking care of herself."

Glancing over at her mate, she smiled. "You've come a long way on your position with females."

He raised his brows. "Did I have a choice? Between your mother and daughter, I was getting more guilt trips than I ever had from my own gran when I was a lad. I mainly changed policy to finally have some peace and quiet."

Lorcan teased her, but Caitlin knew he was secretly enjoying the changes a few female Protectors were determined to bring to the clan, as soon as they finished their time with the British Army.

Patting his arm, she said, "Since I think the changes only brings us closer to your actual retirement, I'm going to thank my family for their harping this one time."

"Because that won't backfire," he drawled.

"Oh, stop. It's their way of showing love and acceptance. If they didn't like you, there would be only silence and plenty of glaring."

"You mention silence as if it's a bad thing."

She sighed. "Lorcan."

He winked. "You know I'm jesting. I'm just partial to your flushed cheeks and revel the opportunity to see them when I can." He leaned over to her ear and whispered, "As well as other flushed parts of your body."

His words only made her face burn hotter.

Her dragon laughed. *If you can't stop blushing at our age, I don't think it's ever going to happen. Prepare for Mam to tease us.*

They approached the last leg to the great hall. *She'll be too busy sitting near Teagan and Aaron, glaring out at the rest of the clan, to notice.*

She may be older, but her eyesight is as keen as ever. Just wait and see.

A pair of Glenlough's younger Protectors stood at the entrance. Ignoring her dragon, Caitlin smiled at each of the Protectors in turn before entering the large, rectangular hall.

Banners in the colors of Glenlough's allies lined the edges of the room. Not only were all the clans in Ireland represented, but also those of Northern Ireland, Wales, Scotland, and both English ones. The multitude of vibrant colors, ranging from blue to green to red, made Caitlin proud. Her daughter had been instrumental in securing each clan's place of honor in the hall.

At the far end was a raised dais, complete with a long table and a series of chairs. Teagan sat next to Aaron, whispering something. Brenna and Killian were on the main floor, talking with Lyall O'Dwyer—head of Glenlough's Protectors—and Dr. Ronan O'Brien. She'd just began searching for her mother when her voice filled her ears. "My daughter is the last to arrive. I'll admit, that's a first."

She opened her mouth to reply, but Lorcan beat her to it. "You don't want to know why we're late, Orla. Trust me on this."

Her mother leaned on her cane. "Oh, aye? Defiling her again, I reckon."

"Mother!"

Orla winked. "There's nothing to be ashamed of. I had my own secret rendezvous at your age. The young think we stop at forty. I think it's because they can't handle the truth."

She sighed. "Can we talk about anything else? How's Teagan doing?"

Waving a hand in dismissal, her mother answered, "Fine, fine. Although Caruso is going to drive her to quitting her position and running away if he doesn't learn to back off."

"Most males are that way. He'll learn. After all, Teagan

isn't one to mince words."

"Do I get a say in how males act?" Lorcan asked.

"No," Caitlin and her mother answered in unison.

Sighing, Lorcan shook his head. Caitlin was about to excuse them from her mother when Molly Caruso—Aaron's mother—caught her eye and waved.

Looking back at Orla, Caitlin said, "Sorry, Mam, but I promised Molly we'd discuss a few things. We'll catch up with you later."

"I imagine so." Her mother pierced Lorcan with a stare. "Try to leave without saying goodbye, and I'll find a reason to visit Northcastle and stay for weeks."

Lorcan raised his brows. "What, and lose your ability to criticize everyone and give orders when you feel like it? I somehow doubt it."

"Cheeky sod," Orla said with a smile. "Now, go on then."

She and Lorcan made it to Molly's side. As Caitlin embraced the other dragonwoman, she murmured, "It's good to see you."

Molly released her. "I'm not fond of big gatherings, but I knew you'd be here. I also want to keep an eye on Aaron, in case he starts to upset Teagan."

She glanced at her daughter and her mate. At present, they were laughing. "Maybe now's a good time to say hello to them, while they're in a good mood. And maybe snag Killian and his mate along the way, so we can have all our children together for a brief moment."

Molly bobbed her head. "Then we can sneak to a corner of the room and discuss ideas for the baby shower."

Even though baby showers were mostly a human thing, Molly had mentioned the one for Evie Marshall back on Stonefire and both females thought it would be a good way to honor their first grandchild.

Caitlin didn't even need to look at Lorcan to know he'd

follow her. He couldn't care less about baby showers and the crafts she wanted to do for it, but he merely wanted to spend time with her.

Her dragon spoke up. *Too bad Georgiana is ill, or we'd have everyone in one place.*

I know. But that just gives me an excuse to invite Teagan, Killian, and their mates to Northcastle.

As they approached Killian and Brenna, Lorcan wrapped an arm around Killian's shoulders and forced him to walk. "Come, son. Your mother wants everyone together."

"She's not going to take a family photo again, is she?" Killian asked warily.

Caitlin jumped in. "Not this time. But once the weather turns better, I want one with all of us in our dragon forms."

Brenna grinned. "I think that's a brilliant idea. Maybe we could even use it as a promotional photo, to show how a family spanning three clans gets along."

Killian sighed. "I can already tell that protesting is going to fall on deaf ears."

Lorcan slapped Killian's shoulder. "You're still young, but you'll learn soon enough to pick your battles."

Killian grunted, but thankfully didn't argue. Her son and Lorcan had grudgingly learned to respect one another over the last few months. She suspected one day, they might even enjoy being in each other's company.

Ascending the stairs of the dais, Caitlin picked up her pace. Spotting her arrival, Teagan stood. As Caitlin held her daughter close, she said, "How're you feeling, darling?"

"I'm fine, Mam." Teagan released her. "No one's challenged me yet and I'm determined to keep my position even after the baby's born."

Aaron grunted. "Bloody too right you will."

Killian nodded. "Say the word, and I'll be back to defend your place."

Teagan rolled her eyes. "I'm fairly good at this clan leader thing." She smiled. "But if I need help, I'll be sure to ask for it."

As Aaron and Killian started planning what they wanted to do to any challengers, Caitlin merely smiled and leaned against Lorcan's chest. His arms went around her automatically and she was content to watch in silence, basking in the warmth and love of her mate.

Her years of worrying about looking after her children were gone. She'd raised two brilliant, fierce dragon-shifters, who now had their own responsibilities and mates to look after. Which meant she could spend the rest of her days spoiling grandchildren and traveling with her mate once he retired.

Caitlin had never thought she'd find a second chance at happiness with a male she loved. While her first mate, Kieran, would always hold a special place in her heart, she adored Lorcan, too. True mate or not, she loved him and looked forward to making many new memories in the future.

Author's Note

I hope you enjoyed Killian and Brenna's story. I was a little nervous because it's so different from my other dragon stories, but my early readers seemed to love it. I hope you did, too. :) And if you didn't catch it, the second epilogue is actually the same epilogue from *Aiding the Dragon* (Teagan and Aaron's story), but in a different point of view. Hopefully it helped to fill in some of the gaps! I don't foresee any more stories about the Glenlough clan members in the near future (if at all). But don't worry, you'll be hearing from them, for sure. I'm trying to think of a way to get Orla and Aunt Lorna in the same room, because that's something I think we all want to see!

There were several new stories set up in this book, but Zain and Ivy's story will be next. A Protector interrogator and a human woman who had been forced to work with the Dragon Knights. Considering what happened to Zain's friend, Charlie, it'll be interesting to see how they get there! I also hope to write about Adrian and Blake in their own books respectively, but I almost never know which book comes next until I finish the current one. Also, there will be a Lochguard foster coming to Stonefire soon, too.

Okay, with that out of the way I have some people I need to thank for helping me to get this book out to the world:

- To Becky Johnson and her team at Hot Tree Editing—you all are amazing. Becky gets me and helps my stories to shine.
- To Clarissa Yeo of Yocla Designs—you yet again

designed a beautiful cover that captures my couple perfectly. I couldn't imagine my series without your talent and vision.

- To Donna H., Alyson S., Iliana G., Sabrina D., and Sandy H.—My beta readers are amazing and provide valuable honesty. Not only that, they catch the little typos that slip through. All of you are appreciated more than you know. <3

And as always, I thank you, the reader, for supporting my dragons this long. While at some point stories about the current generation will have to end, we're not there yet. (Although I *am* eager to write about all the babies grown up!) Thanks a million times from my heart for not only reading, but also spreading the word. Word-of-mouth is more powerful than you think. And if you want a whole new way to experience my dragons, then maybe check out my audiobooks. There's nothing better than listening to my Irish narrator and his take on dragon-shifters for hours... ;)

My release after this book will be *The Dragon Family* (Lochguard Highland Dragons #5), about Finn and Arabella and it will be out on May 15, 2018. However, if you're curious about my alien romance series, *The Forbidden* (Kelderan Runic Warriors #4, about Kalahn and Ryven), will be out in July 2018.

Thanks so much for reading and I hope to see you at the end of the next book.

Coming soon, the long-awaited follow-up story for Finn and Arabella...

The Dragon Family
(Lochguard Highland Dragons #5)

This isn't a standalone story. Please read at least *Healed by the Dragon* (Stonefire Dragons #4) first. I would highly suggest reading the other books in the Lochguard series as well.

For Finlay Stewart, being a dragon-shifter clan leader is easy compared to managing his family...

Finn is trying his best to work and protect his clan on little sleep; having triplets is his toughest challenge to date. But with his mate Arabella at his side, he finds a way to manage. However, as things start to spiral out of control with a pregnant cousin, another cousin constantly containing a mate-claim frenzy, and another driving his eight months' pregnant mate crazy, Finn worries that the clan may think he's incompetent. So his next mission is to find a way to ensure everyone behaves and toes the line. The only problem is that the MacKenzies are a stubborn lot and Finn may be in over his head.

Can Finn find a way to get everyone to cooperate? Or, will he have to give up his clan leadership position to someone unrelated to the MacKenzies?

——————

The Dragon Family will release in mid-May 2018.

The Conquest
(Kelderan Runic Warriors #1)

Leader of a human colony planet, Taryn Demara has much more on her plate than maintaining peace or ensuring her people have enough to eat. Due to a virus that affects male embryos in the womb, there is a shortage of men. For decades, her people have enticed ships to their planet and tricked the men into staying. However, a ship hasn't been spotted in eight years. So when the blip finally shows on the radar, Taryn is determined to conquer the newcomers at any cost to ensure her people's survival.

Prince Kason tro de Vallen needs to find a suitable planet for his people to colonize. The Kelderans are running out of options despite the fact one is staring them in the face—Planet Jasvar. Because a group of Kelderan scientists disappeared there a decade ago never to return, his people dismiss the planet as cursed. But Kason doesn't believe in curses and takes on the mission to explore the planet to prove it. As his ship approaches Jasvar, a distress signal chimes in and Kason takes a group down to the planet's surface to explore. What he didn't expect was for a band of females to try and capture him.

As Taryn and Kason measure up and try to outsmart each other, they soon realize they've found their match. The only question is whether they ignore the spark between them and focus on their respective people's survival or can they find a path where they both succeed?

Excerpt from *The Conquest*:

Chapter One

Taryn Demara stared at the faint blip on the decades-old radar. Each pulse of light made her heart race faster. *This is it.* Her people might have a chance to survive.

Using every bit of restraint she had, Taryn prevented her voice from sounding too eager as she asked, "Are you sure it's a spaceship?"

Evaine Benoit, her head of technology, nodded. "Our equipment is outdated, but by the size and movement, it has to be a ship."

Taryn's heart beat double-time as she met her friend's nearly black-eyed gaze. "How long do we have before they reach us?"

"If they maintain their current trajectory, I predict eighteen hours, give or take. It's more than enough time to get the planet ready."

"Right," Taryn said as she stood tall again. "Keep me updated on any changes. If the ship changes course, boost the distress signal."

Evaine raised her brows. "Are you sure? The device is on its last legs. Any boost in power could cause a malfunction. I'm not sure my team or I can fix it again if that happens."

She gripped her friend's shoulder. "After eight years of waiting, I'm willing to risk it. I need that ship to reach Jasvar and send a team down to our planet."

Otherwise, we're doomed was left unsaid.

Without another word, Taryn raced out of the aging technology command center and went in search of her best strategist. There was much to do and little time to do it.

Nodding at some of the other members of her settlement as she raced down the corridors carved into the mountainside, Taryn wondered what alien race was inside the ship on the radar. Over the past few hundred years, the various humanoid additions to the once human-only colony had added extra skin tones, from purple to blue to even a shimmery gold. Some races even had slight telepathic abilities that had been passed down to their offspring.

To be honest, Taryn didn't care what they looked like or what powers they possessed. As long as they were genetically compatible with her people, it meant Taryn and several other women might finally have a chance at a family. The "Jasvar Doom Virus" as they called it, killed off most male embryos in the womb, to the point only one male was born to every five females. Careful genealogical charts had been maintained to keep the gene pool healthy. However, few women were willing to share their partner with others, which meant the male population grew smaller by the year.

It didn't help that Jasvar had been set up as a low-technology colony, which meant they didn't have the tools necessary to perform the procedures in the old tales of women being impregnated without sex. The technique had been called in-something or other. Taryn couldn't remember the exact name from her great-grandmother's stories from her childhood.

Not that it was an option anyway. Jasvar's technology was a hodgepodge of original technology from the starter colonists and a few gadgets from their conquests and alien additions over the years. It was a miracle any of it still functioned.

The only way to prevent the extinction of her people was to capture and introduce alien males into their society. Whoever had come up with the idea of luring aliens to the planet's surface and developing the tools necessary to get them to stay had been brilliant. Too bad his or her name had been lost to history.

Regardless of who had come up with the idea, Taryn was damned if she would be the leader to fail the Jasvarian colony. Since the old technology used to put out the distress signals was failing, Taryn had a different sort of plan for the latest alien visitors.

She also wanted their large spaceship and all of its technology.

Of course, her grand plans would be all for nothing if she couldn't entice and trap the latest aliens first. To do that, she needed to confer with Nova Drakven, her head strategist.

Rounding the last corner, Taryn waltzed into Nova's office. The woman's pale blue face met hers. Raising her silver brows, she asked, "Is it true about the ship?"

With a nod, Taryn moved to stand in front of Nova's desk. "Yes. It should be here in about eighteen hours."

Nova reached for a file on her desk. "Good. Then I'll present the plan to the players, and we can wait on standby until we know for sure where the visiting shuttle lands."

Taryn shook her head and started pacing. "I need you to come up with a new plan, Nova."

"Why? I've tweaked what went wrong last time. We shouldn't have any problems."

"It's not that." Taryn stopped pacing and met her friend's gaze. "This time, we need to do more than entice a few males to stay. Our planet was originally slated to be a low-tech colony, but with the problems that arose, that's no longer an option. We need supplies and knowledge, which means negotiating with the mother ship for their people."

"Let me get this straight—you want to convince the vastly technologically advanced aliens that we are superior, their crew's lives are in danger, and that they need to pay a ransom to get them back?"

Taryn grinned. "See, you do understand me."

Nova sighed. "You have always been crazy and a little reckless."

"Not reckless, Nova. Just forward-thinking. You stage the play, think of a few ideas about how to get the ship, and I'll find a way to make it work."

"Always the super leader to the rescue. Although one day, your luck may run out, Taryn."

Nova and Taryn were nearly the same age, both in their early thirties, and had grown up together. Nova was her best friend and one of the few people Taryn was unafraid to speak her fears with. "As long as my luck lasts through this ordeal, I'm okay with that. I can't just sit and watch our people despairing if another year or ten pass before there's new blood. If we had a way to get a message to Earth, it would make everything easier. But, we don't have that capability."

Nova raised her brows. "Finding a way to contact Earth or the Earth Colony Alliance might be an easier goal than taking over a ship."

"The message would take years to get there and who knows if the ECA would even send a rescue ship to such a distant colony." Taryn shook her head. "I can't rely on chance alone. I'll send a message from the alien ship, but I also want the technology to save us in the near future, too. I much prefer being in control."

Nova snorted. "Sometimes a little too much in control, in my opinion."

"A leader letting loose doesn't exactly instill confidence," she drawled.

"Then promise me that once you save the planet, you let me show you some fun. No one should die before riding the sloping Veran waterfalls."

Taryn sighed and sank into the chair in front of Nova's desk. "Fine. But how about we focus on capturing the aliens first?"

Nova removed a sheaf of crude paper made from the purple wood of the local trees and took out an ink pot and golden feather. "I'll come up with a fool-proof capture plan, but I hope you keep me in the loop about what happens next."

"I will when it's time. I need to see who we're dealing with before making concrete plans."

Dipping her feather into the ink pot, Nova scratched a few notes on the purple paper. "Then let me get to work. The staging is mostly done already, but I need to think beyond that. Since we've never tried to capture a large ship before, it's going to take some time. I think someone captured a shuttle in the past, but we'll see if I can find the record."

"You always go on about how you love challenges."

"Don't remind me." She made a shooing motion toward the door. "And this is one of the few times I can tell my settlement leader to get lost and let me work."

Taryn stood. "If you need me, I'll be in the outside garden."

"Fine, fine. Just go. You're making it hard to concentrate." Nova looked up with a smile. "And you're also delaying my next project."

"Do I want to know?"

"It's called Operation Fun Times." Nova pointed her quill. "I sense you're going to land an alien this time. You're a talented individual, except when it comes to flirting. I'm going to help with that."

Shaking her head, Taryn muttered, "Have fun," and left

her old-time friend to her own devices. Maybe someday Nova would understand that while Taryn missed the antics of their youth, she enjoyed taking care of her people more.

Still, she'd admit that it would be nice to finally have the chance to get a man of her own. Most of her family was gone, and like many of the women of her age group, Taryn would love the option to start one.

Not now, Demara. You won't have a chance unless you succeed in capturing the visitors.

With the play planning in motion, Taryn had one more important task to set up before she could also pore through the records and look for ideas.

As much as she wished for everything to go smoothly, it could take a turn and end up horribly wrong. In that case, she needed an out. Namely, she needed to erase memories. The trick would be conferring with her head medicine woman to find the balance between erasing memories and rendering the aliens brain-dead. As the early Jasvarians had discovered, the forgetful plant was both a blessing and a curse. Without it, they'd never have survived this long. However, in the wrong dose, it could turn someone into a vegetable and ruin their chances.

Don't worry. Matilda knows what she's doing. Picking up her pace, Taryn exited the mountain into the late-day sun. The faint purple and blue hues of the mountains and trees were an everyday sight to her, but she still found the colors beautiful. Her great-grandmother's tales had been full of green leaves and blue skies back on Earth. A part of Taryn wanted to see another world, but the leader in her would never abandon the people of Jasvar.

Looking to the pinkish sky, she only hoped the visitors fell for her tricks. Otherwise, Taryn might have to admit defeat and prepare her people for the worst.

✹ ✹ ✹

Prince Kason tro el Vallen of the royal line of Vallen stared at his ship's main viewing screen. The blue, pink, and purple hues of the planet hid secrets Kason was determined to discover. After years of fighting his father's wishes and then the ensuing days of travel from Keldera to the unnamed planet, he was anxious to get started.

Aaric, his head pilot, stated, "Ten hours until we pull into orbit, your highness."

Kason disliked the title but had learned over time that to fight it was pointless. "Launch a probe to investigate."

"Yes, your highness."

As Aaric sent the request to the necessary staff, the silver-haired form of Ryven Xanna, Kason's best friend and the head warrior trainer on the ship, walked up to him. "We need to talk."

Kason nodded. Ryven would only ask to talk if it was important. "I can spare a few minutes. Aaric, you have the command."

The pair of them entered Kason's small office off the central command area. The instant the door slid shut, Ryven spoke up again. "Some of the men's markings are tinged yellow. They're nervous. No doubt thanks to the rumors of a monster on the planet's surface."

"There is no monster. There's a logical explanation as to why our team of scientists disappeared on Jasvar ten years ago."

"I agree with you, but logic doesn't always work with the lower-ranked officers and the common soldiers."

Kason clasped his hand behind his back. "You wouldn't ask to talk with me unless you have a solution. Tell me what it is, Ryv."

"I know it's not standard protocol for you to lead the first landing party, but if you go, it will instill courage in the others," Ryven answered.

Kason raised a dark-blue eyebrow. "Tell me you aren't among the nervous."

Ryven shrugged and pointed to one of the markings that peeked above his collar. "The dark blue color tells you all you need to know."

Dark blue signaled that a Kelderan was at peace and free of negative emotions.

"You are better at controlling your emotions than anyone I have ever met. You could be deathly afraid and would somehow keep your markings dark blue."

The corner of Ryven's mouth ticked up. "The trick has worked well for me over the years."

"We don't have time for reminiscing, Ryv. You're one of the few who speaks the truth to me. Don't change now."

"Honestly?" Ryven shrugged. "I'm not any more nervous or worried than any other mission. The unknown enemy just means we need to be cautious more than ever."

"Agreed. I will take the first landing party and leave Thorin in charge. Assemble your best warriors and send me a message when they're ready. I want to talk with them and instill bravery beforehand."

In a rare sign of emotion, Ryven gripped Kason's bicep. "Bravery is all well and fine, but if there is a monster we can't defeat, promise you'll pull back. Earning your father's praise isn't worth your life."

"I'm a little insulted at your implication. I wouldn't be a general in my own right if I lived by foolish displays of machismo."

Ryven studied him a second before adding, "Just because you're a general now doesn't mean you have to talk like one with me."

Kason remembered their childhood days, before they'd both been put on the path of a warrior. Kason and Ryven had pulled pranks on their siblings and had reveled in coming up with stupid competitions, such as who could reach the top of a rock face first in freezing temperatures or who could capture a poisonous shimmer fly with nothing but their fingers.

But neither of them were boys anymore. Displaying emotion changed the color of the rune-like markings on their bodies, which exposed weakness. Warriors couldn't afford to show any weakness. It was one of the reasons higher-ranked officers weren't allowed to take wives, not even if they found one of their potential destined brides; the females would become easy targets.

Not that Kason cared. A wife would do nothing to prove his worth as a soldier to his father, the king. On top of that, being a warrior was all Kason knew. Giving it up would take away his purpose.

Pushing aside thoughts of his father and his future, Kason motioned toward the door. "Go and select the best soldiers to assist with the landing party. I have my own preparations to see to."

"I'll go if you promise one thing."

"What?"

"You allow me to be part of the landing party."

Kason shook his head. "I can't. In the event of my death, I need you here."

"Thorin is your second and will assume command. Give me the honor of protecting you and the others during the mission."

Deep down, in the place where Kason locked up any emotion, a small flicker of indecision flashed. Ryven was more Kason's brother than his real-life brother, Keltor.

Yet to contain Ryven on the ship would be like a slap in

the face; the honor of protecting a prince such as Kason was the highest form of trust to one of the Kelderan people.

Locking down his emotions, Kason followed his logical brain. "You may attend. But on-planet, you become a soldier. I can't treat you as my friend."

Ryven put out a hand and Kason shook it to seal their agreement. "I'm aware of protocol. I teach it day in and day out. But I will be the best damned soldier of the group. And if it comes to it, I will push you out of the way to protect your life."

Kason released his friend's hand. "I won't let it come to that."

"Good. When shall we rendezvous?"

Glancing at the small screen projecting an image of the multicolored planet, he answered, "Nine hours. That will give all of us a chance to sleep before performing the prebattle ritual. You can lead the men through their meditation and warm-up maneuvers after that."

Ryven nodded. "I'll see you then."

The trainer exited the room, and Kason turned toward his private viewing screen to study the planet rumored to host the most feared monster in the region. One that had supposedly taken hundreds of men's lives over the years. The story was always the same—a small contingent of men disappeared from any group that landed on the surface. No one remembered how they were captured or if they were even alive. Anytime a second party landed, a few more would be taken.

Over time, the planet had earned a reputation. Even the most adventure-seeking ruffians had stayed away.

However, Kason dismissed it as folklore. Whatever was on that planet, he wouldn't allow it to defeat him or his men. Kason would bring honor to his family with a victory. He also hoped to give his people the gift of a new planet.

Keldera was overpopulated, and its resources were stretched beyond the limit. The Kelderans desperately needed a new colony and hadn't been able to locate one that was suitable. The planet on the view screen showed all the signs of being a near-perfect fit.

Even if the fiercest monster in existence resided on that planet, Kason wouldn't retreat from an enemy. Death was an accepted part of being a Kelderan soldier.

——————————

The Conquest is now available in paperback. Learn more at: www.jessiedonovan.com

About the Author

Jessie Donovan has sold over half a million books across multiple formats, has given away hundreds of thousands more to readers for free, and has even hit the *NY Times* and *USA Today* bestseller lists. She is best known for her dragon-shifter series, but also writes about magic users, aliens, and even has an upcoming crazy romantic comedy set in Scotland. When not reading a book, attempting to tame her yard, or traipsing around some foreign country on a shoestring, she can often be found interacting with her readers on Facebook. Check out her page:

www.facebook.com/JessieDonovanAuthor

And don't forget to sign-up for her newsletter to receive sneak peeks and inside information. You can sign-up for her newsletter at: www.jessiedonovan.com.

29027793R00183

Printed in Great Britain
by Amazon